a novel

Praise for Darryl Whetter

A Sharp Tooth in the Fur

"These devious and toothsome tales are a black attack on language and lives of smartass desperation. Darryl Whetter's debut is hallucinatory, a new brainscan, an incisor nudging our jugular."
— Mark Anthony Jarman

"He frequently places his characters in a personal cul-de-sac, a very brave thing to do. His combination of theme and style is very admirable."
— Alistair MacLeod

"[H]e can pin down his insights with wonderful precision [moving] from dispassionate perception to an abrupt and moving burst of emotional truth…Other tales reconfirm Whetter's uncommon talent."
— *Globe and Mail*

"Sinewy stories of disquiet and desperation…Plot, character, and dialogue zing along the taut bands of Whetter's language…There isn't a page in *A Sharp Tooth in the Fur* that doesn't shiver with electricity fighting to be free."
—*Georgia Straight*

"If David Mamet were a Canadian 20-something male, he would have put together a book of short stories that looks a lot like Darryl Whetter's debut collection, *A Sharp Tooth in the Fur*…. Whetter has a mean way with a short story.
—*January Magazine*

"Whetter anatomizes the species in unflinching detail…All of the stories are distinguished by Whetter's prose, which is inventive, precise, and vivid. It's the real star of this sly, smart, and gratifyingly original collection."

— Jack Illingworth, amazon.ca

"Whetter's a master of one-liners, a king of openings…He has great instincts for the moment, an excellent ear for dialogue."

—Hal Niedzviecki

"Whetter is an excellent writer, skilled at capturing minutia and investing it with meaning. He writes about arduous physical suffering and the to and fro of sexual ecstasy in an electric way."

—*Books in Canada*

The Push & the Pull

"A brash, vibrant, melancholy, sexy, and finally uplifting book about a mesmerizing father, the son who can't tear himself away, and the women who make them grow up. Whetter is intoxicated with language. He writes like a dream in a quick, urbane, and witty style. His women are gorgeous independent creatures; his men are large and infuriating; and when love happens it's explosive, passionate, and grand. A lovely first novel."

—Douglas Glover

"Brilliant. Darryl Whetter's style gleams like a rare and fresh metal. Here, in a ride we haven't seen taken, is a daunting, all-terrain, solo journey to the heart."

—Bill Gaston

"It's a contemporary quest narrative that never loses its focus. Sexuality, identity, and perspective fragment. But the text maintains its focus…It's this exploration of personal freedom that really gives Whetter's text its power. We can see the potential for tragedy. And, strangely, we hope for it."

—David Adler, *Canecdotes*

"[E]xcellent writing...deeply poignant and resonating...the introspection and adventure keep you along for the read."

—*Atlantic Books Today*

"Whetter weaves life's major issues and cycling together into a journey that takes the reader through difficult but necessary places...Whetter writes like a dream and he deserves our attention."

—*Halifax Chronicle Herald*

"Every paragraph is loaded with sharp observation and the compulsive honesty of a certain type of youth—the restless adventurer who has to learn every lesson for himself."

—*OptiMYz Magazine*

Origins: Poems

"If I may coin a new word, it is ethnoecogeo-science poetry of the highest calibre and may be, like the fossils described, the first of its kind to drag itself out of the tidal water and waddle on this new poetic beach."

—*Halifax Chronicle Herald*

"The scathing 'Privileged Young Men Who Hate Creativity' is a standout. Whetter's critical eye is felt throughout, but no other poem hits this hard... Such unabashed aggression is so refreshing that a reader can't help but hope Whetter stays on this poetic detour."

—*Quill & Quire*

"Whetter's poems are arresting, genuine, full of science and wonder, and reflect the author's tough love for Maritime life."

—Donna Morrissey

KEEPING THINGS WHOLE

[a novel]

DARRYL WHETTER

Vagrant Press is an imprint of
Nimbus Publishing Limited
3731 Mackintosh St, Halifax,
NS B3K 5A5
(902) 455-4286 nimbus.ca

Printed and bound in Canada
NB1096

Cover design: Heather Bryan

This novel is a work of fiction. Names, characters, places, and incidents are either the product of the author's imagination or are used fictitiously.

Library and Archives Canada Cataloguing in Publication

Whetter, Darryl, 1971-, author
Keeping things whole / Darryl Whetter.

Issued in print and electronic formats.
ISBN 978-1-77108-030-9 (pbk.).—ISBN 978-1-77108-031-6 (pdf).
ISBN 978-1-77108-033-0 (mobi).—ISBN 978-1-77108-032-3 (epub)

I. Title.

PS8595.H387K43 2013   C813'.6   C2013-903430-7
                                    C2013-903431-5

Vagrant Press acknowledges the financial support for its publishing activities from the Government of Canada through the Canada Book Fund (CBF) and the Canada Council for the Arts, and from the Province of Nova Scotia through the Department of Communities, Culture and Heritage.

 Social Sciences and Humanities Research Council of Canada   Conseil de recherches en sciences humaines du Canada   Canada *for A., wherever she is*

We all have reasons
for moving.
I move
to keep things whole.
—Mark Strand

Another image for a group of people governed by
such laws is a walled city with a gate at the wall
and an altar in the center. Then we may say, as the
ancients did, that there is a law of the altar and a law
of the gate. A person is treated differently depending
on where he or she is. At the edge the law is harsher;
at the altar there is more compassion.
—Lewis Hyde, *The Gift*

http://www.keepingthingswhole.ca

password: |

Keeping Things Whole

I. Down

1. Send

I'M SO GLAD YOU'RE HERE. The ball's been in your court since you were about seven. Early forties, not a dad, I couldn't tell you how old a kid needs to be to Google *Antony Williams*. I assume seven or eight, though obviously you needed much longer before you typed "Antony Williams" "Keeping Things Whole" and spun the wheel. Much longer and stories from someone else. Apparently loose lips can raise a ship too.

I bought the domain www.keepingthingswhole.ca on your second birthday. Fifteen years has been worth the wait. Other passwords would have worked—*Ambassador, Rowing to Cuba, Peg, William Williams, Cronus, Victor-Conrad, Ontario Farm*—though I'm glad you chose the most obvious: *Medea*. You keep reading, I'll keep waiting and making us money. It's all legit now, I swear. (Okay, no Cuban: I'm sure even your parents dip their oars a little come tax time).

Every story is a staircase. Let me know if ours can only go down. Is there a statute of limitations on gifts from the heart? To the heart?

Anything's possible if you just reach over and click Send.

2. Windsor Rain

THE FIRST TIME I SAW her, she was down by the river, running in the rain. Filly legs. Little show-jumper's ass. The sweetest moment of my 1998 (and, pre-you, probably my life). Katherine Chan, Scottish-Chinese-Canadian. She had this long Iroquois hair swishing across her back as she ran, the tail of a horse that looked about ready to leap the Detroit River and keep going on the other side. All this in a woman willing to pay for what she wanted, not taking rain for an answer. I was driving home after an honest day's house painting. Riverside Drive was thick with traffic and there went determination on two trim legs. She wasn't running in drizzle or a sun shower, but steady rain. Windsor under her feet and ghost-town Detroit hanging alongside her.

The first glimpse I had of her was dedication, self-sculpted legs scissoring through a syrupy September rain. When I drove up onto the sidewalk of Riverside Park, flung open the door of my painter's truck and began running after her—attracting up to two coast guards or police forces—the first thing she knew about me was risk. Or stupidity. Or brashness. But it was that or nothing, probably never see her again. For more than two decades I worked constantly to avoid police attention. At least three generations (the close, the distant, and the unknown) would have rolled in their smugglers' graves to see me hopping up onto the sidewalk like that. Then again, half those groaning ancestors might not be mine.

Fortunately the world has no better shoe for house painting than a running shoe, and I was raised by a yoga-crazy drama teacher who taught me to stand tall and stand on something supportive. I left the truck door hanging open and ran after her in the pelting rain. I kept a wide buffer between us, but saw her head tilt and dart a little as she heard me approach. In went her elbows. I ran abreast, then a bit ahead so she could see me without feeling stared at. "Excuse me, I'm hoping to say hello before I get towed away." I pointed back at my truck parked on the sidewalk with its ads for foolishness and *Victor-Conrad, Windsor's Painter* hanging on the open door. "A self-employed voracious reader who cooks a mean basil peanut chicken. I was an engineering student but didn't want to become a drone."

Not a word from her, just the legs and the nostrils pumping their bit. Drapes of cold rain all around us. A flash of her brown eyes meeting mine.

"I'm trying to be honest here. My name's Antony Williams. Running in the rain like this, you're obviously not waiting for someone to hand you the world. May I get your name?"

Voodoo-the-dog and I had been jogging together for years. Eventually you grow to see running not as a spring from the calves or a reach from the quads, but as music on air. The bottom of your spine and the tray of your hips learn to fly in the airborne seconds between one leg and the next. When two runners pass each other they're weavers unfurling bolts of soul cloth. Tolerance for pain visible in a second. The balance of risk and reward. But she wasn't sharing.

"Okay, sorry. Back to your run."

Only after I'd cut my politely wide J-hook away from her and doubled back did I hear her half-yell, "Kate." She was deep into her run, all oiled lung machine, so she knocked the word out with belly and breath. *Kate* hung in that international air, a slow, aural flare illuminating the river and the growing distance between our backs. I didn't turn around to better savour the fading sound. *Kate. Kate. Kate.* A warm cloth down my damp back.

Of course I couldn't clutch at the stitch in my side, and was prepared, for once, to tell the cops the truth. "Had to do it, Officer. I think I'm in love. Thunderbolt." In my line, you *always* have to be ready to meet a cop.

3. Das Boot

MOM MIGHT ALSO HAVE BEEN a rain runner if she wasn't always at rehearsal, school, or yoga. I grew up on the 4-M plan: mother's milk, music, and martial arts. At five I was enrolled in piano and tae kwon do. Guess which one I stuck with.

A few years before I saw Kate out in the rain, Gloria thought she was hitting me where it hurts when she threw me out. No bigs. My wallet was fine, and moving out improved both my slinging and my dating. I was still a little young when I got the boot, nineteen, though you don't grow up by numbers. You grow up by getting things done and by having the minimum amount of shit done to you. Another hard lesson from Glore. Getting kicked out was the last young thing I did. So I say.

Ultimately, her throwing me out was just more theatre, one of the three Williams family trades—tunneller, smuggler, liar. At university, I'd already propped Gloria's door open by enrolling in engineering, not something respectably useless like philosophy or English. When I quit without a degree, I was practically moving out the first box. As for my truck and ladder work as a painter, well, Mom was right to think that where there was smoke, there was smoke.

She threw me out during a bullfight. Sunday night. We'd been watching *60 Minutes*, and there was a segment coming up on Spain's latest bullfighting phenom. Anyone wants to fight a tonne of horned muscle, that'll keep me awake. This Spanish guy, somewhere in that glorious age between twenty-five and thirty, promise and accomplishment both. And inhumanly gorgeous. Slow-roast a taller Tom Cruise over mesquite coals, give him an accent that strokes you from throat to knee, and you'd have a fraction of this guy's power. Mom let out a little "Hubba-hubba."

The brown eyes, the tan, the dark stubble—Mr. Olive Cruise dissolved wedding rings with a glance. And he was the shit, the reigning Spanish bull tha-hing. Mr. Contemporary doing the traditional glam. His grandfather had been the bull king in his day, same again for his father. But apparently bulls, not matadors, decide when a matador's career is over. Gramps was killed in the ring. Papa got gored on live TV. So his mom dug in, decided to save the son no matter what. Took the boy out of Spain, educated him in America, all the private schools and blonde muff he could hope for. Thrill juice in the blood? Mom encouraged him to ski, got him sailing. Adrenaline management, not prohibition. Had him flying down mountains on bikes and climbing them with thin rope. Anything but bulls. The whole nation had watched his father die. Generation after generation, the only adults in the family that lasted were the women. Bit of a pattern, that. Mom and I didn't share a word after the first ten seconds.

But the Spaniard came home a man, and home meant bulls. Dad and Grandpa gone, how'd he even learn the dance? Who knew, but Don Cojones had the touch. The old leathery men they interviewed, ring rats their whole lives, they all agreed that the kid was even better than his father, closer to the grace of his grandfather. *Mitad toro*, one of them said, part bull, a minotaur with a convertible and dozens of marriage prospects. The kid couldn't stop. To his mom, that was *wouldn't stop*. So she threw him out.

Still he won and won. A villa, a ranch, all from a wave of the cape. He piled everything into the ring. Bought land to raise bulls, personally mated them. Stick around with the smell of spunk up your nose, you know you're in for the long haul. "This is who I am," he told the show's only female interviewer. Everyone—the interviewer, his mom, mine, me— we all knew he was saying a version of that old line: a man's gotta do what a man's gotta do.

Crime. Bullfighting. Enlisting in the army. All these rituals sons invoke to divorce their mothers. I figured this was definitely going to earn me one of Gloria's kitchen-counter notes the next morning. *Antony, you have always been…. X is good about you, so is Y,* but stop being someone I don't want you to be.

Apparently she was done with half measures. She hadn't forgotten about the trebuchets I'd been building for half my life and knew better than I did that much of the Windsor shoreline is just six hundred metres from the Detroit border. She, not I, had met a Trevor Reynolds who drove over the Ambassador Bridge into exile, the Stars and Stripes fading in his rear-view.

Two years before the goodbye bullfight, I'd essentially stopped asking her for money. She came back from an MFA year in Chicago to a teenaged son suddenly keen to pay his own way. She heard me take a lot of brief cellphone calls, and I paid cash for everything, my token rent included. The next time the camera went in close on Don Handsome's face, him again with the *I must, I must,* Gloria turned to me long enough to say, "Get out," then left the room.

I was nineteen. I could have pleaded, showed her the paint freckles on my forearms, handed her invoices. Honest money, I swear. She could have followed me to the next day's (legitimate) job site. But I liked the feeling of an open door in front of me. She hadn't yelled, so I took my time packing a few things. She got the last word, so I went for the last note. *I'll come for more when you're out and leave my key when I'm done. I'd like Voodoo when I'm settled.*

And that was it. No more little boy. Slept in my truck the first two nights. Not at Gran's, certainly not at Nathan's. Kinked the shit out of my neck then ate large breakfasts in restaurants. I already owned a little cooler.

4. Safe Sisters

1998. LIFE BEFORE FACEBOOK. IF Kate had run into my soul even half a decade later, on your thumb-clicking side of the millennium, I wouldn't have been playing my games with the border, and she wouldn't have sent me a paper invitation to *Soup by Safe Sisters*.

Windsor couldn't be Canada's car city without a jillion garages for rent. My painting company rented one, and a mailbox, downtown (each registered to Trevor Reynolds). Before a green punt with the trebuchet, I could be at the garage three times in a single night, ears cocked for sirens and the bark of a sniffer dog. Normally I'd hit the mailbox just once a week, endure the bills and sift the flyers, see who was trying to sell business to my fake business. But after meeting Kate in the park I obsessively checked the mail and phones at work and home.

Her invite called me out to a charity soup sale by some group called the Safe Sisters. Birth-control collective? Feminist satyagraha? No point inviting me if she'd been a nun (with that ass?). Across the back of the card she'd scrawled, *I'll be there, probably not running. —Kate.*

Wa-ha-ha-hell.

The Sisters, soup, whether or not to wear a suit to that bar—her card presented half a dozen questions and plenty to admire. In a stroke she asked me to reiterate my interest in her, clarified we'd be meeting in public, summoned me to her turf and, if the title was any clue, ensured that she'd be surrounded by other women. Protectors and audience both. Friends, colleagues, frenemies—they all get filed under *Female Audience*. With all this blood under the bridge, I truly wish the most accurate dispatch I've ever read from the gender wars wasn't some bitter-coffee

Euro-novelist's line that men want beautiful women whereas women want men who have had beautiful women. Sad but true.

And soup. Good call, Kate. She too was coming up on twenty-five and like me was probably graduating from heating food to actually cooking. It's pretty hard to fuck up soup made from fresh ingredients, and in September Windsor is just bursting with food. We sprout peaches, plums, and cherries, pop out so many tomatoes they're harvested by dump truck. We grow most Canadian vegetables, all with a fine carcinogenic mist from the epicentre of North American manufacturing. Detroit went from being called "an Earthly paradise" to "the arsenal of democracy." In Windsor, we paved paradise and put up a parking lot, a bar, *and* a strip joint. We've got our own modest symphony, but *the Windsor Ballet* has always been local code for our strippers. Strip joints in strip malls, several downtown, even one right off the bridge. Kate and her Sisters will tell you what we do and don't pay for with the local skin tax.

We're within a thousand kilometres of 60 percent of Canadian *and* American manufacturing, yet the thickest section of our Yellow Pages sells the world's oldest service/product. More escorts than car dealers, machinists, and boob-job surgeons combined. So many Sachas, so little time. Don't think this pimping is all underground. Law-student Kate founded Safe Sisters because even the municipal government was stroking a young back for a buck. City Hall took an annual licensing fee off every stripper and escort. The local titty tax risked breaking federal anti-pimping laws, so municipal staff were forbidden to provide info on STIs or sexual safety. Enraged (and self-interested), Kate started up Safe Sisters.

I was falling for a woman, not a girl. With Safe Sisters, Kate saw a winning combination for her CV: a genuine opportunity for social justice work and, by teaming up female law students with escorts and strippers, the near certainty of alcohol at all events. What newspaper editor (or law firm) could resist? In life before social networking, Kate had to tempt the local paper, not her own camera, to take photos of her, Safaa, and a few other law school friends. After one cleavagey article, a few flyers, and a simple, late-90s website, Safe Sisters was born.

All this to say the crowded downtown bar I walked into was thick with the smell of soup and drugstore perfume. Mason jars and Brazilian waxes. What a play. I had to impress her and her friends while simultaneously avoiding the trap of ogling a stripper or escort. Even the soups on sale would show her if I went for gaudy cheap thrills (cream-of-vegetable-something smothered in chalky Parmesan) or slow-roasted goodness (ginger carrot topped with roasted cashews).

No city can have this many Italian then Indian immigrants, a history of smuggling, and a nightlife industry that triples its downtown population without a few good tailors. I wasn't even twenty-five, and my pungent night job had me in a made-to-measure charcoal suit. At law school, her male classmates were reluctantly counting down the days until they wore suits for the rest of their lives. Personally, I was glad whenever I wasn't in paint-spattered day clothes or the ninja-wear from a 3 A.M. punt.

I walked towards her thinking I'd talk soup. *Any gazpacho? Is it cilantro good or cilantro crazy?* When I was two feet from her, a very lacquered stretch of bangs and nails walked her tan between us.

"Interesting friends," I wound up saying.

She leaned in, just a little, to clarify. "Interesting acquaintances."

In Windsor, we've always got an eye on the border.

A few smiles and cosmos later, she finally asked, "If you're Antony Williams and are self-employed, who's the Victor-Conrad of Victor-Conrad Painting?"

"Possibly my grandfather. It's quite a story. You free for a run this weekend?"

5. Sin City

NONE OF US SHOULD HAVE been there, not even Gloria. Windsor, Ontario. Bottom of Canada in more ways than one. Huron Church Road is a roaring line, six lanes of constant traffic right up to the bridge. One truck so close to the next we've got an escarpment on wheels. The Ambassador Bridge, the Ass Door, groaning with freight, pollution, and money. The most commercially vital border crossing in the world, and one of the busiest, yet it's privately owned—a billionaire's plaything.

Click here for a map. There's no denying that we're the crotch of the nation. Delta or prick, take your pick. Sin City as long as there's been a border. Across the river, the drinking age in Michigan is twenty-one. Just nineteen here. Another Michigan law prohibits their strippers taking it all off. Let me tell you what it's like to grow up in a place that gets American college kids drunk and their (part-time) fathers hard. And there's always the American Dungeon Expansion Administration sniffing around, parolling murderers and rapists to lock up pot farmers. The DEA's my reluctant patron, the unofficial sponsor of Canada's $7-billion-a-year weed industry. The export sales of our half-secret national crop exceed wheat and cattle combined, that jagged leaf a more honest flag. Pot's the drug of work, the 'burbs, dating, *and* the dinner party.

Despite all this, Mom stayed in Windsor. Or came back. Stayed on long after each of us stopped hoping for so much as a postcard from Trevor Reynolds, my sire. An educated single mother, a drama teacher, raising a male child. I grew up thinking that plenty got said, everything was out in the open. Other parents didn't tell their teenaged sons why they were teaching them to do their own laundry. But things were far from clear. Only after I joined the local industry and started rowing to

Cuba myself, dipping my oars into the profitable waters of untruth, did I see that Mom had been out on the river for years, that every parent is at the oars. Politically, professionally, and romantically, collusion, delusion, and illusion get us through the day.

The Detroit River: fifty-one kilometres long and often less than one kilometre wide, a pretty but terrifying shade of azure with refineries, factories, and skyscrapers on their side; houses, parks, a distillery, and a casino on ours. It's our side that's lit up, *CASINO* and *CANADIAN CLUB* signs all big red and electric, our nightly sales pitch to America.

A sales pitch on the water and a counterfeit on land. Approach the city for the first time, get off that groaning highway, and it looks like you're coming up on a busy cosmopolitan core. Towers old and new scrape the sky. Detroit's tubular Renaissance Center does its (subsidized) dance of steel and glass. Drive towards our downtown and you see Detroit's, our movie-set backdrop. Actually arrive in downtown Windsor, a downtown of parking garages, strip joints, and bars, and you see that even our skyline is fake. The tall buildings are all on the other side of the narrow river that is an international border, our line in the wet sand, my family cemetery. Take the bridge or tunnel across and you'll also see that many of those skyscrapers are now empty. Boarded up on the ground floor, any remaining windows blackened by smoke.

In North America's car cities you can still see a river making money. Detroit built many of its factories on the shoreline. Ship the gear by day, dump the pollution at night. Turn a corner in Windsor onto one of the many north-south streets running into Riverside Drive and suddenly the horizon, not you, appears to slide on by. The cargo ships, lakers, are two- or three hundred metres long. Boats so big you stop calling them boats. Floating islands. Rusty warehouses on the water. If you're reading this, maybe you agree: sometimes you move, sometimes your world moves.

The official Windsor-Detroit Tunnel was finished in 1930, the first international vehicular subway in the world. An engineering marvel for its dropped module construction and for ramming new air through every ninety seconds (not that the region has known fresh air since Henry Ford paved the family farm). Other, private tunnels were sunk as early as 1920, when the street price of one illegal bottle of whisky would buy a smuggler's next case. That's how Gran and ol' Bill made their pile. And one of their graves.

When Kate arrived in Windsor to study immigration law, she was shocked to find that community halls still existed. The Serbian Community Centre. The Teutonia German Canadian Club. The Windsor Irish Canadian Club (the building, not the drink). Multiple Ukrainian halls. The Franco-Canadians, the Scottish, and the Hungarians. The Canadian Friends of Finland, yes, all thirty-four of them. In Windsor, if they've made a buck and had babies, they've built a hall. Our Caboto Club's bigger and older than City Hall and was founded in 1925 (an auspicious year, you'll hear). To Torontonians like Kate, the very word *hall* was already an antique, never more than a short form for *hallway*. My inherited tunnel under the river, ol' Bill's tunnel, definitely proved to be more hallway than hall.

The one community hall we should have doesn't exist. Eighty percent of all the booze that entered the US during the thirteen years of Prohibition went through our city, yet no brick, statue, or plaque commemorates our wettest hour. With all that booze, all that money, my great-grandparents were the local norm, not the criminal fringe. Strap a single bottle to your belly or thighs, walk aboard the ferry, and you'd make enough to eat out for a week. That tempted *everyone*, and yet nothing around here celebrates the decade-plus of our twenty-six-ounce handshake. Mine wasn't the only great-grandmother to cross the ferry with bottles under her skirts. We've got the slippery touch in our genes.

After the official Windsor-Detroit Tunnel opened in 1930, Windsorites couldn't read or hear the phrase without smiling. Ten years earlier— when tunnelling was done with a shovel, greed, and courage, not an international agreement—police chiefs, priests, and sanctimonious politicians had nicknamed the whole area *The Windsor-Detroit Funnel*. Click back to that map. When we're not the crotch of the nation or its only stiff prick, we're a funnel. Booze from all across our country pouring into theirs at one narrow and populated spot. Glug, glug, glug. Women's voluminous skirts, false-bottomed salesmen's cases, cars on the winter ice, even a submarine cable car—whatever could move the hooch did move the hooch.

Many didn't bother to hide so far from the law, at least not on this side. During Prohibition (or, as my team call it, Prohibition I), it was legal for Canadians to export booze provided the gargle was legal in the destination country. America, no, but Cuba, Mexico, Peru, Bolivia, sure. And the guv enjoyed its cut, $30 million a year by 1930 (roughly $400 million today). When a single man rowed up to Windsor's government docks to buy a case and a permit, both customs officer and rower would agree Cuba, not America, was the destination. Right: a single man was going to row three thousand kilometres to Cuba in a small wooden boat. That he returned later the same afternoon for another delivery was never a problem so long as the feds got their coin. The officers weren't stupid; they were paid, legitimately. And with all their trade, new officers were hired. Promotions. Overtime. Same's now true for the completely failed marijuana prohibition.

You sleep with an elephant, you get on top or you die. Up front we looked needy to America, always noticing them more than they noticed us. But round back we were pouring it down their throats and grabbing cash by the fistful. We got the most powerful country in the history of the planet drunk for more than a decade, and you'd never know it from walking our city today. In a country of subsidized literature and museums funded by three levels of government, nothing commemorates our bottleneck handshake. Where's our smuggler's symphony? Our ode to the Windsor skirt of many pockets? Detroit's waterfront has a huge sculpture of boxer Joe Louis's fist. Where's our bronze bottle? We've got nothing unless you count the Right Honourable Prime Minister Paul Martin Junior's childhood home, the cash drop of former whisky baron Harry Low. The floor tiles and roof slates of a future prime minister's childhood home were originally bought with smuggling money. Kate hit the books at the Paul Martin Law Library not five hundred metres from a river carrying Paul Martin boats that dodged Canadian taxes, yet I was a criminal for moving a plant.

The Detroit River, our umbilical cord of industry. Hanging over it all is the bridge, shuddering with its constant load of trucks. Most nights at least one letter of the glowing red *Ambassador Bridge* sign is extinguished. When the entrance to the nation's hooker capital finally spells out the truth, *ass dor Bridge*, drinks are on me.

When I cross I still prefer the bridge to the tunnel. Despite the trucks and the danger of the bridge, nearly a billion dollars a day in trade tempting every nutter with a bin of fertilizer and a cellphone, I like the view. Get a little perspective on the river, that trough of chopping blue. Between the lakers I can almost see down through the polluted azure to Grandpa Bill entombed there in his lonely mud, bottles smashed around his soaking bones. The fucker.

6. Voodoo Unchained

WINDSOR. WHERE ELSE COULD YOU fall for a Scottish-Chinese Canadian? Kate Chan. Scottish father, Chinese mother, met in Windsor. When they split up, Father Scotsman returned to the motherland, and Mom took baby Kate to Toronto, changing her last name as quickly as she could. Bit of a pattern, that.

I could date her with a drug smuggler's wallet but had to hope this law student could look around the fact that, to her at least, I was just a house painter. She had rocked the LSAT; ostensibly, I rocked a roller pole. A self-employed house painter with deep pockets, but still. I wanted to pull out all the romantic stops from the get-go but couldn't tell her the most exciting thing about me.

A first date. The pre-date. The maybe this is a date, maybe it isn't date. What to do for the exhibition game? A drink or three? Sure, it's convenient and enabling, but if I'd wanted another bar girl, I'd have gone to a bar. A drink is too predictable, every dude's reliable grease. And Windsor wasn't big enough to have nice watering holes where we weren't certain to see people one of us knew. Time for Voodoo to earn his keep.

That's right, *Voodoo*. Part border collie, part attitude. (What colour is he? See, we're getting to know each other already.)

On the phone with Kate, I was instantly tipsy on the cello-y sound of her voice. "You free for a dog walk in Ojibway Park?"

The park was crucial. First and foremost, Ojibway is genuinely beautiful, especially in the fall. Every tube in nature's paintbox opened up. And more than just trees. Think grass but not that cancer carpet you kicked a soccer ball on. Seven-, eight-, even ten-foot-tall grasses, brown by June but standing proud 'til late November, countless stalks clattering in the breeze. And the trees are forest trees, not rakes of ordered pine. Windsor sits in the most treeless non-Arctic county in Canada. What isn't paved is ploughed. With its meandering, mulch-covered trails, the enormous park was a dog's delight, sometimes even frolicking ground for deer. The pumpkiny smell of leaves underfoot. Half-naked branches and tall grasses swaying in the breeze. All this, plus wingman Voodoo.

When Kate agreed to the walk, I pumped an unseen fist above my phone. "Would you like to meet me there or should I pick you up? I gotta warn you: in the car, my dog will sniff your hair."

All week I increased Vood's teeth brushing to get his breath down from dragon foul, then gave him his quarterly bath the night before.

She didn't dress as if nature required a hundred zippered pockets on easy-to-clean fabrics. Ass-music jeans and a soft sweater she was sure to show me was a V-neck before zipping up her vest. Her black hair was pinned up in half a dozen places, a flickering little movie of two crows fighting. The sight of her worn hiking shoes flooded me with interest and relief. For some, the Ojibway Park walk risked being too un-urban, no thump-thump music, no lattes. Not Kate. "Wow," she said when we arrived, "so this is what life outside the library looks like." She stopped to read a plaque I'd never bothered with that claimed the grasses around us were the last preserve of species that used to blanket the entire region. "From tall grasses to tall gases," she joked, and nodded at Detroit's Zug Island smokestacks visible above the tree tops. "Ojibway Park—right. The park's for the First Nations, while the local police force have scabs on their knuckles from the last time they got to write up a Driving While Indian."

When the three of us hit the large and shallow pit Vood and I called the Thunder Bowl, Kate spotted its doggie potential without a word from me. This leafy, dirt-walled bowl spilled down off the trail and was about the size of an Olympic swimming pool. Vood was rarely happier than when he was running in it, around it, or up and over its metre-high dirt walls. "Hey, dog," she called out spontaneously, "you run in here?" And they were off, all chase and feint, old smugsy me bringing up the rear. I didn't get proprietary and call him to me, just joined in the communal chase. I'll get you; no, no, you get me. Only when a panting, ecstatic Voodoo finally rolled over at her feet, her hands rubbing his traitorously exposed belly, did I too bend down and get a piece of Mr. Fluff. Our fingers repeatedly brushed each other's across his soft, white belly fur. We were closer to the ground, catching its mossy smell. "This is where you kiss me," she said, unlocking me with a grin. "Lightly."

7. (This) Ant Farm

NOMINALLY AND LEGALLY, IF NOT biologically, I'm Antony Williams, third-generation Windsorite. This much you may have been told.

Each generation, including the one that brought us here, Gran and ol' Bill, had its war. Peg and Bill started out English, grew up around Manchester, miners and miners' wives. Young widows and a lot of coughing in cramped company houses. The widow part proved true even on this side of the Atlantic. In the Great War, William Williams was a tunneller, a former Manchester clay-kicker exempt from basic training 'cuz Jerry was always digging through from the other side.

There's that scene in *Goodfellas*. No, not the garlic and the razor blade. One where he comes home from prison to an apartment he's been paying for but hasn't seen. Guy's been peddling inside. Decent bread, apparently. He's not in the apartment five minutes before he says, *Pack your bags, we're moving.* Swap the war for prison and across the Atlantic for across the state, and you've got Bill and Peg in pasty-faced England after the guns went quiet. Legend is Bill couldn't come home from thousands of men dying every day to slog out a life no different from that of his parents, didn't want to bring children into the same old mould. So across the Atlantic they went, all hopes pinned to the beaver.

Windsor didn't prove different enough, the automotive assembly lines too much like that insatiable, mechanical war or simply intolerable after it. In the early 20s, Ford personnel managers did evening spot checks on the homes of line workers. Bill had watched bloated rats gleaming with midnight blood eating their way out of teenaged corpses. After that, how was he to endure his employer inspecting his icebox and linen closet? Gran didn't just sit through all this with her hands in her lap. The same Windsor-Detroit ferry that smuggled in America's first copies of Joyce's *Ulysses* also carried my great-grandmother with bottles of whisky strapped beneath her skirts. When she showed Bill the money she'd been making, he quit the line and began digging a different kind of tunnel from their riverside basement. We'll get to that gold mine and grave in a bit.

Then we had our lost generation, Victor-Conrad, my brief, maybe grandfather. Peg and Bill's only child, raised big and strong on New World bounty. His meat-and-potatoes chest caught a bullet in WW II, though not before he supposedly left something behind with a French working girl. In 1946, Gran, already a widow and now mourning her only child, replied to a French curate's letter by sailing to France with a suitcase full of butter, nylons, sugar, and cash. Came home with a baby she had christened Gloria, her glory, survival plan for her grief, and legal if not biological heir.

The wars changed and so did we. Gloria, definitely my mother, possibly Gran's granddaughter, came of age in the late 60s beside, but not quite in, hippie America. Came of age on stage. In her early twenties, Mom was an actor. Don't worry, this isn't fiction: while she could eventually feed herself by crawling around screaming in tights one month then being fake British the next, she couldn't feed us both. Those who can't afford to do, teach, and Mom's been a drama teacher for decades. Half battleaxe, half den mother.

Every story's a detective story, though this memoir (or, indulge me, mem*wire*) starts out with a missing person or two, not necessarily a murder. Immigrant great-grandparents, a bullet-magnet grandfather I never knew, a stern but liberal mother with frustrated dreams, then me. After, of course, a little help.

Trevor Reynolds, sperm smuggler extraordinaire, was an American draft dodger who drove over the Ambassador Bridge in 1969 into a country that would make more art in a decade than it had in all the previous decades combined. Canada's supposed artistic coming-of-age was actually run by any Yank or Brit who could stand. Publishers, actors, editors, professors, broadcasters, journalists, and directors—anybody who could sign their name on a citizenship application got Canadian taxes to tell Canadian stories (however real). Trevor Reynolds was one of them. Actor, director, and a man who found that after he'd left a family and country once, it wasn't so hard to do again.

Then there's my war. Gulf War I? No, no room for small criminals there. Think globally; grow locally: the War on Drugs. Big difference is, those other wars all ended.

I can't separate starting from being able to start. I thought *catapult* long before I ever thought *catapult weed*. Okay, okay, no Cuban: I thought *catapult something to America* long before I ever thought *catapult weed*.

The word *American* didn't turn me into a tinkering little thing-maker. I was already in love with cause and oh-so-visible effect before the A-word got its paternal tooth into me. Show me how something works and my life changes a little. Growing up for me divides into loving moving things, making moving things, and trying to make things move to America.

On our early dates I couldn't tell Kate what little I did know about my sire (possibly fake name, criminal absence of rank, no serial number) without telling her about my science fair projects. Grow up the brown-eyed son of a blue-eyed single mother and you're a genetics lesson waiting to happen. And I'd always been crazy for science fair: demonstrable learning + independent construction + competition = Mmm-mmm-mmm.

I started in grade six with an ant farm, low-rent science coupled with childish narcissism. Antony's ant farm. But learning will sometimes get in by whatever door it can. Vanity may have taken me to ant farms, but wonder held me there. I'd grown up in a house without whiskers in the bathroom sink, had been the only one in two Williams households peeing with the seat up. Then suddenly I was copying out information about ants and their "division of reproductive labour," their "visible overlap of generations working and living together," the "cooperative care for the young" among "sterile castes" (like artists and pot slingers). I had various teachers and a teacher for a mother and suddenly understood them differently when reading about *eusocial breeding*. In eusocial societies, only a few members of the colony breed, yet every member of the colony shares in the parenting labour. At eleven years old, I thought I was copying out facts and diagrams about ants, not my fate. Gran the real-estate queen, Mom the educated parent, and their heir with his different coloured eyes.

Grade six, an ant farm. Grade seven, genetics. Grade eight, the first in a long line of trebuchets (they're like catapults). Notice that Treb. 1 came after a fight with Mom about genetics.

In the late 1800s, as England drew up the Canadian divorce papers it'd take a century to sign, the Moravian monk Gregor Mendel experimented with pea plants and tried to introduce the world to genetics. The world wouldn't listen to Mendel, but his breeding experiments were simple, reproducible by a twelve-year-old, and great ammunition in the family war.

Perhaps you grew up differently. If I wanted to row to Cuba, I'd say I found my values in even-handed play or by purposeful reason or enlightened common sense. As an adult, I've never shot the messenger. That's not true of my life as a kid, not when I had the messenger's blood on my hands and in them.

In tae kwon do, my only female sensei once gave me a koan-like version of *shut the fuck up*. One day when I was too chatty at the dojo she told me, "You're asking questions your body's not ready to understand," then showed me again she could break every rib I had, in sequence. When I'd first started asking Gloria, "Where's my daddy?" I'd been old enough to form the question but not old enough to really hear the answer. Apparently I was also old enough to learn that asking the question wasn't a problem. Until grade seven, I asked with words. Ultimately impatient with mere words for answers, I asked with pea plants and my own version (my first version) of theatre.

Every day I looked at my brown eyes in the mirror and thought of Mom's and Gran's blue eyes I saw the genetic laws Mendel found growing peas. *Pisum sativum*, dinner-table peas, revealed that species and individual animals also have internal and external borders. Even genes move to keep things whole. I sought knowledge and independence with *Pisum sativum* long before I did the same with *Cannabis sativa*. Really, I couldn't make this up. Even the ancientness of the name mocks our recent marijuana prohibition. *Sativus* means sown or cultivated. *Sativus* is masculine, *sativum* neuter, and *sativa* is feminine. Mendel may have worked with *sativum*, but my experiments were hardly neuter.

I now confess that the science fair setting was as relevant as the science itself. I made my confrontation with Mom on my stomping ground, not hers. Sure, she was the taxpayer (bit of a pattern, that). She was a passing acquaintance of a few of the teachers at my school and knew countless others throughout the city. But still, the science fair was at my school, not hers.

Kids are hardwired to love, to lie, and to steal. I thought myself scheming, not cruel, when I told Mom that my science fair project that year was going to be a surprise. Then I was tremendously scheming when I asked to photograph Gran's eyes a few days before I asked Mom if I could photograph hers. Remember the economic law that made my pile: scarcity adds value.

A few times that year I'd slept over at Nathan's when he was at his dad's new divorcing-man's apartment. On his token weekends with Nathan he'd rent us movies with explosions and silicone implants, barbecue us something on his balcony, and, as the empty beer bottles accumulated, toss us pearls of dating wisdom like, "Remember something they like, then invest. All women like money." One night, rather late and related to absolutely nothing, he muted the TV during a commercial and advised us to, "Fuck her best friend." Notice that Mom agreed to be my photographic model once Gran had already posed.

My project combined pea plants growing in Jiffy pots, some placards of dutiful prose (...*hybrids will show dominant parental character*...), a few diagrams with vectors and circles, and a family tree of photographs that still haunts at least one of us. Deep down I'd known the photographs might prove hard to live with. I didn't know how difficult they'd be to actually take.

You kids with your digital cameras savouring the memories of four seconds ago. I'm not so old/vain to suggest that the paper photographs of my 80s childhood were better. Presumably they pollute more than digital photographs do, and back then everyone snapped photos like ocean-raiding fishermen: take several, keep a few. But there was a pleasure of anticipation when photographs had to be developed. Logged in here, maybe you'll agree: when gratification isn't instant, your wants and hopes have time to clarify.

To accompany my pea plants, I tried photographing Gran and Mom's blue eyes and my browns, but I used my kids' point-and-shoot camera. I anticipated seeing more than just eyes in the developed photos but in fact saw far less. The thing about ignorance—you don't know *what* you don't know or even *that* you don't know. I'd seen countless close-up photographs in magazines: a raindrop suspended from a spiky branch, the legs of a bee coated with nuggety pollen. You can imagine the macro shots available over at Nathan's dad's. Close-up photos existed. Cameras took photos. I had a camera and wanted close-ups—*voilà*, yes? *No-là*. Mom drove me to the photo developers then endured my impatience as the film went off into its chemical bath. When we picked up the pictures,

I was crushed before we'd left the parking lot. My intended close-up photos of the variegated tissue in the irises of two eyes were just blurry gobs of possible faces.

Mom waited an afternoon before telling me, "There's a lot more to photography than just pressing a button." By the next weekend she had arranged a photographer to take the photos I wanted, photos which deep down I knew she wouldn't want to see. Emotional maturity is an oven, and nobody is already cooked before they go in. Also, I was drunk on what science calls "confirmation bias." It helped me ignore the fact that Ron, Mom's photographer friend, was no doubt being paid by her in some way. He was one of several stylish men she would collect at busy, productive times in her life. During her *Medea*, there was her director, Vlad. By her *Macbeth*, it was Alain, her designer. If they drove at all, they drove once attractive but now aged European cars. They had outfits, looks, a distinct lexicon of clothing. Small vests on this one, band collars on that one, suits and open collars for a third. Photographer Ron helped me speed away from my guilt by using different colour filters to heighten the blues in the eyes of two of his subjects (Gran and Glore) and the browns in a third (me).

Mendel probably discovered even more about genetics than we know. The vanity of his successor prevents the world from knowing. Part Medea, part Cronus, the new abbot who succeeded the deceased Mendel had *all* of Mendel's unpublished papers burnt upon his arrival. Picture the ashes of decades of paradigm-shifting research drifting down into Mendel's monastery garden, birthplace of genetics. What scheming bastard would be so destructive? A celibate one. My family and fortune know that inhibition and prohibition don't eradicate desire, they just make it more expensive.

My write-up didn't name the eyes in the photographs, just labelled them *Generations A, B,* and *C*. I was pushing boundaries, not trying to kill. And besides, this was science; impersonal, observant science. *The hybrids themselves produce offspring in which the parental characters re-emerge unchanged and in precise ratios.* According to Mendel, Trevor Reynolds's dominant brown-eyed gene gave me a three in four chance of having brown eyes. He was only one-half of my parentage, yet that same gene throbbed in me undiluted and (as you know) gave any child I have the same three in four chance of brown eyes. One drop continued to flavour the stew. I illustrated this combination of probability and heredity through my peas in their Jiffy pots, through blocks of data-heavy prose and, staring back at the viewer, an entrapping grid of family photos.

Each photo was just the eyes, a strip from above the eyebrows down to the tops of the cheekbones, an inversion of a cartoon bandit's mask. I mounted them in a kind of family tree. Where a fourth photo should have been I'd drawn a big question mark.

Gran's eyes

Mom's ——————— ?

mine

I kept that display at school until showtime. The night of the science fair, parents, teachers, and siblings milling around, Gran and Mom entered the school gymnasium still thinking their boy would want some ice cream after his big night. Not so after they saw that meathook of a question mark.

The photos could have been of any three generations, not even of the same family. In ways, they were just eyes, just colour and age. The two people who could spot my fiction within the science weren't likely to say anything. What I had called Generation B (*Mom + ?*) was really Generation C. Generation B was Victor-Conrad, forever sucking his bullet in France.

A decade later I'd better understand Mom's phrase "post-partum depression" for her enervated, doubt-filled crash after a play regardless of creative or professional success. More than just the stress of work and expectation hit her once a show was down. Change also came at her, but in a staggered, limping pace. That night at Science Fair, I was already starting to feel the PPD when Mom and Gran walked towards my booth. I had thought the project would show me more, get knowledge inside me and shake a few more answers out of Mom. But this was science. I should have known that what I wanted to discover was irrelevant to what I might discover. My sire and I had brown eyes, yet my readings and experiments hadn't moved knowledge of him forward an inch. For all my intrusive work with photos, the project was still just a mirror, and I already knew all the people caught in it.

Watching Gran and Mom approach, I suddenly wanted to shoo them off, call it a bust, retreat to familiar ground. Instead, I watched them read my displays, watched them look, watched their eyes return over and over to the cropped photographs of their own eyes.

Gran spoke first. "Very thorough, Antony. There's a place in my garden for those peas if you want to dig them in." When Glore remained silent, Gran glanced around the gym then dipped her oars a little. "Is that Masie Carruthers I see? Excuse me a moment."

Mom's lips were pressing down into their rage line, her nostrils sharp, so, well, strike or be struck. "These are his eyes, aren't they?" I asked. Defiance, not guilt, inflected my voice.

"Antony, someday you'll learn that asking questions is more of an art than a science." She looked me hard in the eye then walked off, pacing her way around another school gymnasium.

8. *Detroit Industry*

BEING IN LOVE IS BEING impressed. Leave your impression here. Arrive faster. Scratch my hidden itch. Be my gravity (my moaning, churning gravity). The L-word doesn't just mean you can't stop thinking *about* her/him; it means you can't stop thinking *like* her/him. When her brain slides into yours, when you think like someone else whether you want to or not, you're either in love or combat.

How to impress Kate, this high achiever with dimples that lit up when her smile shifted from fourth to fifth gear? I knew I was in trouble when I was haunted by parts of her I wouldn't normally think of as high action. Okay, yes, there was her chest, always, but also her long black hair a hundred times a day. The boomerang of her jawbone hit me on the way there and again on the way back. I could think of her smooth, endless back for an afternoon of painting, the way it spilled down into her hips but also paused at that planar triangle, neither large nor small, above the hips but not of them, that shovel into me. Mascara transformed her eyelashes into these black little frogs' paws I could watch dart around all day.

I wanted to hand her my best story, my golden fleece, yet this future lawyer couldn't afford to leave her fingerprints on it. I was just shy of twenty-five and made serious cabbage catapulting weed into fortress America. If only you could have seen me slinging the green. With the truck version of the trebuchet, I could fire my reeking load to catchers down near Zug Island then drive off in eight minutes. The back of my painting truck and some PVC pipes earned me a quarter of a new car every time I punted a load. Investment bankers aren't self-made men. I am. My trebuchet. My contacts. My (untaxed) pay.

Show me the non-geeky law student who doesn't smoke weed. Kate wasn't so young she'd be impressed by my breaking the law, but, secretly, I had independence in spades to offer. House painting wasn't exactly the best car in my showroom. For five solid hours of painting I'd go over and over the fact that I could not, could not, could not tell her about my punting weed. Then I'd fantasize endlessly about taking her out for a 3 A.M. lob with the trebuchet. I pictured her hair in braids beneath a black watch cap, my own opera Viking. I wanted her to feel the infectious thrill of letting the treb fly, feel something I designed and made kick and pitch the quarter-ton truck it rested in. We'd feel bound together as we watched the load fly, catching a faint whiff of green instead of Zug Island's acrid waft.

Until I met her, I'd loved working in secret—Dr. Jekyll and Mr. High. I'd gotten the swaggering bad boy out of my system selling loose joints to the American bar pilgrims as a teenager then learned discretion from dealer/lover Claire. With Kate half in my hands, humility and silence only seemed admirable in the gentlemanly abstract, not in the competitive day-to-day. How could a bright, achingly gorgeous law student with dimples that lit up like she was spitting a hundred dimes want to date a house painter? But I could not tell her about the punting—for her and for me.

I wanted every inch of her. Hour after hour, our mutual devour. But in my line, a rat was far more likely to get me caught than anything else. Loose lips sink ships and great-grandfathers. Feel flash, blab about your scheme, and you create a witness. Growing up at a supper table with Mom, conversation included gems like the fact that *Romeo and Juliet* is regarded as a "lesser tragedy" because the mechanism of tragedy is an accident. R & J are undone by a letter late in the mail, not an emotional outgrowth, not two competing desires held in the hero's sweaty hand. At sixteen, this was pork-chop conversation. Who knew it would also be prophecy?

I needed Kate to see I was smarter than the average bear. Bay Street financiers weren't the only people in the province who took risks and won. I desperately wanted to tell her, only her, that betting on yourself and winning is the second greatest feeling in the world, maybe even the greatest if you count how much longer it lasts.

At first I simply bought more time. You hungry? Let's pop into Grill, my treat. Bottles of lacy, chewy red every time she turned around. A kitchen gadget here, some roasted nut, bunny-loving eco body lotion there. The CD she liked at my place on Friday would be in her mailbox by Monday. It probably would have been cheaper if I'd just bought a lingerie store, not all that biweekly gear. Some nights I'd arrive at her apartment with a whole date of gifts. Roasted organic garlic and a pinot swirled into that spiralling MOMA decanter. A baguette younger than the day to be smeared with St. André (don't live too much longer without trying this: is it cheese or is it butter?). And of course a finger of organic indica for an appetizer. Smoke that and the whole world's pressed to your tongue.

I tried to let all my non-smuggling attributes stand a little taller. Not just the money but the independence. The free thinking, the eclectic reading, my painting days full of audiobooks. And with Detroit, we had a second chance for a second date. The second date is a lot like the second song on a CD. It has to be everything the first one is, yet more. Higher energy but also more latitude, casual elegance. Those early dates, you dress so carefully, wash clothes two days in advance, wipe the dust off your ironing board, all with the hope of tearing each other's clothes off. But how was a house painter supposed to compete with future lawyers? They had just twelve to fifteen hours of class a week. With painting and punting, I sometimes worked that in a single day. I had to hint about the math, indicate but never state that her classmates were advertising potential wealth but actually spending credit. These future lawyers who propositioned her daily, yes, they were eventually going to make money hand over fist (smooth hands, unscarred fists). But how many of them were actually going to run law firms? The world has employers and employees.

I was general of a gift army. Books that would make her want to curl up with me for a half-dressed hour. Nothing Canadian, obviously: no sex please, we're *fake* British. Get the ladies books, the right words, get them where they think and feel at the same time. If she loved a novel I gave her, she'd eat it up, would ban me from speaking while she finished it at the other end of the couch. With the novels, I was definitely my mother's son. I'd grown from being read to by Mom to reading to her to reading beside her. Eventually I noticed that books allowed Gloria to be alone but not lonely. With Kate I knew, but couldn't quite say, that if she were to date a law student, odds were better than not she'd find a TV in the bedroom, not novels, a TV bought on credit. She may have been fine dating a novel-hungry house painter when it was just the two of us, but no woman dates an island. I had to go the dinner party distance.

We needed another big date, not just a communal read, more than just another bottle of wine and wandering hands. Where to go in Windsor if you really want to impress someone? One afternoon I called her from a job site. "You can cross the border, right?"

"I'd be a pretty fucked up immigration lawyer if I couldn't."

Detroit, plague city. Pockets of action amidst long stretches of blackened chaos, buildings abandoned or razed to the ground. People actually walk around on our side, multi-ethnic shoppers during the day and white drinkers at night. Our downtown, undeniably smaller but fattened by American coin, is centralized, one playground of sin. They have boarded-up or burnt-out nineteenth-century mansions abutting empty lots or chic new restaurants. There's no such thing as an empty lot in downtown Windsor. Every purchasable metre is a parking lot to some degree, even just a guy with a flashlight, a plywood sign, and a pocketful of bills. Anyone walking in Detroit is either moving from building to parking spot or is wiped-out poor, almost certainly homeless. Our downtown is surrounded by short blocks of run-down houses, slack-jawed aluminium siding, plastic toys, and rusting car parts littering four square metres of overgrown lawn. But they're still homes: roofs, running water, shelter from the river wind. Not Detroit, where you see the homeless every time you cross. They shuffle or push shopping carts past steaming sewer covers. I'm half an engineer and still don't know why Detroit sewers steam and ours don't. Even Canadian shit's self-effacing.

Detroit doesn't just have abandoned buildings; it has abandoned beautiful buildings, the world's best architecture of the 1920s. Before it sat empty for decades, the eleven-hundred-room Book Cadillac was once the tallest hotel on the planet. When the car-body Fisher Brothers gave Albert Kahn a blank cheque and carte blanche to design their headquarters, they were part of the betting pool that picked Detroit, not New York, for the capital of twentieth-century American commerce. All that decadent architecture from between the wars, Art Deco's last, glorious gasp, was lost to social failure in half a century. Throughout the smoking city, custom-made chandeliers were sold, abandoned, stolen, smashed, or left to fall unseen and unheard into marble carpeted with dust. Hand-carved marble balustrades and curlicued wrought-iron railings now protect, present, and divide nothing more than fetid air. Decadent hotels now decay, the Fort Shelby, Lee Plaza, and the train station's hotel sit empty in a city with ten thousand homeless. The same city that launched not one but two postwar musical sounds, styles as diverse as Motown and techno, now has theatres with perpetually fallen curtains: the National, the Adams. Office buildings officiate only dust and crack deals: the Kales Building, the Metropolitan, the Farwell. Every other Detroit building is the architectural undead, neither dead nor alive. When the wind is up it blows through their smashed-out windows, stirring an elegiac howl for siblings lost to the wrecking ball: the Statler Hotel, the Madison

Theater. When Stalin was dynamiting churches for intellectual progress, Detroit was doing the same due to social ruin, St. Cyrils and Jefferson Baptist lifted unto heaven with a blasting box.

We were both stimulated by that jagged landscape of failure, the flush boom and charred bust. For our first trip over, I planned the datiest date ever. First stop was the Detroit Institute of the Arts, that escaped former tsar now huddling among the crack houses. The DIA has the best Van Gogh collection in America. His self-portrait with the corn-coloured hat is held hostage in the ruins. They've got a colour drawing Giacometti did of his wife that is the very picture of love—adoring, respectful, and slightly terrified. Most alluring for us were the Diego Rivera murals.

For a big date, we didn't go to Windsor's art gallery. When the Ontario government finally admitted they couldn't keep their hands out of gambling's busy till, they permitted one then two casinos, Windsor and the Rama First Nation (because Ontario cares). When the casino company (American, of course) needed to jump into temporary Windsor digs while they built their custom gaming house, the old Art Gallery of Windsor was an obvious place to start. On the water, broke, needing both cash and exposure, the AGW was handsomely paid to be temporarily relocated (to a mall, how Windsorian) and got coin for a new building. Shortly after all the international, interpersonal, Kate-Antony dust settled, one of Canada's newest art galleries was built to stand watch over the river not far from where the local rowing team used to line up for their crates of Cuba-bound whisky. Architecturally, this may be why the new gallery has a glass boat sailing through one side and out the other, (another) bow bound for America.

Date number two wasn't going to be at the Windsor Mall. Plus, I had a quasi-religious relationship with Diego Rivera's *Detroit Industry* murals. When Kate and I strolled into the DIA's Rivera Courtyard, with its painted, thirty-five-foot walls and numerous skylights, I stared up at Rivera's sprawling, living machine for probably the thirtieth time. I was just eight when Gloria first took me to see them. To my surprise, Kate was a Rivera virgin. The skylights and Rivera's metallic palette give the room an aquatic light. Kate treaded water then finally dove under.

We didn't speak for at least fifteen minutes, an eternity on an early date. Surely couples go on art gallery dates because, unlike at the movies, they can look at something but still talk. I cut her all the slack she wanted, her spine stretching in front of one wall, my chin climbing up another.

Like this memwire, the four painted walls of the room are undeniably linear in ways—one wall flowing horizontally into the next—yet each is also layered vertically, a strata of industry and human life. Ford's iconic assembly lines pulse with undeniable vitality. You gotta keep the line moving, keep it whole. Suspended rows of inert steering wheel columns lend depth near unattached car doors that roll as linearly as the boxcars of a train. Shafts and blades of orange and red sparks fly off whirring grindstones to occasionally brighten the sallow-faced workers in their drab aprons. All this beneath images of the body's own assembly lines. High on one wall, scientists in lab coats and masks hold up test tubes, while on another a baby swims in paisleyed utero.

I first saw all of this long before I'd met Kate, and it was in that same spacious gallery courtyard that Gloria had told me how, where, and mostly why Grandpa Bill had died behind us in the river. When Glore drove us back over the bridge Rivera's workmen lingered behind my eyes as I looked down at the alien blue of the industrial river. I imagined Bill entombed and Gran riding a ferry with a skirt she hoped the law wouldn't raise. Halfway across the bridge (in suspended, international air) Mom knew what I was thinking. "Always remember, Antony, he didn't have to die."

In the date I'd planned with Kate—gallery, followed by drinks and paninis followed by a trip to a record store followed by another drink— I'd thought I might reach for her hand and maybe more, get some gallery hip, a little polite ass. But after twenty minutes in front of the murals she grabbed my hand like she was falling off a cliff. Hers was no faux-accidental brush of the fingers as each of us crossed from one wall to another, no delicate interlacing as we stood, heads canted for quiet talk and steady wonder.

She'd been living in Windsor for more than a year and could have been to the DIA any number of times, alone or with another stubbled schemer. Apparently not. She put a hand to my arm. "No one, including me, has brought me here." Her eyes roamed the walls constantly.

We circled and circled, stared and shared. In the middle of the room we sank to a bench to sit beside each other but facing opposite directions. I told her about my family, what I'd been told in that very spot. After she emptied her lips of mine, she looked me in the eyes. "Get me home."

9. Trevor Appleseed

PATERNITY IS ALWAYS A STORY. Ask the Bible or every other Victorian novel. Subtract dad, add story (the ol' shell and Mendellian-pea game). Paternity is something you get told, not something you feel. Not in the beginning, anyway. (And, for some, not ever.) All those monthly cheques written because of paternity: contracts, petitions, detention lines. A woman feels maternity, lives it. If science doesn't tell her first—little chemical strips changing colour, a positive sign coming up whether it's positive or not—nature eventually will. The sore breasts. Darkening areolae. Dizziness. Morning sickness isn't a cliché to the person running down a hallway.

When you're the child of a single mother, you don't ask immediately. Babies are animals long before they're linguistic, mewling birdies in the nest, membranous little things, the hair like a stain dripping off their cantaloupe skulls. A baby fresh from the oven will open its mouth reflexively, regardless of who's holding it, the will to survive written in the rooting little lips. Every baby needs a tit. It might, *might* benefit from a father, Mr. Errand, Mr. Stockboy, possibly Mr. Provider, but it needs a tit to survive.

I have a few memories of life from before I started seeking (inventing?) my own paternity story. Kate, not me, put two and two together and realized that Gloria had enrolled me in taek just before I'd start to get teased at school for not having a dad. We were both single kids of single moms and traded stories about those early years when we hadn't even thought to ask about Dad Vader. You don't really care until around the age of five, when you're at school, when other people want you to care. Between three and five there was no trauma in the questions, and I have zero complaints about how Glore told me about Trevor Reynolds.

"Where's my daddy?"

"You don't have a dad, just me."

"But who was my dad before?"

Really, she was great about all this, would set her book down or pause scrubbing something in the sink to look at me. She didn't even cast blame (that bit isn't so saintly: she just waited until blame could cast itself).

"Your father and I separated before you were born. This family is just the two of us."

"And Gran."

"Right, and Gran."

For a while, that worked. But by six it all snagged on a single word. This story wouldn't exist if one adjective was very much not like the others.

"I want to go see my dad."

"Antony, you don't have a dad the way some kids do."

"Well, where is he?"

"Nowhere around here. I haven't seen him since before you were born. He left without telling me where he was going. I'm sure eventually he went back to the States. He was American."

America, the land across the water, a very thin strip of water. Eventually I'd put that narrow river to use, connect my history to the continent's. If you've ever had a toke, you've held the country's secret immigration in your lungs. Canadian pot, which is now recognized globally as truly killer shit, originated in imported strains of hairy American *sinsemilla*. That's Spanish for "without seeds," and for the years I knew her Kate loved the stuff. She taught me the verb *cornerstone*. "You know, when you want to turn a corner sexually but need to get high to do it. *Cornerstone* your way into the bonus tunnel."

Green-keen Kate loved all the matriarchal weed lore. Once as we prepared to smoke she said, "Such a human plant. When it gets ready to bloom the males grow balls and become useless, or a threat, while the females get hairy in the crotch." Later she contrasted the female marijuana plant to her Safe Sisters: "That rare single mother that doesn't need subsidies." Another time she asked, "If the valuable seeds were *masculinized*, not *feminized*, would it be so illegal?" At online seed catalogues, somewhere between the spelling and grammatical mistakes (ah, my peeple), you'll find two lists of prices. Feminized seeds are guaranteed to produce smokeable female plants, so they're at least double the price. This is a story of how I got feminized (at least for a while).

When it comes to weed, Canada's only marginally smarter than the US. Canadians spend as much on weed as we do on tobacco, though none of it gets taxed and most sales go into gang coffers. But here at least drug crime is just another crime. In the US, drug criminals, including pot farmers, are handled with all sorts of unique legal pressures. Minimum sentencing, no parole, sentencing by the prosecutor's office instead of a judge, and convictions for nothing, and I mean *nothing*, beyond someone's word against yours. Rape a woman in front of multiple witnesses, leave DNA smeared everywhere, and you'll serve much less time than if you're rumoured to have carried a bushel of green.

Cannabis has been tripping the light fantastic for as long as humans have been farming. The plant is ancient; its prohibition is very recent and as American as atom bomb pie. George Washington and Thomas Jefferson had hemp farms. Some say the US Declaration of Independence was drafted on hemp paper. Mind you, others say Rudolf Diesel designed his engine to run on hemp oil but was assassinated by the petro-chemical industry so they could co-opt the tech. These theories are usually launched around 4:26 P.M.

The US federal government has subsidized the growing of hemp or has even sewn it directly to make blankets or ropes during the war *du jour*. Once your start seeing the overlapping borders of prohibition and inhibition you'll notice that *Virginia* passed America's first marijuana law. In the 1600s, the virgin state required every household to grow marijuana.

Government-sewn ditch weed still grows wild in Indiana and Illinois, though industrial hemp and mind-bending smoke are about as much the same plant as a Pomeranian and a Doberman are the same animal. The mind-smoke has been illegal since the 1930s, and its prohibition is about as unflattering a portrait of government as you can find, ours and theirs.

In the 60s, Canadian hippies smoked American or even Mexican weed. Three decades later, BC Bud was trading pound for pound with cocaine, the grown on par with the cooked, raw lumber as valuable as finished cabinets. Contrary to the image of bountiful BC, our market parity of bud with marching powder is all a consequence of how lightly the gavel comes down out West, not soil or climate. North Americans chase BC Bud as if it's the product of the sweetest growing spot in the world, as if every stone has a *goût de terroir*. Fact is, most of the export crop is grown indoors. *Goût de* basement. *Goût de* closet. *Goût de* the one place in Canada where judge after judge doesn't hammer the gavel over green. A pot bust in Canada is an endurable cost of doing business. In the US, it's the end of your sorry life. Yet they, not we, have the highest per capita consumption in the world.

During the Vietnam War, Canada became home to a different kind of American Green Beret. Draft dodgers brought pot seeds, grow-how, and a crucial dose of chutzpah to a Canada that had been importing, not yet growing or exporting, its marijuana. When the war was over and amnesty finally declared for its resisters, some of those hippie farmers went back to the US; their strains, me included, didn't.

Confession No. Something: I like my drink, a bit of the Windsor lifeblood. If I absolutely had to choose forever between my vices/ birthrights, it would be drink over pot. A bottle of wine is the fuel cell of dating. With smoke, you're high in four minutes. What do you do for the rest of the date (other than listen to the best CDs you have and find something else to put in your mouth)? But still, I like to talk *while* stitching together my buzz, not just after. If nothing else, and this is reason enough, I'd go with the sauce not the green, even though weed's better for me, because I can read with a glass beside me. Judging from the length of this memwire, apparently I can type with a tipple as well. High, I just want to feel the rusty texture of a guitar line, do spontaneous yoga or make dubious combinations in the kitchen. I absolutely promise never to make you my guacamole fettuccini.

Another picture we need to reframe. I say *Johnny Appleseed* and what do you see? Classrooms all across America—and Canada when teachers are lazy and/or bending a knee south—hand out colouring sheets or pictures of Johnny Appleseed sowing apples all across the New World. Striding around barefoot with a bag of seeds (bit of a pattern, that), he brought sweetness to the land. True, but the apples were for hard cider, not eating. Johnny Appleseed was the first liquor baron of the New World, not a wandering farmer. Ah, lies in school. Any more questions on why I sling?

No matter what they spend on their war on drugs, another of their false wars, their rich-get-richer wars, we will win. They win battles; we've already won the war. Every dollar spent on prisons and workplace drug testing is waste, vicious waste. Never, ever forget that we could be beautiful. What we spend on guns and prisons and big-dick missiles could be spent on the mind, on health, on the future.

"Exactly," Kate eventually replied. "Spend your money on the future."

I'm trying, girl. I'm trying.

10. Rolled & Ready

NO SINGLE EVENT LED ME to the green. Just growing up really, growing up where and how I did. This punctured, hybrid, half-dead, and half-rich land. My family of rowers and bounders. The end of faith in government (by everyone). As a teenager, getting then quitting a job in the fast food industry nudged me along—pocket money for treb parts plus a long, greasy look at the McIdiocy we all bankroll. Reading helped. My genes on both sides. Plus the education at Mom's knee, not that she'll admit it. She claims to condemn what I do, but our holiday meals were at Gran's, a riverside house built with smuggling money. Italian marble floors and walnut wainscoting, all with the sound of the river nibbling our ears. (Plus Zug Island up the nose when the winds weren't kind.)

Windsor's downtown is a mouth, an open mouth. Bar, parking garage, bar, strip club, bar, falafel joint, parking garage, bar, casino, bar, bar, strip club, bar. All take, all sell. Indignity at night but a pocketful of cash come morning. A wet mouth, our oracle at Delphi. Downtown tempted me away from the treb at thirteen then sent me back to it at sixteen. On a weekend night, our population increases by up to three thousand people, everyone there for a vice, drinking, gambling, or whoring. There were a few non-licensed oases for the underaged, cafés where my teenaged friends and I could watch, endure, or deride the American herd. In January, you'd see visiting American girls in open-backed shirts smaller than handkerchiefs shivering in line outside a bar. C'mon. Jess, the first girl I liked more than just sexually, was a bright girl with great hips who really got me by snorting, very audibly, as a pair of these frozen bar girls clicked by in their heels, backs cut open by the cold night, skirts the size of belts. Jess was wearing boots and a toque, cool boots and a darling little toque, but still, boots and a toque for January. Later that night she slid my hand under her sweater and she was warm, warm, warm.

Sixteen, seventeen, unable to drink in the bars ourselves but equally unable to not watch, not be there. Eighty percent of Canadians live in the 20 percent of land closest to the US border. Sure, that's also the warmest part of the country, longest growing season, cheapest heating costs, and closest to the big market, but still. Noses to the candy store window. Maybe our loyalist blood keeps us close to the border, all the former Americans who came up glancing back ASAP. When we glance back, my team turns into pillars of green, not salt. Was Trevor Reynolds still glancing back? Or maybe, once in a while, glancing north again?

Downtown Windsor on a teenaged Saturday night. The official border stretched out behind us and other, unofficial borders were drawn all around us. We stood a little closer to the candy store, had one foot in it. And we were overrun with candy shoppers, sticky fingerprints on our glasses and Sachas. Too young to drink, too bored or incomplete to avoid downtown, we were there most weekend nights as teenagers. Compiling censuses of derision, sure, but there all the same.

For decades now, every weekend night I've been downtown I've seen some drunk dude, usually a blond, corn-fed Midwesterner, pausing in his stumble across the street to bellow at the top of his lungs. Invariably this feat of genius cracks up his dude posse, leather jackets, dental work, and misogyny yucking in the night. Four seasons a year in Windsor's weekend inferno you can cock an ear and wait, certain that soon enough someone will bellow out this half-local mating call.

We heard the idiocy and saw the industry. Every downtown block had its mega-bar. SWAT-team bouncers, a coughing smoke machine, rapier lights. When you're on the outside of that looking in, watching cash get pulled from the small pockets of tight jeans, all that can make a thinking teen question alcohol. If you have to huddle behind a back-alley power transformer to chase your buzz or hide in the shadows around the abandoned armoury, why bother with bottles, glasses, and all that gear? Why spend twenty-five minutes to do a job with cumbersome liquid you can get done in five with some herb? I'm certain more Windsor teens choose this same route in the molecular garden of forking paths, THC not -OH, precisely because of the weekend carnival. Go figure if a few of us turn pro.

What words do I use to describe the first joint I sold, the first September night Nate and I cruised the bar lineups muttering, "Joints rolled and ready. BC Bud. BC Bud"? *Eventually* isn't adequate. I didn't just *eventually* start selling. Jess and other friends had grown up with the same sham borders. They didn't *eventually* start slinging. And *change, change* is also too small. My first pre-rolled stroll felt like I was chopping off a finger, not just changing. Chopping off a finger then gaining a whole other hand.

I lost my literal virginity two months after I popped my criminal cherry. There was no condom involved in my selling, and I could do it for more than ninety seconds. Well, no rubber condom. There isn't a day goes by I don't thank Mom, at least mentally, for enrolling me in tae kwon do at an early age. If you think of the taek as a tool, or, let's stay the oars, a weapon, then I've used it all of once in my life. But every day I've used the feeling that the tool is there if I need it. And I'm not overstating my protection. One of the big lessons in any martial art is that there is always, ALWAYS, someone else who can kick your ass. Someone faster, more fearless, or more gifted in the hurt. You feel that in every tournament, a smell stronger than B.O., soul knowledge. But of course those high priests of the hurt generally weren't out drinking on a Saturday night. The crowds were fine. My problem was Jess.

I conceived the Handshake of Nations plan and was arguably my own best defence, but still. I wanted a partner, someone with my back. Nathan was large (which matters visually but not practically), less clever, and, in the beginning, not a chronic pothead. But in Jessica's eyes, he lacked one crucial qualification: he wasn't her.

Happy Weed versus Fight Juice. I knew (then) not to go anywhere near the casino. Aficionados of the Windsor Ballet also had zero interest in an introspective drug, so we ignored the strip joints and concentrated on the Monopoly board of bar lineups with its cash-fat Americans impatient to chase a buzz. Our product also had another advantage: what white boy can dance without weed?

Back in the early 90s, a gram cost $15 Canadian and would yield three decent joints, no blunts or cones, but not all pinners. We'd sell each joint for $10 US. This was before the oil patch wars had bankrupted America, so $10 US was $14 Canadian. One joint to cover costs. One to bankroll the next g, and one for profit. That should have meant that getting ripped off over a single joint didn't matter, though of course by the end of the first night money was only part of the glow from my green lantern. "Pot rolled and ready. BC Bud. BC Bud," we'd mutter, prepared to say *Kelowna Hydro* or *Okanagan Valley* about our Brampton Closet green. Good product, good service, but a little Cuban in the pitch.

More shameful than the marketing was the wigging. I knew the TV word *wigger* long before I ever read my Québecois quarter-countryman Vallière's phrase "white niggers of America." Sell drugs in the age of TV and you sell counterfeit blackness. Our bars were full of white kids up from as far away as Ohio. Whitey was on a tear, and oh the fake blackness this created. Nathan'd say, "Handshake of nations here, brother. Cash to me and product from my man." Every handshake was choreographed for the Hollywood ghetto. Oullette and University became our Compton, our El Barrio. Just saying hello, Officer, being sociable and all. A vertical bumping of fists with the Ohioans, one potato, two potato, or some slides and pulls of the flesh, a bill or a pin tucked beside the thumb.

You might do something (or someone) once out of curiosity. Twice is an investigation. By the third time you're at a crossroads: is this who you want to be? The first stroll Nathan and I did with loaded pockets was a lark. Six joints on a warm September night. Could it be done? We sold out in ninety minutes, and other friends were nearby as soon as we walked off work. Steven, Emil, and Adria lingered at a café table with a fuming Jess. Being night muscle generally isn't the best way to impress your vegetarian, ad-busting, Blackspot boot-wearing, sometimes maybe hook-up girlfriend, but I had secret money in my pocket and a new high under my wings.

One of the fundamental facts of the bud business—excuse the obvious—we were outside the law. There was no police or Better Business Bureau for us. That was oh so clear as we tinkled a different kind of ice cream bell up and down the bar lineups. "High sticks. BC Bud. Loose jays." Cash first, no exceptions. Many a frat boy wanted the deal otherwise, all liquored up on Jaeger and stronger beer. "No, no, no," Huey, Dewey, or Louie would say, "we get the product first."

"Look around, Magellan. We've got more customers than you do suppliers. Buy or bounce."

But Jess was right. All of that was unnecessarily risky, each transaction too close to a cop-summoning brawl. Genuine accounting concerns what to measure, not how or when. Out there in the No Assholes Land between the cops and the bouncers, we were risking everything, including a stomping from three different directions, all to make $7 each. The bouncers were the biggest, the customers almost always drunk and in groups, and no one fights as viciously as a cop, all that sanctimony and self-mythology coming at your ribs. (Two things about bouncers: one, empirically, scientifically, muscle size does not necessarily indicate muscle strength. And two, no matter how big a guy is, he has a nose, and it's a blood faucet if you can open it.)

Jess almost got me. "Why do you only ever seem to proposition assholes? Make money or pick your little fights. Don't do both."

"A customer's a customer," Nathan claimed, half-satisfying me.

"No, every customer is a risk," Jess shot back. "Choose your customers. For a start, you should look for couples, not packs of guys. As for looking for smokers, just find the people with the best shoes."

If we'd been selling in Vansterdam (aka Bongcouver), we would've had to worry about getting stomped for selling on someone else's corner or having to protect our own. In fact, our first and only competitors were the very friends we'd left behind. Next weekend Emil and Steven strutted around saying, "Unbleached paper. Get high and don't die." Not to worry, theirs was a passing thing. Nervousness was written all over Emil's face. If he kept it up, someone was going to read it back to him.

My hands did little more than float in front of my chest for two years selling weekend street weed. The only nasty thing I ever had to do was pose a question. Eventually one frat fuck thought he'd try to give me a shove, a posturing move which happens to be the dumbest way possible to start a fight. Hey, shove, I might hurt you. I answered by sweeping both his arms aside and tugging his own shove forward so that he half-fell across my raised knee. I tapped him, literally tapped him, on the back side of his exposed ribs. "How hurt do you want to get?" I let him hear me breathe, fuelled the sweep and set with a very trained exhale.

Whatever we were becoming, it sure beat working at the mall. Nathan and I quickly graduated from smoking for free to making a little side scratch to increasing our profit margin. Buy in bulk and save. The first time we bought an ounce, we were half-terrified and half-elated at the sheer volume of the icky. None of our friends had ever bought more than a quarter of an ounce. Too few Canadians are completely bilingual with English and French, but most are fluently bimetric, switching between the imperial and metric systems without even noticing. An ounce, an oh-zee = 28 grams. (FYI, acting and painting majors, a "half-quarter" is an eighth.)

Niche marketing. Customer satisfaction. Risk analysis. Accounting. Turns out the biggest surprises were in human resources. Sure, I wanted

Nathan there in the beginning, but my original 50-50 split on my own idea quickly became rebukingly childish. Big Lesson No. 2: management is vigilance, though I needed more watching than Nate. As a criminal, you've got to keep an eye on what adrenaline does to you. Our revenue and our profits kept growing, so I had to be careful not to race home and immediately dust the cobwebs off the trebuchets in Mom's basement. My self-inflicted resentment over the 50-50 split with Nate spared me any temptation to tell him about the treb, but it also meant I was even itchier to use it. And I was young. I didn't want to show him the treb, but I seriously considered showing Jess what I could do with PVC plumbing, physics, and smuggler's genes. And there, finally, I saw my own drug problem. Adrenaline either exhausts and terrifies you, or it makes you higher than your customers. Per hour, I'd have made more money working as a busboy at one of the busy Windsor restaurants affluent Detroiters feel safe enough to dine in. But jingling my green bell—that money was all mine, my paper valentine from the visiting Americans. No boss or official had any piece of it.

Who knows? Landscape alone, not politics, family, or history, may have taken me down to the shores of the river with a pocketful of green. Rivers aren't borders by accident. How did Julius Caesar announce he was promoting himself from general to emperor? By crossing a river, the Rubicon. His senate decreed that taking their/his army over the Rubicon was passing into treason. Caesar crossed that river then many others, most of them bloody. We know his name, not those of his senators. The Detroit River was my Rubicon, my family cemetery and half an altar. The lying, Cuban press natters on about *gateway drugs*. The Detroit River is a fifty-kilometre gateway. And grave.

11. (M)otherwise

WHEN POSSESSION IS THE CRIME, best keep the shit moving. My job involved juggling a female plant. Apparently I'm not so good at holding onto the ladies in life, either. At the end of high school, Mom unintentionally accelerated my street slinging, and ultimately proved to be as important in my career selection as border-dodging Gran or the straight-dealing Claire. Without Gloria's own American invasion, would I have become what Kate did and didn't want nearly a decade later?

Gloria, a tough freethinker who cries at dance movies. For a while during her self-appointed school campaign against uptalk—young people? almost always girls? making every statement sound like a question?—I foolishly tried to be their supper-table defence attorney. "Why can't they speak how they want to speak?"

"They can, but only once they've broken out of how they've been trained to speak. No one can want to sound so flagrantly uncertain."

At her high school, Gloria created a one-teacher campaign she called Down with Uptalk. She transformed a little brass desk plaque so it read *The ~~buck~~ uptalk stops here.* In Mom's class, if not at their parties, young women could finally protest the misogyny of hip-hop lyrics. She knew she couldn't win over the uptalking girls by herself and that many of her so-called fellow teachers would be less than no help (oh the church ladies with a B.Ed., oh the MRS grads). To win, she had to first win over a few girls, the right girls, and then, as in any fiefdom, have them police their peers. She'd pull an uptalker aside or send her a note. *Natalia, I'm certain you're bound for university and could, with application, aspire to any number of meaningful careers. Today, however, the intelligence of your comments on Juliet were undermined by....* She'd never go toe-to-

toe with the popularity queen herself: no one wins a land war in Asia. Instead, she'd go for a lady in waiting with a wart on her fanny. Not the brightest lady in waiting—too easy a convert and too easily resented by the others—but the ambitious one, Iago in knee socks. One converted uptalker would turn another down, and so on. No doubt she felt her ends justified her means (what else could?). Eventually I agreed with her and was proud to tell these stories to a Kate who once returned home from a Safe Sisters event groaning, "Nothing but thongs, Frangelico, and uptalk." As for Gloria's campaign of onesies, Kate was fine with the craptards when they were just a story.

If you want to see maternity leave in action, go to an Ontario public school. Their union has more members than some provinces have people. Their pension fund owns a chunk of the local shopping mall and the country's biggest newspaper. Unlike at universities, corporations (excuse the redundancy), and law offices, a public school teacher meets no quiet penalties for mat leave. Promotion isn't slowed or capped. Research isn't threatened. Seniority doesn't stall. So the broodmares waddle in and out.

The same conscientiousness that had Gloria never forget a teacher's partner's name (it's not so hard: she just keeps a list), littering hellos at Christmas parties and June barbecues, the very politeness that had her query correct spellings, allowed her to present pregnant fellow teachers with a custom printed onesie with a hyphenated last name stencilled on the front. An organic cotton, clay-dyed, eco-wonder with *Franzen-Carey* or *Griebel-Aitken* emblazoned across the chest of a baby she knew full well was only going to carry its father's name. These scorecard onesies may never have been worn, may have been a waste of time, money, and pollution, but not a single colleague returned one as inappropriate. Mom was the first to confess that she wasn't well liked because of the onesies. She was respected, and the few friends she had at her school loved her dearly, but she too was willing to pay for what she wanted.

Given her uptalk campaign and the damning onesies, how would you take Gloria going off to do an acting MFA during my last year of high school? She left during my last year or, as I really suspected, *for* my last year. It was a pre-emptive strike, of course it was. Oh sure, she wanted the degree—thwarted ambitions finally realized, better intellectual company, blah pension blah. But just as obvious was the fact that she left me the year before she thought I'd be leaving her, left me to fend for myself and care for Gran (watch where that one got her). To her, an empty nest was a theatre of war. I don't blame her for leaving; eventually you'll see that. Better still, I admire her. Best acting I've ever seen her do. Still, even Mom and I broke up in stages. For the first email I sent her in Chicago, I had changed the default name on my account from Antony Williams to Trevor Reynolds. She didn't say anything about it and, point made, neither did I.

In my second-last year of high school, mail from various universities began crossing our threshold by the pound. All that curling ivy and all those multi-ethnic smiles were just for me, right? The computer labs in the brochures never had the broken chairs, flickering lights, and booger-studded keyboards of real life. Young, photogenic professors at University X sat amidst a handful of students, while in actual classes his ESL teaching assistant stood at a microphone in front of four hundred paying customers. All that education sold with photographs of gyms and exercise equipment. The StairMaster, seat of learning. A few years earlier, a national news magazine had rescued its revenue stream by handing out an annual report card to Canadian universities. Their hard-hitting pedagogical inquiries are illustrated annually by a young piece of fuck on the cover. A new cover girl each year, all dental work and blowjob eyes. Her representation of academic life in Canada, with its chilly September-to-April calendar, usually includes a robust tan.

Until late high school my career as a mail recipient had been pretty limited, though not without potential. Until I was about ten, Mom and/or Gran always mailed me a birthday card from across the city. More than just a tender little surprise, these cards were designed to distract me from the one letter I waited for every weekday and prayed for constantly throughout the month of my birthday. Every day, day after day, year after year, I looked for an envelope with an American stamp addressed to me in Trevor Reynolds's phantom hand. By grade two, I already knew mail days from holidays. Oh, the wasteland of a long weekend. Return address or no, I wanted him to trace all the letters of my name. I clung to the idea of that thin hello.

When I told Kate of that aching young hope for a letter or a birthday card from a man I should have despised, found words so easily for this in our muzzy dark, she recognized that I wanted a letter because it was contact at its least confrontational or demanding, none of the awkward air or hanging silence of a phone call, none of the towering threat or paunchy disappointment, the balding, moustachioed weirdness, of a physical meeting.

No high-school student can think the pile of university mail at his door, often with his name misspelled, is sent to him as an individual. I got so used to these bulk mail-outs I assumed anything mailed to our house from a university was for me. The Chicago School of Fine Arts taught me (m)otherwise.

I swear my opening Mom's envelope was just dumb habit. But Mom had a point: being inattentive is hardly an admirable defence. Even pre-MFA Mom knew that habit is the enemy. Honestly (I think), hers was just one more envelope I opened while inhaling a mini-pizza after school.

Dear Ms. Williams,

We are delighted by your interest in the Acting MFA program at the Chicago School of Fine Arts, one of the premier art and performance colleges in America…

Whoops. The fuck?! Whoops.

Have that classic mixed lot of high-school friends—the rich kid, the muscular guy, the musician, the chick who doesn't eat—and someone will have totalitarian parents who open their kid's mail. Pure Stasi mind slap. Yet there I was, Mom's envelope open in my hand. Equal to my guilt was electric, protean shock. And selfishness. An MFA? What about me?

I was contrite, but I was also sixteen (and, you might say, male). When she got home, something leapt in front of my apology. "Looks like they've got the wrong Williams over in Chicago. I opened this accidentally, I swear."

"What, you *accidentally* thought you were me?" She hung up her coat, set down keys and bag.

"No, I just—well, it's a school. When would you be going to Chicago?"

"Ant, my going is far more a question of *if* than *when*. I'm just testing the water here." Finally she directed me to the couch in the next room.

"At its least attractive an MFA would increase my pay. Each and every year. That means more money now, more money ten years from now, and more in retirement." Uh-oh, a reassuring hand on my shoulder. "Canada has very, very limited graduate programs in acting. Why bother connecting our education dollars with our arts dollars? But listen, Windsor Community Theatre isn't exactly the best reference I can hope for. I have to be prepared to be rejected, especially the first year I apply. If I get to go at all, it's almost certain to be after you."

But what's certain?

12. We Safe Here?

WHAT COUPLE LIVES WITHOUT DRUGS? Alcohol, yes. And how does the day start? Coffee. The wake-up drug. The be-smart drug. It too was once illegal, vilified by a status quo nervous to see people congregating around the foreign coffee merchant's counter instead of the altar or flagpole. Behold the maddened eyes of the coffee drinker! Smell his demon breath! For years, Oxford and Cambridge students were forbidden to enter coffee houses. Students without coffee! Only when the increases in productivity were observed were the copy clerks allowed new stains on their sleeves.

Coffee is the official drug of work. What's the official drug of relationships? Used even more regularly than wine? For all the talk on those early dates, no question is more significant than *Are you on the pill?* You can get every stitch of her clothing off, have lowered, chased, or baited her body into every conceivable offer and exchange, be chased and baited, yet nothing reveals like this yes or no. With drugs, we are indisputably and quintessentially human, especially in this most animalistic of acts. Voodoo and I were never more clearly on opposite sides of knowledge versus sensation than whenever I had to shove a pill down his throat.

Are you on the pill? This information, the revelatory, data-rich syllable of her answer, a sliding yes or a grounding no, can be more arousing than anything in her bra or pants. I want to see here, here, and will you show me here? Let me glimpse your pharmacy soul. Show me which risks you avoid and which you're willing to take. I agree, the price of pleasure is always risk. No risk, no rise. Yet another drug to keep things moving, or whole. Or both.

In the early tumbles with Kate I was no smarter than my customers' customers. As with any drug, part of what you're chasing is a romantic idea. In my—forgive me—tunnel vision, I would forget that many women take the pill for regulation or now even to avoid the monthly carnage altogether. I'd hear a *Yes* full of slutty sibilance because that's what I wanted to hear. Delusion is always the meta-high.

For all the times I've stood in a grocery store lineup flipping through *Cosmo* (that primer for speaking Tramp), I've never once seen a poll or graph describing the context and location in which a man first asks a woman if she's on the pill. Much later in a relationship a very different question may get popped, but that first big question is usually dropped. Sure, it could be posed in a bar, car, or restaurant. Email might make it another digi-confession flying through the ether like this one. But I'm sure I'm not the only one who waits until the plane's taxiing down the runway before asking how high we're going to fly. *We okay here? We safe?* You get to know each other pharmacologically as you get to know each other biblically.

From what I've been told, I was less of an asshole than most about birth control. A few years before Kate, true, I didn't always steer so safely away from disease, but from pregnancy, always. I may have rattled the key in the lock a little first, but at least I'd ask. *We okay here?* In relationships, I'd suit up or pay for the pill. (How do women tolerate guys who don't?) Nothing could save a guy more money than paying for the pill, or half of it if that's the brand of Feminism™ going (though it almost never is). With Kate I wanted to do everything right, originally at least. I planned on the full, adult dating trajectory of latex, testing, then abandon, not its younger, worried inverse.

I loved those early dates with her. The weekend outfits planned all week. The polished shoes. Six months later we knew every shirt and sweater, each article of clothing from tip to toe. We'd watch clothes getting purchased, would wash, hang, and fold them, picked them up off shared floors. Eventually, I'd see all her shoes ranked in our hall closet, pairs of fighter planes grouped into formation on the deck of the aircraft carrier HMS *Taste*. But nothing compared to those early dates when each shirt was cut from whole cloth, each zipper an unknown pathway.

Foretalk, those early dates were all foretalk. The restaurants, the parks and wine bars, they all built up the sex, each declaration, question, and answer more wood for the eventual fire. But she wasn't planning her date underwear half a week in advance and shaving her legs every other day just to chat.

"Talking with you is so great I almost forget I want to kiss you." I meant it, I did, but it was also a line. Kate's Safe Sister Melissa confided that her strangest clients were the ones who tried to seduce her, who had hired her, she quickly saw, to build confidence. Again, all of this is different because of the Web. Melissa's clients found their pickup lines online, so she often heard the same ones repeated by big-bellied Nigel and skin-condition Paul.

Aside from keeping my green secret I was effortlessly honest on those early dates. In just a few conversations with her I was getting to say things I hadn't fully realized I needed or wanted to say. Only she understood my excitement about working for myself, even with the house painting: the whiff of the deal, the hints I'd drop, the hooks I'd reel in. Gran had cared, but family care is always a little proprietary or conscripted. On other dates I'd tell women that I ran a painting company and they'd ask what else I did. Right, like only concert cellists and neurosurgeons normally ever got a hand in their pants. And with Kate, I got to ask the question other students usually asked me. Why Windsor? In one of Canada's last lunch-bucket towns, citizenship is always a question. What do you get to offset the pollution?

"Toronto's fine," she said at the end of another restaurant meal. "I'll probably go back. But for immigration law I want to be at a border. As we sit here, van doors are being yanked open by jerks with badges and flashlights. I want clients who have more at stake than waiting a little longer in their Richmond Hill apartment."

And she didn't take any shit. When I mentioned Windsor smuggling Joyce's *Ulysses* into the States she said, "Admire the smuggling, not the writing." At last, clear-sighted honesty. A skinny American singer once described irony as "the shackles of youth." I disagree. Indecision shackles youth. Indecision or insincerity. Irony deepens with age. Everything gets layered. I wanted the whole layer cake of her. She could do the sauciest little grin, was curator of my lust.

Doggie Vood saw me off on every date, not caring at all for my exposed shirttail, V-neck sweater, and blazer combo. At first he wasn't exactly the welcome wagon when Kate slept over, wasn't above dragging a hundred-dollar bra back to his crate for a chew. Sexually, maybe even romantically, who doesn't envy his dog? Live with a dog and you see that they have just three reactions to other dogs: yes, no, or maybe. Fighting or fucking, they sniff aft, middle, and fore, twirl and circle about, and they let you know: I'll fight you, I'll let you sniff or see my crotch, or I'll leave it undecided for now. Why do we pretend we're any different?

Early on, clothes strewn from one end of her apartment to the other, smirched wine glasses and stubby little roaches smeared in candlelight, I was asking for more than just information, more than just that deepest invitation. *Are you on the pill? We safe?*

Yes and no. And apparently I wasn't the only one who realized it was question time. When we were getting ready to sleep one night I opened the drawer of her night table to drop in the little packet of green we'd been sampling.

She reached out and laid a hand on my shoulder. "You sell it, don't you?"

She'd finally exploded the underground mine she'd been digging for weeks, showed me where the charges lay, shook my muddy ground.

"Let's just say I know how it's grown. It's organic. It's not biker bud. I want that for you."

She rose up on one elbow. "Antony, you either spend every cent you make trying to spoil me or you make a lot more than a house painter should."

"Define 'should.' Do you know any other painters? I price the client, not the job."

But she reached up and sealed my lips with her finger. That might have been endurable, would have been just a smart future lawyer hedging her bets. It was the shake of her head that got me. A finger to my lips then a slow shake, side to side, a Kate eraser rubbing away at me.

13. McTreb

PART OF THIS IS A war story, and in war there's always a catch. Sometimes a feeling gives us a phrase and sometimes a phrase gives us a feeling. Catch-22—you know the phrase even if you don't know its war, Victor-Conrad's war. In our teens, we can't get sexual confidence without sexual experience, but we can't get sexual experience without sexual confidence. Kate really got me, stirred me between the shoulders and ears, not just the hips, with a simple little card, a scene of slashing Japanese rain daubed with red lanterns. All she wrote was: *I don't love you, yet.* Later, she amended it with a speech.

"No doubt we've both wasted the word in the past, used it on people who didn't deserve it. I'm not going to do that with you. I also hope, if love does bloom, I never say *I love you too*. If it comes, it's not going to be a contract, or an exchange. It's going to be admiration, respect, helpless attraction. I don't love you, yet. But, well, I'm knocking on your door."

The vixen. Half-love. Potential love. And a very adult admission of doubt. Catch-Not Quite 2 + 2.

At fourteen, you can't get a job because you don't have work experience, yet you can't get work experience without a job. Catch-14. Well, you can't get a job you like. Let she who lives without embarrassment cast the first stone. When I was fourteen and wanted parts or tools to build trebuchets, I signed on at McDonald's. I couldn't envision an improvement to the treb then not try it, and I'd outgrown doing extra chores around the house to earn a few dollars off Glore for hardware store money. One night over supper I announced, "I start next week at McDonald's." I hadn't mentioned the application or interview.

"Your first job, congratulations." After another mouthful she added,

"Wash your uniform after every shift. Grease and polyester won't be good for your skin." No questions about when I applied or who my references were, just a little salt in the congrats.

"It's the one off the bridge. I'll be able to bike there."

"Good. Good for you. Try to resist the free food, though. You wouldn't eat a handful of free get-fat-and-sick pills, so don't eat the food."

McRaunchie's. So easy to blame them, their chemical warfare of sugar and fat, their propaganda, but they're us. Everything they've done, we've voted for with our dollars.

Two weeks in I was already hoping it'd be the first and last time I wore a uniform, yet every month for fifteen years I could have gotten myself zipped into a prisoner's uniform. Those orange jumpsuits are freezer bags: you never come out as fresh as you went in. A decade after my McJob I also gladly buttoned up a valet's vest at Casino Windsor. *Uniform.* One form. In uniform, the soldier is no longer an individual, but one spoke in a mighty wheel. I wore a uniform to fund a trebuchet I had no clear purpose for other than touching America.

Don't let me sound naive, America=bad, Canada=good or even =all right. An early adopter on gay marriage, sure, but the tar sands and an asbestos export industry. And no Windsorite, not a one, is content to sleep beside the elephant without occasionally stealing his peanuts. Whatever water Mom and I have under the bridge now, I'll always treasure the second education she gave me at the Detroit Film Theater and the Motor City's pair of art-house cinemas. Classic film (Fritz Lang's *Metropolis*), French New Wave (*Bob le Flambeur*), international movies old and new, good and bad. A lush Korean guilt-fest or Kurosawa's *Throne of Blood*, that Japanese *Macbeth* (you'll see that one touched us equally). In Detroit, but not Windsor, we could actually see Canadian movies in a cinema. Kate and I caught Montreal bands in Detroit, not Windsor. I was never more my young self, yet also less so, a non-me, not me but just awed life, than when Mom took me to see a vintage print of

2001: A Space Odyssey on the big screen for my thirteenth birthday. If anything, that movie put me into the McUniform.

If you're wondering why I still live part of the year in Cancerville, even now when the money's clean, there's one answer: mega-city art (courtesy of the D) but Windsor housing prices. I first saw *2001* in a cinema, not on a TV screen, saw that bone club rising up and smashing down, a bone twelve feet long on a public screen, not twelve inches long in my living room. Bone=club, here we are at a space station. A-fucking-men, Brother Kubrick. Every tool is a lever moving something. The stirrup. The compass. Gunpowder. Movable type. The bicycle. Detroit's cars. People tinkering away, turning the old into the new, individual and species changing in the process. The personal computer. The pill. The hanging, half-public library of this Web.

In the parking lot after *2001* ended, Mom reached for my shoulders, each of us noticing how she no longer had to bend down to hug me. "I knew you'd love it." We drove home over the bridge. I was beside Mom, guide to my splendour, yet thinking as never before of a trebuchet's buck and swing. The air hanging beneath the bridge was international yet familial. Some of my genes might have been buried beneath the bridge while others had come over on it. Archimedes said, Give me a place to stand and I'll move the world. *2001*, my McJob, Windsor, my family, and especially Gran were helping me learn that if I could stand near a border, I could move the world's pot.

Normally Gran was even less likely to say something to my back than Mom was. In her late nineties, the woman was 105 pounds of scar tissue in a 110-pound body. She and Mom always fired straight from the hip. Only when Kate began complaining of Melissa and her "passive aggression" did I even begin to consider that aggression could be anything less than direct. Imagine my surprise one day when Mom and Gran dropped me off at work and Gran spat a wad at my back. Her timing couldn't have been accidental. "A uniform," was all she said, but she said it in the brief interval between my stepping out of the limomom and my shutting its door.

I heard and reheard that little taunt of Gran's while I worked the job for eighteen more months. Her poke and a history essay I wrote about the influence of World War I on North America's fast food industry eventually helped me quit. History teachers must lead exasperated lives, with 99 percent of their students not giving a damn about anything other than themselves or young celebrities. Worse than being in the other 1 percent of those who cared and were willing to work, I had scores to settle, empty chairs at the dining room table.

We climb a few mountains in life, and we're always different coming back down. Everything in my life to date had led me to that essay on the war and fast food, yet I felt so different having written it. Snakes and lobsters have something going. We too should shed our old skins. I quit the Mick by leaving a copy of my essay for the manager.

After I quit, Gran waited a week before she offered to pay me to paint her house. She let me stew a little, gave me worry before a reward. But I'd made her proud with every gob of dirt I'd flung in the essay about mechanization, centralization, and fake uniformity (of soldiers and meat, excuse the redundancy). What was Mom's big problem when she found out Gran hired me to paint her house? I called Gran as soon as Mom backed out of the driveway.

"She's on her way over."

"Of course she is."

When Mom got back home, I felt like the fuming parent for a change. "Why don't you talk to me instead of Gran about my quitting my job?"

"Family isn't business," she said, announcing some previously undiscussed law.

"You always hated the Mick."

"And I still do. But you should have replaced it with a real job, not taking your grandmother's money."

"One, I'm earning her money, not 'taking' it. Two, the place does need painting, and some splasher and dasher might rip her off. Three, isn't this between Gran and I?"

"Gran and *me*. No, this isn't just between the two of you. I'm between the two of you."

"What about all those burns you'd told me I'd get? What about the environment?"

"Work outside the family, not in it."

A good exit line, I had to admit. It didn't stop me from painting Gran's house, but it sure drew a few lines in the sand at Mom's. For a start, I bought my own painting gear rather than use hers. Splurged on the brush, cage, and pole, saved on the drop cloths and rags (thank you, Value Village). As unpleasant as it was, Mom's disapproval also forced me to second-guess that near universal delusion that I already knew how to paint. People all think they're funny, have good taste, and know how to paint. No. No. No. Anyone can get paint onto a wall, not everyone can do it well. With Gran as my customer and Mom as my critic, I took out books and videos from the library, perfected the W-method of rolling, learned how to slide then draw my brush. Tape was for amateurs. Eventually, we'd all have to wonder if Gran wanted me to work on her house to get to know it better. Maybe that was Mom's problem.

14. Family Pride

ABOUT TREVOR REYNOLDS. I'LL TELL you in the order I got told.

I could probably recognize four poems. The rhyming, hurry up and shag one; the rainy chicken wheelbarrow; Ginsberg's "Howl" (because of the drugs); and the Larkin one about parenting. Larkin's opening sounds just like talking and is bang on the nose: "They fuck you up, your mum and dad." Wisdom of the ages there.

Full-term single mothers, those alone, aloof, or abandoned from the get-go, have two to four years to rehearse answers to the question everyone's been thinking since they first slid into a pair of stretch-front jeans. For once, the cramming and the exam are far apart.

As parent, teacher, actor, and director, Gloria planned, planned, then planned some more. She did the groundwork and only then let spontaneity blossom. Trained intuition. With Toddler Antony growing up into a question, she rehearsed her lines, assembled her props, and waited for the inevitable but unscheduled showtime. Her MFA wasn't her only contingency plan.

For the start of her dad campaign, Mom gave me a child's illustrated dictionary and introduced me to puns. *The Book of Spells*, she called it, and showed me the difference between spell as a verb and spell as a noun. Har har.

By the time she sat me down for act one of the dictionary dad show, I'd already asked my way through the basics. *Who is my dad? Where is he?* Six years old, seven, I was graduating into the most explosive of those quick questions. I knew the when and was the what. To a degree, I had already learned the who. When Mom sat me down at the kitchen table with the dictionary, I definitely had no interest in the how. But even then I knew that the real question was why.

All of this one evening over the kitchen table, Mom, her props, and her plan.

"All right, Antman, let's see if you've been paying attention in school. Boats without motors are powered by…?"

"Sails."

"Sails. One point. A *sail* is a noun, a thing. And when we see sailboats out on Lake St. Clair, we say they are…?"

"Sailing."

"Sailing, right. A *sail* is a noun and *to sail* is a—"

"Verb, Mom. I know this."

"Then let's move on. Look up *dad*." She nudged the dictionary towards me. "Let's see whether *dad* is a noun or a verb. Just look for the little *n* or—"

"It's a noun." I'd interrupted her twice without reproach. That should have been a clue.

"Now look up *father*. A noun or a verb? Keep breathing, we're just looking up words here." Her hand encircled my shoulder, cupped its little ball.

The crawling letters and words marched straighter than ants. "Both," I finally answered.

"That's right. *Father* is a verb and a noun. A dad is someone doing a job, like a doctor or an electrician. A dad and a father can be the same thing, but look again. Sometimes *father* is just a verb."

Suddenly I was the only Canadian grade three student not in French immersion who would always distinguish verbs from nouns.

Mom dug library books out of a large tote bag. Little purple and pink flags marked several pages. "Here, look at these penguins. Sometimes in nature being a father is a job. Male penguins, they're dads. They keep the eggs warm just like the moms do." She opened another book. "And the Darwin frog carries the fertilized eggs in his throat. You like Darwin."

Even within this swirl—*dad, father, dad, father*—I recognized that "fertilized eggs" was classic Mom. I'm selling her short if I say that was Mom the teacher. There are plenty of lax teachers out there—union drones, babysitters, lifers. Not Mom. *Fertilized eggs*: her voice an excited label on a diagram.

More of her pictures. A snarling wolf and, nearly identical, a coyote, curled their lips high over gleaming teeth. "But honey, for many mammals the male does little, or little good, beyond impregnating the female. Even in a single pack, male dogs are not monogamous. They mate with various females and don't know or care which puppies are theirs." The next image was of two bears fighting, patches of gelatinous blood slick on their brown coats. "Male bears—sorry sweetie, this isn't nice—male bears have been known to eat their young. When a male lion fights for control of the pride, he usually kills the cubs of his rival. These animals father children, but they're not fathers to them. They aren't dads." She put an arm around me, but not tightly. "These fathers are just verbs. They don't make being a father their job."

I held one edge of a glossy page beneath my finger and thumb so I could curl and uncurl it, covering and uncovering the lion's roaring mouth.

"Antony, you can't ever, ever feel this is your fault. Your father left before you were born. That shows you that his leaving was all about him and had nothing to do with you. Your father wasn't a dad kind of animal."

She didn't try to hold my hand or ruffle my hair. She was beside me, breathing very steadily. Eventually, she rose to tidy the kitchen counter yet again.

"If a lion fights for what?" I finally asked, pretending to still look at the book.

"Control of the *pride*," she said, half-turning around. "A group of lions is called a pride."

Years later, for the kitchen table sequel, she'd show me an entire note, not just single words.

15. Who Knows the Guy

WITH MOM AWAY FOR MY last year of high school and my regularly being handyman over at Gran's riverside house, I stared daily at America and the narrow Detroit River. A castle market with a river for a moat. How could I move beyond slinging street joints? Mom hadn't been in Chicago more than a month when Gran broke her ankle. Suddenly I was there at least twice a day to carry her up and down the oak stairs. Looking out her windows, trying to picture ol' Bill's tunnel beneath the street and the park at river's edge—how to find a bigger dealer? The drug industry is feudal: prices drop and quantities rise as you climb the fiefdom, but you can only climb if the guy above you introduces you to the guy above him. In a secretive industry with prices inflated by the scarcity of illegality, who's going to do that?

I was about to graduate high school, but I couldn't graduate beyond slinging loose joints, a kid's game. Pot dealers aren't listed in the Yellow Pages. As for any Green Pages, you crazy? We don't write anything down and we've got better things to do with paper. Generally, it's a who-knows-who industry. And the business dialogue always starts in person, not over the phone. Plenty of meetings in large parking lots or abandoned buildings, cellphone batteries left behind. Click here for a *Time* article about the ECHELON project, the multinational surveillance effort that snaps to attention if your emails or phone calls include *jihad, Allah, bomb, infidel,* or *weed*. (What about *truth, beauty, wisdom*?) Look, I couldn't make this up: the software that runs ECHELON is called SIRE.

Version 6.0 of the treb was assembled and reassembled from PVC pieces that fit into the trunk of Gran's car. At 3 A.M. on Remembrance Day I shot a kilo of birdseed onto Detroit's Belle Isle (as Cuban a name as Antoine de la Mothe Cadillac's "Earthly Paradise"). Belle Isle wasn't very close to Chicago and who knew how close to phantom Trevor, but still. My payload hit an empty field in America. Unlike later versions that could be strapped into the back of my truck, Treb No. 6 had to be braced against the ground with giant U-spikes. Inserting and removing those took time. I knocked them in quietly before the shot then pried them out in a frenzy after touchdown. When I drove over to Gran's for the morning shift, squawking seagulls mobbed that end of Belle Isle for my feed. Go, my bright cheerleaders. For three days my stomach was a parade ground of squirting fear.

Officially I was leaving one school and preparing to study engineering at another, all the while staying close to the border. For years I'd concentrated on the treb's engineering: material strength, shot reliability, set-up and take-down speeds. Then in actual business I atrophied for want of better human resources. No contacts meant no product. No product, no market. Only female plants get smoked, and as our man sings, "No woman, no cry." Battle cry. Call to prayer. Open for business.

By now I have met every manner of smoker: career moms, physicians, software developers (why not? they can't spell *or* add), teachers before they have their babies, and calorie-counting women and athletes. But at eighteen, I knew only casual smokers and the local basement bong freak.

"An*tone*," Simon greeted me as I stopped by his basement apartment one Saturday afternoon. He sleepily scratched at his sideburns, muttering, "In brother, come in."

Stepping inside Simon's I tried not to look at the wall-sized Bob Marley flag and assured myself (inaccurately) that the song he was cuing up on the stereo couldn't possibly be Ben Harper's anthemic "Burn One Down." He poured himself onto a couch blackened and hardened with grime. Several grams of weed were no doubt sprinkled across its dark cushions. The bud he began grinding up was as red and hairy as a Celtic swordsman. I hoped that the karma in which he no doubt believed meant

Bob Marley's grandkids would grow up wearing T-shirts emblazoned with Simon's face. The slit-eyed grin and halved IQ he turned to me had never made a straight career look more appealing. Bring on the banking. Hello, London insurance industry.

"Sy, think we could talk a little business before we blaze? I know a ways-and-means guy looking to move something across the river. Ask your guy if he's interested in unloading."

He nodded but went ahead lighting up.

"I'm told there's a sack in it for you, things work out. A big sack."

Herculean lungs expanded before me. Industrial bellows drew blue smoke.

"It's all music," Simon eventually replied.

Wonderful.

I proved to be a much better engineer than I was a fisherman. I had to make similar visits to Dave, Luke, even art-school Slyvie.

"Tell me again why I'm doing this," I implored Slyvie as she moved a green dreadlock aside to stare through a tripod-mounted video camera. I was standing on a milk crate holding up a sheet of Mylar in one hand and a square metre of chicken wire in the other.

"The usual," she replied. "Fight the power. Free the subconscious. Antagonize my prof. Okay, action!"

I swept the chicken wire toward the Mylar.

"Cut," she called. "Can't you get it to curl a little, like a wave? Be the wire, Antony. Be the wire."

Middlemen. Brokers. Agents. As the months until Mom returned from Chicago slipped through my treb-ready hands, I grew to see all of those glib little commercial parasites standing in the middle of every industry, skimming their cut. Consultants. The strip club managers who make money without having to spread their legs (or other even more intimate parts). Some musicians sign contracts to always pay the guy who introduced them to the guy who makes records. I couldn't get myself a product, so delivery didn't much matter. All I had were pointless costs, wasted time, entrepreneurial fantasies.

This is one of the last industries where "business school" remains an oxymoron. Genuine business is a mirror: it shows you what you're made of. You make money by character, ability, and chance. No digital slide show, group work assignment, buzzword, or accounting software *du jour* can change your stripes. There's no business school for drugs and, irony of ironies, America's War on Drugs is a war on capitalism at its most pure. What other product continues to sell with zero, and I mean *zero*, marketing? Some fraction of every sticker price you've ever seen in a store recovers money spent trying to convince you to buy. In most provinces, ours included, the state pays to market alcohol, printing posters and magazines for their liquor stores then cutting cheques for the hospital down the street. The Grateful Dead couldn't own stocks in the Love Potion No. 1 or Blueberry Tea seed strains. Half of the Canadian narcotics economy is in weed. Seven billion a year and *nothing*, not a dollar, has ever been spent on marketing.

With the treb, a key of birdseed, and a car I didn't own, I'd gotten around the actual border, but I was stuck at the borders in the local pot-clouded heads. No one was willing to introduce me to the guy who knew the guy who knew the guy who grew. All right, sure, there were risks, layers of extra heat (two police forces, two coast guards, two border patrols—all that competing gun dick), but this was pre-9/11. We could all see that America did not spend federal dollars on Detroit. Every low-level dealer who refused to take me upstairs was insulting local history. We'd all heard stories of great-grandparents skating across the frozen river to sell booze. At parties, we'd smoked weed someone swore had been smuggled over on a windsurfer or a kayak. Where was their civic pride?

I even tried following the tomatoes. Thirty minutes outside of Windsor is Leamington, tomato capital of Canada or maybe the world.

Ketchup in Kansas or Idaho or Manitoba starts in fields just down my road. But the road suddenly lengthens if you actually want to cut up and eat a local tomato. Come Labour Day, if I walked into a big grocery store to buy "local" tomatoes, I was buying tomatoes that had been trucked from Leamington four hundred kilometres to Toronto, sold to a distributor who then sold them to grocery store chains, including my local stores, before trucking some of them four hundred kilometres back to Windsor. *Eat local* indeed.

So off to Toronto I went, cash in one pocket, three phone numbers in the other. I had to party with an old friend for a day and a half before he'd hear why I was really there. All I wanted was a meeting, a meeting to see someone who sells a product and therefore likes customers, but oh the grief. *I don't know. He's really touchy about new people.* All I'm asking is for you to ask. I drove home empty-handed and almost maudlin enough to sing that ever-available Canadian chorus: Toronto only helps Toronto.

In the end, by chance and then heavy payments, tae kwon do proved more helpful than anything else. I'm currently embarrassed to say that at eighteen I wouldn't really have noticed a thirty-two-year-old woman anywhere outside of a taek class, black belt or no.

One of the big sexual delights in life, surely in the top three, is surprise. Most of us meet the standard fare early on, and those pleasures'll last as long as the libido does. Much later, you find your hidden desires. Or are shown them. Claire d'Entremont was a thirty-two-year-old whose ass caught the eye I should have kept focused on the coil of her elbows and her lightning back foot. If you're thinking about anything other than the moving bodies, the taek instruction went, you weren't working hard enough. But oh for Claire's sculpted ass. I lingered on the sight of it while we sparred, lingered just long enough for her to brake a hammerfist two inches from my nose. As I registered my shock at that fist hanging off my face, she said, "But thanks." At the end of class she asked me home to her place. Ah, thirty-two.

Claire's first lesson (or second, if you count the sparring emphasis on paying attention): girls get fucked; women fuck. Once after class, then again, then a long naked Saturday. Eventually, Claire would use words like *work, meetings,* and *clients.* She took a lot of brief cellphone calls but never punched a regular clock. When I asked her what she did, she replied, "A couple of fitness classes here, some promoting there. I get by." As the sweaty weeks grew, I never saw her carry a briefcase, never heard her say *office.* And she always had a sack of the most pelvis-dissolving green. Once when she reached for her pungent little bag, I asked, "How can I get you to introduce me to your supplier?"

She shook her head before we lit up. "We fuck or we do business. Not both."

Then pass me my gitch and your Rolodex.

Claire proved to be the smartest dealer I have ever met. Aside from sex, I learned three other crucial lessons. One, don't dress like a criminal or a pothead. Her clients were lawyers and office workers, and she dressed exactly like them. Yeah, yeah, yeah, dress codes are relaxing all the time, millionaires in jeans, but you know what I mean. Shave. No *Smoke the rich* T-shirts. Easy on the piercings and tats. Claire also unpacked the rhetoric of greed for me. You want to improve your standing with a dealer? Be on her call list when times get lean? Then don't expect her to light you up for free during the deal. For whatever reason—the cannabis camaraderie, the illegality, contact high—some people want, need, or expect to smoke while buying. Maybe potheads are looking for parity with the provincial liquor stores and their army of slim fake blondes dispensing free samples. Point is, many buyers like to smoke during the deal and those that think they should be getting a freebie won't be on speed-dial when times are tight. And my last lesson from Claire—genuine learning requires humility.

Who knows what you really want the first few times you drop your clothes. Two weeks, three, four, the phone a silly piece of plastic in my hand, I finally admitted that what I wanted in Claire was a master, no other word. You know that martial arts myth about the bridge? Two warriors step onto opposite ends of a narrow bridge. The weaker will step aside to let the stronger pass. I did my bit with Claire, dedication here, some young muscle there, but she had me outclassed, outskilled, and outgunned. We both knew that she was giving me skills for life, would be with me in every new woman I met.

And I suppose there was always this. A few months after Mom's thesis production of *Medea*, I was invited to a June barbecue at one of her friend's places. I strolled into the backyard with Claire all swishy and fit beside me. "Mom, I'd like you to meet Claire." A summer dress on each of them.

At the end of August, just before I was to start university, just before, as Claire knew, I'd be meeting ten new girls my age every day, she made me a proposition. "This isn't about weed. It's about money. No introduction is free in this business. The two of us will meet someone in a parking lot. Normally I buy half a key. Thanks to you, I'll be driving away with a full one. I leave, you can stay behind for your chat. You cross that threshold, though, you no longer cross mine."

Deal.

16. Draft Age

FAMILY—WE RARELY SAY WHAT we know. Every family speaks a little Cuban, some a lot. Kate had dared to ask and half-invited me to tell her if I sold weed, but then she also brought us closer again two days later. She left me another card on the breakfast table. The front was Van Gogh's *Wheat Field under Threatening Skies with Crows*. Inside she'd written:

> "What is beauty but the beginning of terror?"
> —Rilke
> *I think we're beautiful.*

Within days we found ourselves in one of those unplanned, ridiculously hypothetical yet somehow inevitable discussions couples have, debating the merits of Rilke as the name for a child. I know, I know—I should have noticed the writing on the (vaginal) wall. *Wheat Field* was the last painting Van Gogh did before he shot himself.

She was my gravity. If you do anything beyond breathe in physics class you learn that gravity isn't necessarily a force that pulls things down. Gravity pulls mass together. The Earth just happens to be very massive and beneath us. In a vacuum, mass doesn't fall; it gathers. That's gravity's big deal: things want to fly together, join, coalesce. Love is gravity. Helpless. Endless.

That fall, Kate and I were crazy about each other. Our clothes dropped as steadily as the leaves in Ojibway Park. Evenings in the D. A weekend walking Chicago's dozen little bridges. And daily life. The supper chat. Nights reading at opposite ends of the couch. As a student, she had a roommate. As a self-made criminal, I didn't. She started November co-opting half of one of my dresser drawers and finished it with the whole thing, camisoles abutting panties, T-shirts squat in a corner, bras collapsing and expanding as sullenly as caged ravens. One night in early December when she stood in front of my hallway closest, she was both accurate and a little scheming when she said, "I never see you wear most of these jackets." By Saturday my off-season jackets were stored in a bin beneath the bed and a small army of her shirts had colonized three-quarters of the closet. I was possibly too generous (or, more honestly, ostentatious) when I had a birch dresser custom-made for her for Christmas. I let her run her hands back and forth over the curved drawer faces—Go ahead, stroke the Dutch hooker—before I slid out one drawer to show her its old-fashioned dovetail joinery. "No glue. No nails. No screws. The drawer holds itself together, wood biting wood." I ran my finger down the flared, hugging dovetails, enumerating "You, me. Me, you." Finally I slid the drawer shut and got her into my arms. "Live with me. Live with me, you gorgeous slut."

She wanted to hear this and she didn't. By then she almost never slept at her apartment, would complain about paying bills for her "off-site closet." And yet my jokes about our living arrangements didn't always get laughs. "Why do I need a better iron? Why don't you just move yours in?" Because, as her gift iron implied, Kate was an escape-route kind of woman. (Can you get a genuine education and not be?)

Yes, I was showy with the handmade dresser. While I gave her a big, flagrant thing, the jewel in the crown of my/our bedroom, she gave me a thin, stained, and tremendously ugly used book that nearly took my knees out from under me. When she handed me the present wrapped in a new tea towel (no disposable paper for her), it had the height and width of a book, but not much thickness or weight. Oh no, I thought as I untied the ribbon, please not some local poems or a student literary magazine, not some saddle-stapled slice of earnestness. Yes and no. The thin, thirty-year-old book had a stained cover barren of images save a small red maple leaf.

Except for the title it looked as sober and boring as an old government instruction booklet. *Manual for Draft-Age Immigrants to Canada.*

"It's the little book that could," she explained. "A new press run by hippies, yet sales of this book doubled every year. It was put together entirely by volunteers, Canadians and Americans in Toronto basements, then mailed all over the US. More than 65,000 copies."

And stapled to my heart. Of course I'd told her plenty about Trevor by then—Mom's dad-vs.-father speech, my science fair work with genetics, his goodbye note—but still her gift shook me, made me feel instantly smaller to have only concentrated on the physical with the dresser.

"He'd probably have used a copy," she added. "Most in the exodus did."

I held her to me, and not to hide the moistening of my eyes. "This is the best present anyone's ever given me. Live with me even more."

"*We're* the best present anyone's ever given me," she said. "Well, most of us." But then she did stroke the dresser again, lingered on its beautiful curves.

Ideas don't believe in borders, and once they so much as glimpse a bridge they're keen to get across. Neither the tomato nor the noodle is indigenous to Italy. The New Testament golden rule is a verbatim retelling of Confucius. Despite the Korean flag that hung at my taek dojo or the smattering of Japanese any *karateka* learns, many martial arts are as cross-pollinated as cooking, architecture, or fashion. Sweat in enough dojos and someone will eventually tell you about *tai sabaki*, the ancient art of getting the fuck out of the way. While a few black-belt masochists train to gladly take the first (but only the first) blow, a tai sabaki practitioner steps aside at the last minute to let your first slide by his chest, avoiding your blow and ready to turn your arm into a handle (or lever). For sparring, dodging the blow needs no sales pitch. Romantically, tai sabaki is impossible. If you're always stepping aside at the sight of movement, you might have some kind of relationship, but not love. To be in love is to be a target.

17. Courage Atlas

IN A NOVEL, YOU WOULDN'T believe that the skyline of Detroit, failed Motor City, was bookended by an enormous, abandoned municipal train station at one end and by a police station/courthouse at the other. Every single one of the six hundred windows of Michigan Central Station is smashed out, and none ever emits light. The marble-rich station and hotel, once the bright smile of the city, has six hundred missing teeth. With its vaulted ceilings now home only to pigeons, and its acres of marble abandoned or covered in five kinds of feces, the ghostly station is the city's tombstone for the death of public transit (or, to many a Detroiter, public life). Only dust, birds, and the mad commute within it now. The skyline's other end is 1300 Beaubien, a courthouse and police station filled, not emptied, by civil strife. Together, they're the bookends of the Detroit riverside. A failed way out at one end of my horizon and a lockup at the other: I couldn't make up my life. Can you? (Have you?)

Borders: here vs. there. Cross from Greece into Turkey and you'll meet every manner of bureaucratic intrusion, five pairs of hands going through your passport and half a dozen yelled insults demanding to know why you would ever want to leave beautiful country A for that dog's asshole of a country B (that dog's asshole of a country with, at the border crossing, an identical landscape). Snarling soldiers stand in towers and behind painted or fenced lines, hate and machine guns ready. Greece and Turkey. Haiti and the Dominican. Bosnia and Croatia. Windsor and Detroit have none of that. Our hands are too deep in each other's pockets (pockets of various kinds) for anyone to raise a fist. But still, every border does its fictitious *here* and *there*. As Kate used to say, then finally showed,

"You see a jurisdiction best at its edges." Too true. And in the D, most of the edges you see are black.

Everything I'd done with weed in Windsor was meaningless over in the D. The profitability of my loose jays, the connect I'd paid for through Claire, the flinging treb—small change in the wrong currency. And let's call a non-spade a non-spade: in the D, I was cracker white. Over there, my skin said more in advance than I ever could with my mouth.

Windsor's as multicultural a Canadian city as you can get. With war, kleptocracy, and drought spinning a changing planet like a roulette wheel, every generation of immigrants that Canada has ever attracted has settled in Windsor. Meanwhile the D has been losing one colour for fifty years.

Polite Canadians (excuse the redundancy, and the Cuban) want to say that race is irrelevant, a non-issue, a source of national pride not problems. Right: we're all one race, all white, rich, and liberal given the right chances. Some part of you knows otherwise. What percentage of your lovers have been of a different race? Can the adventurous even claim 10 percent? How many Canadians know that Canada also had a slave history? While I'm at it, did you know that John Newton—the man who wrote "Amazing Grace" and led, against all odds, Britain and arguably the world's fight against the slavery of blacks—was a daily opium user? Prohibition chases inhibition.

Anyone who believes humanity is just one race should visit their nearest correctional facility. The plaque at America's Statue of Liberty, that "Mother of Exiles," famously reads "Give me your tired, your poor / your huddled masses yearning to breathe free." Those tired, poor masses have disproportionately high representation in prisons, pharmacies, and morgues. When I wanted to smuggle pot internationally, a courthouse was a job fair.

I was a white Canadian looking for pot dealers in Detroit. With 1300 Beaubien weighting down the skyline, I could let someone else round up the applicants for me, all without a headhunting fee. Even the street name had elastic borders. *Bow-been*, we'd overhear locals say in Detroit's clubs and restaurants before we drove by street signs our school French had us pronounce *Bow-be-en*. *Goodwell Street*. Not for most of the people there.

Every defendant was black, and the only white people were judges and lawyers, a few police. The bailiffs were black, the stenographers, most of the cops and lawyers, the families of the accused, all the custodians. Walking from public courtroom to courtroom I could hear complete resumés of crime. Young Tyrell Jones minored in assault before moving on to major in armed robbery. Jephrey Johnston joined the court one day after three busy seasons with community programs. Strapping young Wardell Jones was no stranger to moving keys of green, but he liked to crack jaws and ribs along the way. I skipped lunch to hear more about Lester Davis, a promising green prospect, only to find that two of his former places of legitimate employment had gone up in flames. On my third day I got a glimpse of Carter Stewart, a man neck-deep in drug and gun charges. The weapons charges didn't stick, so Carter stayed in my sights. By then I'd sat through so many dockets and listened to more than three centuries' worth of incarceration get handed out. When a visibly terrified witness finally changed his testimony, Carter was found not guilty and already knew his way to the exit. I followed him out through the large courtroom doors.

There are places where your name is the last thing you want to hear. I caught up with Carter at the elevators. "Hi, Carter, I'm Trevor Reynolds. I wonder if we might chat a little." I was another white line on the road telling him to stay in his lane. He took a long look at me, eyes as static as coal. Still, no place where he was more likely to keep his hands at his sides, and at 1300 I could be certain a prospective employee wasn't exercising his right to bear arms.

"How about I show you some ID," I said before the elevator even arrived, "show you which team I'm *not* working for?" I slid a passport out of my pocket, cover out for him to read. *CANADA PASSPORT/*

PASSEPORT. I'd never been more grateful for official bilingualism, that capital *E* a big glowing sign saying, *Not from here.* I shrugged and slid the passport back into my pocket.

Carter and I remained immobile until the elevator finally arrived. I stepped inside first, was grateful and terrified when he clomped his Timberlands in after.

"I'm Trevor Reynolds, a Canadian looking to talk a little business."

"Man, what this shit about?"

"Weed, Carter. Pounds of Canadian Chronic."

We walked out into a parking lot in one country and looked over at another, greed, etc. driving each of us.

"C'mon, I'll buy you a beer. Propose terms."

That courthouse networking was done long before I ever met Kate, yet when we were together I burned to tell her about it. You only get courage by doing something that tests your courage. I felt every hair on the back of my neck as Carter and I stepped into an old bar, peanut shells on the floor, pressed tin ceiling above us. To you I admit that I've generally put my courage into making money, not relationships. (Until this blog, anyway.)

Kate did the opposite.

18. The Foundry

LIVE ON A BORDER AND the new year has twice as many places to start. Or to grind to a halt. My Christmas *live with me, live with me* invitation didn't win the response I'd been hoping for.

In Windsor, we all grew up with carloads of afternoon smuggling. Everybody had "border shoes." When your runners ran down and split apart, you'd set them aside rather than throw them out, saved them for the next crossing. This pair was only to be thrown out on the other side, crammed into some fast-food restaurant bin, so you could come back with two new pairs, one on your feet and the other hidden in the car to avoid duty. Local moms prided themselves on how large an article of clothing they could fit into their handbags. Everyone followed the Clark Kent dress code and would drive home with newly purchased American clothes under the old clothes they'd gone over in. Otherwise safe and conscientious parents would remove spare tires from the bottom of trunks to better stash dog food or new power tools or sporting equipment. Now I say spend it where you make it, buy jobs when you buy products. That wasn't the local lesson.

Immigration law and Kate's having been born here weren't the only reasons she came back to Windsor. Detroit was the third. No sense training to be a lawyer outside the country where you'll practise law, but how else could she make her second degree different from her first? As she joked, "If I can't study abroad, I'll study abutting."

I'd always been over for movies and concerts, then was over even more for the Kate dates. Restaurants there meant less likelihood of bumping into someone we knew. We made regular trips to the Rivera murals, swore we saw different colours in different seasons. Once we toured Barry Gordy's original house, birthplace of Motown. Not a replica, not an architectural homage—the actual house. In one upstairs room, singers had been placed beneath an opened attic hatch for a more echoey vocal track. When I told Mom and encouraged her to go see it, I had no idea that echoey Motown attic would become a hidden hatch in her own tunnel offensive.

Initially Kate and I also did a little cross-border shopping. Somehow a city with a perpetually draining population still has a better lingerie selection. After I proposed we live together, Kate took us over for some cross-border stopping.

At Christmas, when I first said *live with me*, she'd been a puddle on two legs, all wet love. But as soon as the new year got under way and I tried to discuss our looking for a place together, she clammed up. Only when she emailed to say she'd be spending the night at her place one Tuesday did I acknowledge that she hadn't returned my calls all day.

What? I replied.

I'm studying.

The cold e-shoulder. That night, as she deigned to send one brief reply to every three emails or phone messages from me, I fell into one trap after another. I felt fair and reasonable sending off *Don't I deserve to know why we're fighting?* then like a maudlin little eunuch when her response quoted my own question. *At 11:13 p.m., Trevor Reynolds wrote...*

Then: *I need some time to think. Respect that.*

Right, my asking why we were fighting was another infraction. My insensitivity. My barbarous lack of telepathy. By the time I was finally fighting mad it was too late to head out, yet because of her I couldn't concentrate to read. Everywhere I turned in my apartment there was some little thing of hers. Boots and belts. Her dirty travel mug. Fucking hairpins. My place was our place but her place was just hers.

The next morning—no email from her, no messages—I was merely a house painter. The tedium of it, moving molecules, fighting time, bandages for entropy. I wasn't stupid enough to accelerate my next lob with the treb just because I was in a romantic spat. Back then, my first three rules of business were: (1) make money, (2) make it so you can keep it, and (3) stick to rules 1 & 2. A drop because I was bored? Pissed off? Dissatisfied? Please, I am my mother's son (and possibly the great-grandson of William Williams, tunneller near-extraordinaire). The grow must go on. If you have a brain and self-control, crime isn't chaos. Just because you step over the legal line doesn't mean you step over the rational line. Should be the opposite. Crime is pure adulthood, life without insurance. Only you look out for you.

After her second night away I didn't need a morning coffee to shoot my blood up the thermometer. I asked her to live with me and she got mad? Now I was pissed off, doubly. Bring it on.

As always, the fight went meta, yet another fight about fighting. Communication, emotional goals, change—all of it gave way to trench warfare. Duck, rise to fire, stay alive. I'd rehearse insults while painting. Careful with that 10-megaton *Parent-pleaser*. Easy with that heat-seeking *Drone lawyer*.

Work, just work. Fourteen hours painting a swivel servant's living room in "wild sage." To me it was the colour of bile mixed with toothpaste, but hey. Over lunch I used a germy payphone to send and receive four coded messages and arranged a drop, schemed my way to a month of Mom's salary for forty-two minutes of work. Fuck Kate. Stick with the money, the privacy of profit, that narrowing mirror that showed only me. Or so I told myself until I got home to her email.

Can you meet me tomorrow in the D? 7:30 @ The Foundry.

I went to bed extra horny, sure that my arms and bed were only temporarily empty. I was half right.

19. Listening Posts

ANOTHER DIFFERENCE BETWEEN A LAW student and a student, between a second degree and a first, is twice the experience with men. Date someone close to twenty, and she'll probably have met nothing but takers, baseball cap dudes who'll barely undo their own pants. These doofuses (doofi?) think, *Cunnilingus is that toga senator guy with the sandals and shit.* Mid-twenties, a woman's more likely to be getting the sex she wants. (You won't believe me yet, but mid-thirties is usually more accurate.)

Kate's men. Blair, her high-school dude, her hunk of football youth, her life-support system for a hemp/coral/shark's tooth necklace. Christian, her (first?) bad boy, her emotional criminal, the man who taught her, however negatively, that selfishness is part of life. If she wasn't devoted to herself and her clit, why should anyone else be? Then Charles, her *sensitif,* her attentive and caring partner who encouraged her growth, a growth so unencumbered she eventually discovered she needed more than safety and someone who cleaned up after himself. Inevitably, for her at least, a pet artist: David was good with everything, except the rent. Computer programming, soldering, video editing, handmade pasta—he could teach himself anything save the fact that the world didn't owe him something. Ryan, her scholarship pirate, her challenge junky, her bounder. Richard, her older guy, bit of money (as amateurs go), but he had too keen an eye on appliance deals and shared too much of his intricate knowledge of income tax.

Me? Well, don't we always think our current lover is an amalgam of our past lovers? Accurately or not, we see a chain, not isolated, possibly ill-fitting, links. Thing is, chains end. After three days of near silence and

zero sex I was keen to test the strength of our chain, but not so happy
to do it in a Detroit restaurant. If our Foundry date was to be a genuine
reconciliation, all shaved legs and strategic underwear, why complicate
a race home with a border crossing? (Isn't make-up sex one of the secret
reasons couples fight?) And the border would throw off my relationship
radar. Arriving separately, what would be fashionable lateness, a border
delay, or manipulative spite?

Kate was the second thing I noticed when I stepped into the crowded,
mid-sized Detroit restaurant. She was there and dressed to induce cardiac
arrest, flesh here and tight fabric there. The spiky cascades of hair I loved.
She smiled slightly in my general direction before edging her nose into
a fishbowl-sized glass of red. The colour of her shirt matched the wine.
With a pair of crisp black pants, the burgundy shirt made her look like
a waiter or a hit man with tits. The sight of her was multiply inviting, so
clean, so together. Memory and fantasy both tickled my palms with the
curves of hip and breast I could see twenty feet away.

She stirred me entirely, but the half-packed restaurant did not. At each
table around the perimeter of the room sat a well-dressed woman with a
glass of wine and a pen. Sheets of notepaper sat stacked in front of them.
A three-sided bar thrust forward from the rear of the room. I gravitated
to it, not Kate. Men in adult pants who didn't live exclusively in running
shoes huddled around the bar. Everyone was older than we were, thirties,
forties, almost exclusively white.

Three waitresses in white shirts rode herd, ushering late arrivals to a
table or the bar. Eventually one of them stepped to the centre of the room
and addressed us. "Good evening, silent singles of Detroit."

WHAT!?

Kate did an excellent job pretending to be interested in anything other
than my incredulous stare.

The emcee marched on. "You've no doubt read about silent dating in
Manhattan or Chicago. You certainly didn't *hear* about it." The younger

staff chuckled. "Now it's time for the Motor City to quiet down. Quiet down so we can let romance be heard. We all live with so much noise. Ring tones stabbing at us. TVs blaring. Cars with their thump thump. You're here tonight to quiet all that down and meet others who want to hear better things in life, who want to quiet down before we open up. Welcome to Detroit's chat room with bodies."

"And drinks!" the bartender yelled. Relieved laughter sloshed around.

Kate's eyes found mine across the room. Prosecutor's smile. Little duellist's toss of the chin.

The emcee stepped back to throw a thoroughly condescending look at the men. "All right, the rules. For the next ninety minutes, *all* of your talking will be done with a pen. Silence. Silence. Silence. Exchange notes, exchange looks, exchange anything you can with a pen. Now go on, mingle. Enjoy each other's quiet."

Crossing towards Kate I tried to be a sport. Fine, we'd make up with pens. *I'm sorry. / No, I'm sorry. / You're even prettier than I remember. / Let's get out of here.* But I wasn't the only bee flying towards that burgundy flower. I got cut off by some button-down hustler keen to fill the passenger seat of his Stock-Market Utility Vehicle. And she was all smiles. For him.

Let her cross her Rubicon. I didn't pause what had been my walk towards her but pretended to be intent on getting paper. This was war, so I sought out the most attractive blonde that could keep me in Kate's sightline.

Hi.

Hi.

What else do you do for fun?

Glore often joked about my "taxi-metre brain. " She never did get me stuffed into an actor's pair of tights, but that doesn't mean I hadn't learned from the countless rehearsals I got hauled to as a kid. Like it or not, I'd endured eighteen million household conversations about stagecraft. Blocking. Floor plan. After scalping my blonde I went with a classic stage trick: I found a woman (older; line-of-credit hair) who was facing Kate so I could sit with my back to her. By hiding my face from Kate, she would have to infer how much and how well I was flirting by looking at Ms. Salon, not me. If my table companion gave me a bedroom smile, it would ricochet across the room.

I'm not actually looking for a date. Should I move on?

Lady Manicure checked the traffic, then scribbled.

Not yet, but you'll understand when I ask you to leave. So what are you looking for then?
Get my girl back. She's behind me. The long black hair.
And the chest. So what did you do?
Asked her to live with me.

I'd heard about silent dating on NPR and thought it pure twaddle, another Moleskine fantasy. We scribblers all. Actually trying it, though, I put honesty in and got honesty back.

Asked without a ring?
We've only been together six months.
Would she say only? You asked one question. Maybe she wants to hear a different one.
I don't really think she's the marrying type.
Is there another?
Yes, I was raised by one.
A bit hard, was she?

You date by exam, you learn a few things. Around us the confessional allure of a chat room was shaken liberally with the eye and body work of a bar.

Oh, you're off. I see a fresh divorce walking around.

I headed for a drink, trying not to notice that the oak bar was crowded almost exclusively with men. Even at the bar, silence reigned. The dude to my right, oh so very sports TV, nudged me to reveal three separate notes. *2 bad we cant cut and paste* read the note in his left hand while in his right he carried two identical notes, each of which read, *Looks like you don't need help getting dates at any volume.*

Finally I got my place in Kate's royal court. I began with invitations.

Do you want to
a) tell
b) hear
c) ask

She laid a note over top of mine.

Hi. I'm Kate. What do you do?

Kate but not my Kate. The old re-seduce me game. Right, let's pretend we don't already know what's beneath the zippers.

Buy low. Sell high. Lived in Detroit long?
Live near here, not here. You guess where? 'Buy low, sell high.' You mean stocks?
Buy everything low. Sell whatever you can high.

I tried to squeeze out some time with my pun. Could I guess where she was from? Running me all over the court. Who's ever going to guess Scottish-Chinese Canadian? Maybe she was trying to bait me into posing that contemporary racist question, *No, no, where are you* really *from?* Was she a Kate I didn't know or a new Kate? Kate 2.0?

I think I know where you're from. The State of Gorgeous, right?

Lethal little half-smile.

Maybe did your undergrad at Articulate and Intelligent U.?

A dismissive reach for her wine glass.

Now you've got your first apartment alone in a little loft district called Likes to Laugh.

Stonewalled.

Not afraid to travel on the Fighting Expressway if you need to.

Actually @ law school across the water. Live in a district called Definitely Not Jail.

They have parks over there? I have a scampish dog.

'Have' or 'am'? No, no parks. Not a lot of green in the area.

That's too bad. Have never met a law student who didn't like her green.

Nice place to visit. Wouldn't want to live there.

What's a home without plants?

So, what, you lie on a bed of poison ivy every night?

People live more lies than they tell.

Let's step outside and talk about lies.

Let's step outside. A line from a parking lot nose-breaker. With fists, at least you know when the fight's over.

I didn't hide the fact that I gathered up the pages of our silent date and tucked them into my suit jacket as we exited. Always destroy the evidence, even the fake evidence.

"So have you finally agreed to talk to me?" I asked as the doors swung shut and the cold January night clamped itself around us.

"And then some."

"Look, you don't return my calls, you drag me out here for some charade all because I asked—"

She whirled and came at me. "Because you might go to jail, you liar."

Our eyes locked, not pleasantly.

"I don't *lie* to you, Kate. I keep things from you, yes, but I do not lie."

"You're clever and careful to not tell me exactly what your 'night job' is. But if you ask me to live with you, I need to know, and you need to tell me," she jabbed my chest, hard, "whether what you do could put you in jail for a decade."

I glanced around. Abandoned stores. Some chute of pitted freeway visible in three different directions. Billboards advertising anti-anxiety prescriptions and HMOs. Of course. We were in Detroit not for romance or adventure, but because it was a different jurisdiction.

"Kate, I want us to live together. In a bigger apartment." Up and out went my hands. Pale invitations. Peacemakers.

This time she hammered me in the chest, no more jabs. "Never, ever, ever—god damn you—ignore what I'm saying. Could your 'job,' your 'work,' your *you* put you in a cage? Try, for once, to be honest."

That brought me off the ropes. "*Honest?* You want *honest?* Yes, the life I live, the life I want to live, could put me in jail. Just like living here"—big theatrical inhalation—"could give us cancer or entomb us in the 401 or throw shrapnel through our skulls if some nutter buys a van and some fertilizer. You want to talk about *lies?* You and your friends all smoke dope. Judges, lawyers, cops—the whole profession is chrons. Everybody drinks. That drug's okay, but mine isn't? What emergency room, what courtroom, isn't fuelled by alcohol? Legal, illegal, sold by the state, policed by the state—don't tell me about lies. Pharmacies sell opium. We run a plant harvested by some of the poorest people on the planet through some of the richest corporations, that's medicine. We grow a plant, that's a drug. Sell muffins at a local market and the law requires you to list what's in them. Your classmates swill pitcher after pitcher of factory beer with no idea what it's made of. Why? Because the government makes tax selling it. The war on drugs is a war on truth."

I could feel my voice fading in the cold air. You think something five hundred times, it sometimes comes out in a bundle.

She hooked her fingers into the back of her pants and threw some jaw at me. "Yes, yes, yes. You don't eat bullshit for breakfast, that's abundantly clear. But you say *live with me*, you've got to acknowledge that some day our door could get kicked down. We pretend otherwise and *we're* lying."

"No one's going to kick our door down."

"Sweetheart, I always do the homework. Queen and Rowbotham— twenty years for hash, just hash. Queen and Raber—the first thing the police did after they kicked the door down was shoot the family dog, dead. This was at the afternoon birthday party of a seven-year-old. Three bullets, one dog. You think they're going to kick our door down then talk soothingly to Voodoo?" Her eyes were a little shiny, but her voice wasn't.

"So what," I asked, "we shut up and obey? Everybody has pot. But don't sell it, no. Be another obedient Canadian! Or maybe just let someone else do our dirty work for us. Pay the immigrant to clean my toilet. Let the hog manure ruin a distant water table so long as my bacon's cheap. The more people smoke, the more likely we'll collectively choose to end this ridiculous prohibition. You're not the only one who does homework. We spent ten million dollars putting Rowbotham away, and our taxes market booze."

"Choose your battles. I'm talking about us."

"So am I. Think of how many people make money in shitty ways. Insurance. Consultants. Let's say it, some of the law—how much of this is rationalized piracy? Oil. Chocolate. Diamonds. Purposefully obsolete electronics—"

"Stop. Stop, you asshole, and listen to me. I have spent weeks not even knowing what I'm feeling. I stare at *shower taps*. I have suddenly forgotten terms I knew before I even started law school. I worry my professors must know why I'm not concentrating. I am afraid. I'm afraid to love you."

You should know this, she grabbed me by the throat. Slowly, and not quite crushingly, but she wasn't stringing a necklace. "And if you're half as clever as you seem to be," she tightened her grip, "you'll want me to want you to stop. Don't you expect me to find the same faults in you that you do?"

"Stop and what? Shuffle paper? Write blistering memos?" I leaned my Adam's apple into her thumb. "You said it yourself. *What is beauty but the beginning of terror?*"

"That's just the beginning."

She kept shaking her head as she walked to her car, as she drove away from me. Kate of the tail lights.

20. Me Too

NO MATTER HOW OFTEN I'M in the D or how much money it's made me, no matter that half my blood's American or that eventually my real-estate deals there were much larger than those here, I always hit a point when I want to come back. Legally, politically, socially, architecturally—eventually the D fucks with my shadow. Let me back through the gate.

After our parking-lot fight, my desire to repatriate hit the second I saw her bumper pull away. By the time I squeezed onto Detroit's riverside Jefferson Ave., I soured back into indignation. Clipping my wings, she wanted to clip my wings. *Don't you expect me to find the same faults in you that you do?* Yeah, but the same virtues too. Risk, yes, but life full-sized every day of the week. Ask a dance movie, ask an incandescent novel: a life half-lived isn't worth living. At times I think Victor-Conrad must have preferred young glory to an aging fade, especially if he got to make that genetic deposit in France. Ol' Bill survived one international tunnel then died in another, but have you seen the tunnels that get forcibly opened in an old age home? Trench warfare all over again. What did Kate really want—me in a useless job pegging my life to two weeks' vacation? Centenarian Gran excepted, I come from the young dead, not the dead young. Worker drones. Shopper drones. No thanks.

But her hook was in. Kate had jabbed me in the chest and now a version of her voice kept on jabbing. Would Gran agree that her dead husband and dead son had lives worth living? Crossing back this time, I took the tunnel, not the bridge. The disapproving voices of Kate and Mom came into my car like radio I couldn't turn off, radio that didn't crackle and fade as I poured down into the greasy tunnel, all that family water pressing down above me.

By the time I had crawled out on the Canadian side and turned into the five-lane lineup for Customs, I was suddenly exhausted, resignedly contemplating a life without Kate, her intelligence, or her legs. As I glanced to the crowded lane on my left, I saw her just one car ahead. She quickly saw me too. We managed about a metre of pursed lips and the pretence we could ignore each other in this international purgatory of brake lights. That sham dissolved when yet another delay in her lane (some uppity black thinking he could cross the border without a hassle) and acceleration in mine (whites in a minivan, whites in a minivan) brought our cars abreast.

The chance flow of cars, the whims of the border guards, the fluke that had put me to her right not her left and the days we'd just spent apart suddenly gave new use to the back sides of all that silent dating paper in my jacket pocket. I fished a marker out of the glove box and scrawled GUN RUNNER ↗ on one oblong sheet. I held it up to my window and pointed at her, rising in my seat and batting my head around in mock indignation. Her dime-spitting grin lit up her face before she could shake her head at me. I got so caught up in my tattler's mime, eyebrows sanctimoniously raised, shopping her all 'round, that I failed to notice her digging in her bag. Up she came with a piece of notepaper and PUBLIC ENEMY thrust out the entire length of her arm and pressed my way on her passenger window.

Here, finally, we both said no to drugs. The truth was the one weapon we weren't going to use. If we had been trying this stunt on the way into the US, which we *never* would have done, I would have had infinite ammo. *COMMIE. VEGAN. DYKE.*

STU LOAN FRAUD, I accused as our cars inched forward.

TAX CHEAT, came the counter charge.

I'd never been more prone to a 3 km/h accident than there juggling paper and slander, the laughs all the more irrepressible for our physical separation. With the fire of rage finally extinguished, I re-heard her parking lot tirade more clearly. "I'm afraid to love you," she had said. There it was, the L-word, table-sweeping trump. The chuckles drained from my face. Fake sanctimony fell from my eyebrows. The woman I thought about more than I'd ever thought about another human was busy nailing up false charges to the window of her car and tempted to love me. Her lineup advanced, giving me time to scrawl ME TOO before I pulled back alongside.

We were then just three cars away from the Canadian border guards, and my ME TOO note clearly didn't make any sense. She raised her last card with furrowed eyebrows. PORN HOUND, said her window, but not her face. Another car advanced.

I tried recalling her line, writing AFRAID 2 LOVE U then again holding up ME TOO. Her frown and the resigned nod of her chin and the attention she returned to piloting her car to the guard's quadruply marked stop line all told me she thought I was saying that I too was afraid to love her.

"No," I said aloud, rolling down my window, my voice already strange after the frantic writing. She tried to keep one eye on the impatient guard looming in her window. "Kate, I love you," I called quickly, seeing just a glimpse of her before she rolled forward.

Flashing cameras recorded our licence plates. I, and no doubt she, stared up at a Canada Customs officer made furious by our irreverent propaganda war and our inability to find them intimidating. Yes, we were hauled out of line for the extra nasty talking to, the repeat showing of ID, the standing and waiting for torture by bilingual forms. So what. We'd known from our first inky volley that we were Canadians returning to Canada, just Canada. My hand found hers in front of a scuffed melamine desk. She squeezed back.

21. The (R)evolution Will Not Be Televised

AFTER KATE AND I WERE finally released from Canada Customs—our love definitely something to declare—she returned to my apartment. We made up for lost time that night, but come morning she reconvened the debate. She made tea, not coffee. Tied her hair up and sat me down.

"*What are you?* People have asked me that all my life, usually bluntly. Put Scottish and Chinese into the blender, this is one version of what you get. Mixie. Half-breed. Fusion that isn't welcome outside a restaurant."

We were becoming the Web generation, but this was still life before Facebook (back when friends weren't virtual). She couldn't search for groups devoted to "the ethnically ambiguous." No photo- and emoticon-rich collections of the Danish-Kenyans, Indo-Russians, or Swedish-Brazilians awaited her.

"As a kid, people were at me all the time. *What are you?* Somehow *Canadian* was never an acceptable answer. To the whiteys, sure, I look Asian. In high school that meant I was expected to be good at math and a geeky virgin. But get raised Chinese and they know in the cradle if you're a mixie. I could spread around all the orange New Year's gifts I wanted to my aunties and uncles, but still. During wedding games with my cousins I was never the bride, because marriage meant two Chinese kids, not one-point-five.

"When I was about fourteen, Amy, a 'full-blooded' friend, and I had a code word: CHIN-ez, not chai-KNEES. If something was Chinez, it was still Asian but we were a little…*ashamed* is too strong a word. Just keeping it close. *Chinez* was for the world between home and school. The food we wanted to eat but were a little embarrassed to shop for. For a while there, Amy claimed to envy me because I was half-white.

"Point is, I've kind of just got myself sorted out, have just gotten over not being one or the other. Now with you it's doubt all over again. Doubt and/or impermanence. I love you, but I shouldn't. I love you, but I can't."

"Who says you can't?" I reached for her hands. "Imagine making money and doing good at the same time. The money's tempting enough, but I'm also out pitching my load because it's right. The better part of the green team, we're revolutionaries."

She withdrew her hands from mine and tucked them beneath her knees. For the rest of that eventful year she'd come back at me with a series of retorts. "Other people will always be willing to fight this revolution." Or, "So you're Ché. Everything inside the revolution, yes, everything outside it, no?" In the pallid light of that January morning her actual response was much more pragmatic. "Do you honestly think for a second you'll win?"

"Did the suffragists win? Is abortion legal? In a few more years, when every baby boomer is either in chemo or loves somebody who is, yes, Canada stands a chance of legalizing. The US? I'm not hopeful."

"Which just happens to be good for Windsor business, right?"

"Those rules I didn't make, but yes. Every North American who's ever been sixteen knows this is a completely failed prohibition. The law— those dolts. My side's not losing the war. We're bleeding them out in a draw. They waste money while we make it. Even when we're not winning, we're winning." Damn me if I didn't smile.

"I need to go for a walk."

At the W-word, Voodoo shot up and trotted over to her, a black arrow of intent. He gave her his full repertoire of manipulative pleading—the short-range pacing, the whines and snorts, his little ears rowing forward and back.

"You don't have to take him."

"Him I'll take."

Go, Ambassador Vood.

I left her a sandwich and a note then cleared out before she returned.

Sweets,

I hate seeing you upset, upset because of me. Feel free to study here or maybe you'll go to the library. I've got my cell and am going to do a little (honest) work for a few hours. Call me if you'd like to eat here tonight.

Yours,

—Ant

But of course it wasn't just a Sunday night supper I was proposing. She did stay behind for the afternoon, half in her clothes, half in mine. I wasn't in the door two minutes before she was drawing up a contract.

"You say *live with me*, that's gotta mean none of your *work* ever comes home."

"Other than what we smoke, none of it ever has or will. You won't see it or smell it. I'm not some idiot with a pungent tub beneath his bed."

"Let me get through the fine print. We're twenty-five, not twenty. I'm not going to hide the fact that essentially we're shopping around here. My sun's not going to rise and set on you, but I also don't want to see this—us—go to waste."

"Hey, I'm not just putting in time here either. All love involves vulnerability, right?"

"But elsewhere the price of admission isn't as high. Yes, you're smarter than the average bear, but you're also more expensive, much more expensive."

I hugged her low and hard. "And you're here precisely because you know that sometimes you get what you pay for."

She smiled and shook her head simultaneously. "All right. Get your pants off."

A few nights later we planned dinner out, in Windsor, to ceremoniously launch our hunt for a new apartment. We'd never been closer. The hanging, just detectable sense of reproach we/she had for me lent us an air of depravity and indulgent punishment. We enjoyed a couple's post-affair sense of increased closeness without the attendant doubts and recriminations. I even got a smile when I referred to her as my partner in crime.

We purposefully changed the sheets before heading out and wore enough clothes for a walk along the tinkling January river. On cold nights the river's million little pieces of irregularly sized ice bobbed and tinkled, supplying a constant, erratic music. Returning home we held mittens, trudged together in a shaving cold past the gaudy, busy casino. Walking beside her, my brain drifted in coupley neutral. No conscious thoughts, just plenty of images of how we'd spend the next twenty-four hours. I longed for the cold on her skin, for her skin warming against mine in the clean sheets. Visions of our usual bedroom routine danced in my head: sex, reading, sleeping. But then inspiration struck its fangs into me. The casino was bright and busy behind us. In front of us, on the bridge, the red thread of American-bound tail lights was sewn and resewn into the night. Shit.

Mom claims every story is a staircase. Maintain then change. Maintain then change. Well, Mother, what do you think smuggling is?

After years of painting and punting, I was bored with the treb. Really I'd outgrown it by the fifth successful lob. I liked the coin and the late-night fuckoffedness of it, but even I could see I was stuck in a boys-with-toys rut. Sure, the treb made money and it helped seed the weed—*Overgrow the government*—but basically I made my living with a large slingshot.

Thing is, business is about making money, not kicks. I knew I was bored with the treb, but knew also that boredom was to be used, not fled. Play the game but think of the season. Move your strategy, not just your chess piece. Don't say no until you can say yes to something better. Actual business—not inherited money or branded nothingness or the Bay Street country club, class with an income attached—actual buying and selling is all juggling. Ball 1: the product and/or service, the thing, the saleable. Ball 2: the current customer. Ball 3: the next customer. Each is vital.

My day job was proving just as immature as my night job. When a team of contractors carve up a new house, bragging here and robbing the client there, the sole consensus going is that painters are the boys of the site. The only time the electricians and plumbers stop insulting each other is when they mock a painter. *House Boy. Hey, Paint-by-Numbers. Deco Fag.* Generally, all that ribbing was water off a well-paid duck's back, but still.

Month after month, year-in, year-out for nearly five years, I tried to think of something better than punting a load over the river at three in the morning into some abandoned Detroit factory lot. I chewed this over before Kate and especially after we met. Infiltrate Shipping and Receiving at a busy auto parts factory? Sea kayak nightly? Bribe some of the Chinese Americans who came over every weekend for better Asian groceries? Only after I popped the half-question to Kate did I finally see the light(s).

On the bridge, that steady red line of tail lights, gamblers returning to Detroit—that red line was the devil's big grin. Eu-fuckin-reka. I didn't need to smuggle, I just had to have American sin-tourists smuggle for me. Time to play shepherd.

At least 75 percent of the cars leaving the casino were returning to the States. Cars are made of metal. Magnets stick to metal. Circuits open and close to power electromagnets. Looking at the casino and the red line of tail lights on the bridge, I saw ons and offs and green.

A bright new idea throbbing through me, I broke both my sleep-on-it-rule and my tell-her-nothing rule and drew Kate into my arms. Lights from two countries reflected off the tinkling, jostling ice and danced in her eyes. "I'm thinking of getting out of painting and wonder if you would still tear my clothes off if I wore a valet's uniform? The money would be *very* good."

Mistake.

22. Take It

IN ROMANCE AND REAL ESTATE, only hindsight is 20/20. How did we survive Kate's chest-pounding accusation that I was a heart-breaking criminal? With love and a really gorgeous apartment.

Weekday nights and Saturday afternoons we were getting ready to move in together, yet I finally had the smuggling idea that would raise my game. I promised not to lie to Kate about work if she agreed to accept "I can't tell you that" as an answer. I know, I know, my side sounds like a philanderer's dream, but that wasn't an issue. We never had enough clothes on to worry about fidelity.

Over the years I've heard two and a half good pieces of relationship advice. One, the cliché is true, communication is the key. Sexual communication, emotional disclosures, the crap about in-laws—get it out, but constructively. Communication isn't whining or complaining. Tell me what (y)our problem is and, ideally, how to solve it. Two, as Kate wrote in the first card she gave me in the new place, *Love is a behaviour, not a feeling*. Genuine respect takes work, effort, sacrifice. And the half point: marry your sexual obsession. Mom once told me how shocked she was when Janice, the art teacher and regular set designer of her school shows, confessed that despite two kids and after a dozen years of marriage, she was incapable of being alone in the same room with her husband without having sex. First and foremost, we're looking for a mate. Then again, Rules 1 and 2 aren't always compatible with 2.5.

Lest Kate sound like a gold-digger, put yourself in her funky and attractive shoes. She went into our apartment hunt adamant she'd pay fifty-fifty, that we'd stick to a budget. For all the bad press single parenting gets, kids in single parent homes often receive a better financial education.

Two parents talk to each other about money. Single parents still need an audience for the money chat, so single kids grow up learning that *have*, *want*, and *need* are three very different categories.

We had essentially three rental options. Contemporary apartment towers of soulless pre-fab with wafer-thin walls and cardboard doors, paper houses more written than built, contracts with doors. Better but still flawed were the fallen old places from between the wars, once-nice apartments that had come down in the world. One apartment had a genuine claw foot tub, but it had been painted, not re-enamelled, and its grey bottom was the colour of Spanish flu. Hot water tanks had been dropped into already cramped kitchens and sat as ominous as unexploded bombs. Down in the distillery district there were also the renovated money sinks for newlyweds and junior lawyers. Kate tried to hold out, but then we saw a place with two balconies (one for breakfast, another for cocktails). What were her defences compared to a granite counter and cherry wood cabinets? After the landlord showed us the heated bathroom tiles I let him stroll over to the windows without us then squish-hugged her up against the shower stall. Through her hair I cupped the back of her ear like we did to Voodoo then gave our joyous doggie command. "Take it!"

Leave it is a great, all-purpose command for managing your dog. *Leave it* should be enough to keep your dog away from some trailside pile of rotting putrescence, another dog (meaner, more vulnerable, or across a busy street), or, ideally, anything at all. Gloria and I, then Kate, trained Voodoo to "leave it" by first having a treat in our palm. *Leave it* and the fingers close. *Leave it* again the next day and the palm can stay open. Finally, he'd get to hear *Take it* and eat the waiting treat. Snorf, gobble, snorf. By the time Kate was living with Vood, he already knew a jackpot awaited him if she laid little cubes of cheese up his sphinx-pose legs. *Ooookkkayyy, take it!* Snorf, snorf, gobble, snorf.

"What are you doing to me?" She tapped her forehead against mine.

"I love you. Let's live where and how we want."

She, not I, walked out of the bathroom to ask for the lease. True to the spirit if not the letter of her budgetary laws, she has since saved me tens of thousands in housing costs.

What got easier when we moved in together, the sex or the talk? Or, that third overlapping circle, the sleep? I took us shopping for more bedding to celebrate the household merger, bought sheets with a thread count so high they were practically bullet proof (a joke I didn't make). We'd just spent nearly every night together for four months, yet we told ourselves the nights were different now in our own place. Our nightly nights had no end in sight. In bed, four lungs lay in a row like a small shelf of your absolutely favourite novels. The body mingle. In the waking hours there was food, the protracted, healthy arousal of into your body and mine. This local cider, these fresh eggs, cheddar half as old as we were. A live-in lover doesn't just cut the bills in half; she cuts the boredom of paying bills in half. Heat was no longer just heat, but our relaxation, our sprawl. The electricity bill said *reading lights, long shaving showers, frozen organic tomatoes.* I'd already courted her with a dozen kitchen gadgets, now I finally got to live with them.

Most notably, you're hunkering down with another body. You'll never really know someone else until you live with him/her. This gender fieldwork may be the third most compelling reason to cohabit. You see the other face much more than you see your own. Your man. Your woman. Not a possession but a subject, an area of expertise, a library book on renewable loan. On the couch one Sunday she groaned all the way up from her hips. "Agh, day two of my period—my version of tunnel war." Tightening my jaw and thrusting out my bottom lip once while shaving in front of her, I claimed, "Every man is Mussolini when he shaves."

And of course the body itself, that distinction in bone and flesh, the similar yet different chemistry swirling there beside you. How did her skin always stay so soft, so smooth? When I went without shaving, her thumbs, palms, and fingertips would trace over my cheeks, neck, and jaw with the same curiosity mine had for the reliable smoothness of her cheeks, the programmed curve of a breast. Our bodies so close yet so different, hips boxed or arced, strength and resilience variously mapped.

Lovers generally graduate from dorm rooms to apartments to houses as their bodies, not just their bank accounts, allow. Put us in the smallest space when we are most beautiful. Give us more room as we need it. Inevitably, apartments remind you that the body can alienate as much as it can arouse. The kitchen may be the heart of a house, but that's rarely true for apartments. There, the heart shifts between kitchen, bedroom, and bathroom, locus of good times and bad. The bathroom—epicentre of the abject. Part pharmacy, part operating theatre, the room of flow, of taps and drains. Even the towels—folded by Kate into rectangles she assured me were more attractive than the rectangles I made—were in constant flux, their stack depleting, their crisp edges rumpling with our wear. There in the in-and-out room, that thin architectural envelope full of half-secrets, nothing was more important, more life changing, and more alien than Kate's little strip of birth control pills, that credit card for a sexual shopping spree.

Tired one chilly night, we dropped our patience for taking turns in the bathroom. We left the door open and grinned through a bobbing choreography of rinsing, brushing, and spitting. The one body chore she had that I didn't was reaching for her oblong packet of pills. She held the pill out on the tip of one finger to say, "The centre of our home is very small but very powerful." Then, bless her, she widened her eyes and pressed the nightly dose to her tongue.

Several times a week I'd overhear the horsy squirt of Kate peeing. The pill and her vitamin supplements made it more drugged than that of a racehorse. She told me that roughly 85 percent of Canadian women go on the pill at some point. Our sewers swim with excess estrogen. Zeus's father Cronus ate his children to circumvent a prophecy that would have him overthrown by one of them. Since 1964, women have been pre-emptively eating their children. Science versus nature. One nature versus another. One of the tricky trade secrets Melissa shared about escort and lap dance work is the fact that skin workers who don't take the pill make more money. No matter where they are, cold climate or warm, post-industrial or college town, skinners with an undiluted cycle clean up in tips. The whiff of them. Yet who needs to control birth more?

Another cohabiting surprise were the unexpected midnight chats in bed. We didn't lack conversation elsewhere, but there was something about the darkness, comfort, and ease of our shared bed that tugged out one casually honest conversation after another. She'd often save her most stimulating law school highlights for bedtime. I'd parcel out my inheritance, the Greek myths, the acting legends, and, always a gamble, even a little from my childhood comic book obsession.

"There's this guy, Cyclops, who has this red ray that shoots out his eyes."

"Of course he does."

"A special visor allows him to check the deadly rays when he's in costume, and some custom red glasses do the job when he mixes with the civvies."

"And then one day…"

"He falls in love with his teammate, Phoenix—"

"Who moonlights as a van art model."

"Totally: all tits and cascading red hair. She has the twin powers of telepathy and telekinesis."

"So she knows what you want to watch *and* she can get the remote from across the room."

I drew her in even closer to my chest. "So at some point her powers get augmented, through the roof. She knows what you think and can control your body better than you can. The rest of the team just take up space on the plane. But even the omnipotent need romance. Off she goes with lover man on a picnic. A hike in the woods in a cotton sweater. Let's forget about global evil for the afternoon. After lunch, she asks if she can stare into his eyes. He can never stop those deadly rays, only control them. Until now he has always felt a bit like a monster."

"Which we pick up from the name *Cyclops*."

"With her heightened powers, Lady Van Art can control those rays, can hold them back with her mind. Remember this is all done in comic-book frames: face-to-face master shot as she reaches for the glasses then in tight on his swirling red peepers. Picture love, fear, and wonder in red, picture terror and gratitude as she stares into a force that normally kills. To me, that's the pill."

"Kills?"

"You know what I mean."

Spooning in our darkened bedroom I couldn't see her face. Nor she mine.

23. Paper Clips

I'M TRYING TO COME CLEAN, ugliness and all. My next bit of housing wasn't nearly so nice.

All managers should have dogs and try a stint as a criminal. In addition to the dozens of small lessons you learn actually doing things, not just swapping buzzwords, run under the law and you come smack up against the fact that every employee is just one threat or temptation away from becoming chief witness for the prosecution. Unless you're the lead dog, the scenery never changes.

My casino plan (Operation Roll the Dice) kept those two classic commercial gauges, time and money, perpetually in front of my eyes. Of course it would have been cheaper to try the casino legitimately— get hired as a valet, win over a crew, do my thing quietly with just a little grease. But it would have taken forever just to get hired. And the nepotistic union was all grease anyway, so what was a legitimate hire? Cousin X and Nephew Y would have beaten me to every valet job that came up. Even if I did get hired, there'd be the unpredictability of who I'd be working with. Business Lesson 4 or 5—fuck chance (especially when the money clock is always ticking).

People like Gloria, steady job, steady pay, they only reserve uncertain spending for life, not for making a living. For most, love, parenting, and maybe real estate are the only areas where they go in spending then keep spending indefinitely. For entrepreneurs, uncertain spending can be daily life. One roulette wheel or another is always spinning.

Worse than hemorrhaging money, the casino plan would no longer allow me to work alone. Every co-worker is a witness. With the house painting, I had always tried to know my crews a little. Where they lived.

A bit of their past. Their family. Work is one long character interview. At my busiest, I'd be running five guys, most of them sub-contractors, four-handed painters who could coat a wall faster than you can measure one. Reese was with me the longest, a local boy who was there because he wanted to make money with his body without sacrificing it, which you absolutely have to do in full-scale construction. Bye-bye, knees. Reese had that bristling physical energy best tied to a paycheque. Send him up the highest ladder with a sheep (a roller with the deepest pile) and he'd finish the climb with one leg stretched out to balance the arm he was reaching well beyond sanity or comfort on the other side. He never minded a little dirt on his hands.

For the casino, I needed to run the valets when I wanted, how I wanted, and with my own crew. My recon included a little money lost on the tables and then plenty of hello tips for the valet staff. Say, who's your manager? Samir Hussein.

Samir was in the phonebook. Moy Ave., first block off Riverside. Easy to find, quick to leave. His house was in Walkerville, not too far from our new apartment. In the 1920s, Hiram Walker knew the lay of the land: legal booze on one side of the river, more customers and higher prices on the other. Walkerville was a classic company town. Sewers courtesy of Big Man Hiram. Local cattle fattening on the spent whisky mash. In Windsor, we're always moving something, and Canada's first electric streetcars ran between Walkerville and Windsor proper. That tram got people to and from work but was later ripped up so workers would buy the cars their neighbours were making at Ford, Chrysler, and GM. Take a VIA train into Windsor today and you still get off in a station called Walkerville, towering distillery silos all around you. When the wind is right and the boil is high, you can smell the fermenting rye anywhere in the city, like the smell of Grape Nuts and so thick you want a spoon.

Samir's house had signs of work everywhere. New windows throughout, and that surely meant a loan. New siding. Fresh white plastic sewer cap on the lawn announcing a redig. Here was the old real estate advice in action. Buy the cheapest house on a nice block. After a few strolls past the house with Voodoo, I saw Samir step out of a used BMW. I wanted to run over and lick the hood ornament. Instead I walked to the nearest pay phone and called City Hall. "Hi, I just moved in on Moy. When's the next recycling pickup? Thank you very much."

At the end of the next day's painting, I took Reese out for a pitcher of beer.

"Next Wednesday, you want to make fifty bucks picking up a box?"

Reese was one of those guys of seemingly inflatable size. Not too tall, 5'9", big enough one minute, compact the next. Round, simian head, meaty shoulders.

All week I'd been loading a new fine-paper recycling box with flyers, junk mail, even blank sheets. At 3:30 in the morning on recycling day, I drove by Samir's place in a rented van with Reese crouching by the side door. He grabbed Samir's recycling bin off the curb and switched it for the dummy before the tires stopped. Back at my garage, I got to know Samir. Three credit cards, a personal line of credit, car payments, and a heavy mortgage—another North American dangling from a long rope of debt. Aside from the bank statements, I burnt what paper I didn't need.

Putting the touch on Samir was as complex, as variable, and as challenging as designing and building the mule bags I'd invite him to make money ignoring. The human element, always tricky. Should I tap him on the way to work or coming home? Carrot or stick? How much stick? I knew he needed money, but not how he'd react. Need's enough to start.

I'd already logged thirty hours watching Samir by the time I sat down on a park bench with a clear view of the casino's employee parking lot and his Beemer. Thirty unpaid hours plus thirty hours of opportunity cost plus operational costs plus a significant risk of exposure. This was the casino—cameras everywhere. Rest assured that a disguise is the only time I wear a baseball cap. I sat with a decoy book open on my lap while actually listening to an audio book with earbuds.

When Samir finally stepped out into the parking lot I kept up my library poker face. I waited a little after he drove off then pretended to check my watch and strolled away. Only when I rounded a corner did I begin to hurry, unlocking my bike and racing through the ghetto streets that run parallel to the riverside street he'd be taking home. (That's right, *bike*. Cars have licence plates.) He had traffic lights and Windsor's version of rush hour to contend with. I only had a few stop signs to breeze past.

Honestly, I would have preferred to catch him at work. Talk business at business and never risk looking like I was threatening his family (which was the last thing I wanted to do, personally and commercially). But the casino was designed to look for exactly the kind of move I was trying to make. Sorry, Samir.

Mutual self-interest. All I've ever really tried to sell is mutual self-interest. Greed's a much better fuel than fear. Fear can be numbing. Greed stays fresh.

I had just enough time to lock my bike and get myself in front of Samir's house as he parked. I wiped the sweat off my brow before I approached. "Mr. Hussein, I'm Trevor Reynolds." I gave him plenty of room. "Could I give you my business card?" I held out the fake card, a brown C-note paper-clipped beneath it. As he took it I made an obvious half-step back while he weighed the card and the cash. Commercial tai sabaki.

"My number's there. I'll walk away now and hope for your call. Perhaps we could meet sometime for coffee."

After a day and a half with a phone practically glued to my wrist, Kate joked that my business was shady enough she never had any doubts I was waiting for a call from another woman. No sooner did I say, "I'm legit in places," than Samir finally rang.

"What is this about?" he asked immediately.

But he and my C-note already knew what this was about. "Mr. Hussein, I wonder if we might meet for coffee. Wherever you like."

Time bombs have counted seconds less dramatically than I did waiting for his answer. Marriage proposals have received less exciting replies.

"I won't be alone," he finally said.

"I most certainly will."

One of the few feelings better than holding an ace in the hole is winning without having to play it. I went to our meeting with Samir's groaning line of credit statement tucked into a blazer pocket.

We met at one of the ex-Iraqi restaurants down Wyandotte. During Gulf War I, every use of the word *Iraqi* had been covered over with *Mid-Eastern*. Vinyl banners were hung over their exterior signs. Laminated paper printouts were taped over the coloured, curving script of their hand-painted window lettering. The menu was stippled with tiny white stickers, tissues on so many global shaving cuts.

The restaurant had three public dining rooms, four (visible) men, and a few hundred mirrors. Every other surface was reflective. Mirrored tiles the size of your thumbnail curled around a pillar. Silver beads hung draped in door frames. Each of these tiny mirrors showed me that once again my greed made me the only white guy in a brown room. Samir sat in the innermost dining room with his back to the wall. Three younger Middle-Eastern men paced between a bar and Samir's table, tracksuit, wrist hair, gold chains, and cellphones on each of them.

I asked if I might take a seat. "Mr. Hussein, we have mutual business which could be mutually profitable." I'd anticipated a list of his possible responses and got the best one. Not *I already have a job*. Not *What makes you think I'm looking for business?* Not *If this is about the casino, forget it*. Instead, golden silence. Then, even better, he nodded at the 'waiters' and said something in Arabic (or pig Latin for all I knew. *We will garrotte this limp faggot in seconds*). They retreated to another room.

"I'd like to become nighttime valet manager, and I'm prepared to make that worth your while."

"You think I'm stupid?" he asked.

"Just the opposite. I'll pay you a third of what they pay you." Beat. "In cash." Half beat. "Weekly."

"And what am I to do for two hundred dollars a week?"

I smiled. "We both know that one-fifty a week is a third of your salary. We're here because neither of us is stupid." I could have showed him his bank statement, but that might have scared him off. "Six hundred extra dollars a month, cash, to hire me and then just keep doing what you do. You do your job, I'll do mine."

"Why would I risk my job for only a third of its pay?"

"Because right now you're already losing a quarter of your pay to interest."

I got a little eyebrow for that. "So obviously I can't afford to lose my job. Nine hundred a month. And a five percent raise per year."

We shook hands on $750. After the shake he confessed, "I don't have total control over hiring. There's management *and* the union."

Fine. In Windsor, we were all brother$ in the union.

24. (Beneath) the Belly of the Beast

THE CHIEF COMPLAINT—KATE'S COMPLAINT, Mom's, yours?—is that I saw things too technically, that I solved problems without seeing what problems my solutions created. The punting money had been good, but my life changed with the mule bags I slung out of the casino. Like most fortunes, it was built on the backs of others. Or, more accurately, their undersides.

Guilty as charged: when I sent an electromagnetic bag of high-test off under some white Michigander's Lexus, well, I wasn't risking a mirror pole or sniffer dog myself. I still claim I didn't take from Kate or my family, that anything I received emotionally was freely given. But with the mule bags, yes, I took from others. My profit, their risk. But we all take something. To be alive is to take. Romantically, takers never become givers, yet you can't love someone who only ever gives (or pretends to). Admit you're alive, or you're not really playing the game. The organic coffee farm I run now is only possible because I once had dirt, and blood, under my fingernails.

First getting the bags over took months: infiltrating the casino, earning the trust and fear of my crew, learning to wire bags that would drop off at the press of a button. Once I had error-free bags and a casino crew who didn't know their associates on the other side from the Detroit Pistons, sorting out who looked for what when couldn't have been easier thanks to Blogspot. You might not believe this, but there are multiple websites devoted to car poetry. Pimpedridepoetry.com wasn't the only site featuring tripe like *Oh Fiesta / my little blue siesta*. On mine, I'd number the poems to show the numerals in our mule's licence plate and sign the poem with the poet's initials for the letters. State or province of poetic residence. Go, mule bags, go.

I'm trying to be honest here, not another male braggart: by the time it was up and running the casino work quintupled my take-home income. I wasn't quite the Montreal Angels, no half-mil a day for me, but by spring I was doing better than I ever thought I would. In those first heady months, Kate was only human.

As others have said before me, if you're going down on the *Titanic*, at least sail first class. At the casino, my hours were actually more reliable than when I'd been punting with the treb, and the pay was much, much higher. Kate caved. Our apartment quickly had more Danish end tables than a Copenhagen furniture museum. Reading was Pleasure No. 2 for us, and our living room had an armada of reclining chairs and sofas, each with its small, attentive light. Living across from the D also meant living across from an American airport, and we were off to a new city every long weekend. San Francisco. Rainy, potty Seattle. Houston on a Rothko pilgrimage.

If you think Kate more spend-happy with my money than she had originally wanted to be, realize how tempting actual cash is, especially cash that will never see a bank account. Kate had made vows of self-sufficiency when we looked for a place, but those campaign trail promises didn't survive into the backroom legislation, at least not at first. In part, she was ruined by the physical, untraceable cash, such a rarity in these days of direct deposit, credit cards, and Web transfers. Each of us was just old enough to remember whining in huge Friday afternoon bank lineups as our mothers and half the city waited to deposit their bimonthly paycheques.

I had multiple safety deposit boxes around town and steadily laundered money through Reese and the painting company he was now running for me. Still the paper piled up. Restaurants, groceries, bookstores, folding money for work—all greased by cash the government wasn't counting. If I spent extra living with Kate, our kitchen outfitted in more stainless steel than a microbrewery, that was joy, a happy tax I was willing to pay. All the same, she wouldn't accept any donations for Safe Sisters. Some restorative smoke, sure. A nice warm place to come home to and surgically programmed, morning cappu-organa everything, yes. But no slices off my green brick when it came to hooker justice.

Perhaps because my life had no official scorecard other than my pile, I was extremely interested in her exams and assignments. She was two-thirds of the way through law school, halfway to becoming a lawyer and willing to spend the summer with me in life-threateningly humid and polluted Windsor. I kept celebrating. In addition to travel, there was a fleet of new wine glasses and some Boreal forest protected in each of our names. I threw some cash at a foster-family, goat-adoption, third-world guilt something and got Voodoo's teeth cleaned. Popped corks all around. Yet one of the best ideas I had didn't feel right to share. Loving Kate, I also wanted to do right by Gloria.

Before, during, and immediately after Mom's Chicago MFA, sure, doing it had seemed like a great idea. Her artistic renaissance. Her professional expansion. A test of who she was and who she could be. I certainly never lived around her in the same way after her starring performance in *Medea*. If my mother hadn't played a tear-jerking, respect-inspiring Medea, would I have so readily followed a woman who ran in the rain? But a high IQ and artistic vision still have to get through the work week, might still care about a pension. She had gone off to Chicago a high-school drama teacher and in large measure she came back a high-school drama teacher. Her MFA had been a peak, and invariably there was a valley after it.

Head over heels in love with Kate and lamenting Gloria's funk, I registered a new company without breathing a word about it to either of them. Shortly after we came back from a May trip to Barcelona, Cronus Holdings Ltd. was a paper entity. A week later it had a rented mailbox and a website full of soft-edged clip art. Clear skinned women with shiny ponytails wore telephone headsets. Fit, multi-ethnic office workers exchanged documents and grave but determined looks. Translucent numbers collected in one corner of the screen like lucrative snow.

Gloria would never have taken money from me directly but needed production dollars if she was ever going to do more than produce gymnasium plays scheduled around volleyball tournaments. Sometimes generosity is more generous when it's anonymous. I side-hired a low-level bean counter at my accounting firm to answer cellphone calls and emails from me or Glore and to offer her financial backing for her next production. That Kate and I would invariably see such a production didn't dissuade me from keeping quiet about my donation. The play, not its backer, should have been the thing.

25. Getting Her Spine

THROUGHOUT THE SPRING AND MOST of the summer I invaded the American mind via the undersides of Lexuses, Lincolns, and, the obvious target of choice, Cadillacs. Come the heat and stink of August, Kate reminded me of how many other packages I'd also let go.

She's right, I was indeed "less observant" that August, at least on one crucial front. Windsor is an absolute inferno in the summer, nine circles of smoggy hell. We spent half of July up north at a rented cottage, but the grow must go on. I was the only link between my Windsor crew and the Detroit team, and I had to keep it that way. The Safe Sisters and I knew that so much of good business is like safe sex: you'll never have to pay for costs you don't incur in the first place.

Come August, Kate and I were back in the inferno living on iced everything. Between the iced coffees, iced green teas, and ice water with cucumber we endured smears of days with a temperature constantly above 30° *before* the humidex. Kate claimed it was too hot for booze. Gone, suddenly, was my gin-and-tonic partner, my Orvieto comrade. One night I wondered aloud if this new teetotaller with a shiny forehead wasn't an impostor. When she once again declined a drink I fake-shook her shoulders and asked, "What have you done with Kate?!" I could've handled annoyance or disapproval, but her response was simultaneously squishy and sharp. She looked at me with such a bottomless sadness I was terrified.

"What is it? What's wrong?"

"You're less observant than you once were," was all she said before she headed off to bed early (again).

I let it drift, blamed the constant and cumulative heat, the drain of her summer job reading photocopies at a law firm run by yucking men. Every day was another day in the oven. Sure, she was irritable and despondent, but then we had our hours of fit and gulp.

Given how the fight started—Kate leaving and letting me know by sending me flowers at work—you might be thinking I'd settled down with the second theatrical woman in my life, Sigmund Freud the casting director in life's rich pageant. Gloria claims we all already speak theatre, that drama only uses the body language, exchanges, and emotions of life. Look at the manipulation and spite Kate wrapped around a dozen red roses.

Usually when she bought flowers at the market, shooting a little colour into her life of grinding study, she chose jubilant, multicoloured things. Fat discs of Gerbera daisies or zinnias, or waxy, spherical blobs of rudely homogenous colour. That or an arrangement of spindly, gawky beauty, papery Icelandic poppies. But to get me at work she chose a dozen arrow-like roses, all crimson blood and uniformity. I didn't think of this at first, but if she came back, roses would still be alive and strong after a weekend away.

When I watched the flower delivery go through the casino doors then come back out toward the valet kiosk, I somehow knew they were for me. Even when the bouquet was handed to me, I didn't for a second expect to read a card saying, *I'm at my mother's, --K.*

Here, see for yourself. (When our grandchildren ask why we chose to make scanners, bigger TVs, and computers that didn't last as long as a shirt instead of renewable power, drinking water, and sustainable food, what will we tell them?)

I'm at my mother's. For the second time in my life, I read a short note in which each word was a stepping stone away from me.

The mother moat. The drawbridge is up and you, Mr. Penis, won't be getting across. As intended, I was consumed by the phrase. It became my instant mantra, my state propaganda, my doublethink.

And let's not forget that the target for Kate's crimson missiles was my work, not our home. The next, lonely morning a fresh meaning poked me awake. If she had said, *I've gone to my mother's*, there may at least have been the possibility of her *coming back*. Damn it, I deserved a *because*. *I'm at my mother's because....* Because you are or because you did or because I need. That would hurt, alarm, disrupt, it would be just as fucking inconvenient considering the 12k drop I had planned for that night, but it would still resemble a little something called common courtesy.

I tried her cell even before I'd had breakfast. I had to pace around the apartment to endure its shrill ring and caught my reflection in four or five mirrors. My hair looked like Voodoo had been licking it all night. It was the hair of someone never getting past his lover's voicemail.

So I'd been working a lot. It wasn't as if she didn't regularly work fourteen, sixteen, even eighteen hours a day during term. Sure, some of that was in the home, but that's not necessarily better. Working from home can be great for the person doing it. Fewer germs. Comfy clothes. Caffeine and snacks at hand. But what a drag for the other cohabitant. Textbooks open on every table. Having to use headphones if you want to listen to music. Dirty coffee cups and plates with toast crumbs everywhere. Half-eaten tins of soup abandoned on the counter. And where does cohabitant lust squeeze into a twenty-page paper on intellectual copyright or tort law exam prep?

Lust isn't welcome in fury. Nor doubt either. Damn her. Without a proper note, without a solid accusation to debate or some taunting intonation to replay, I had to reconsider *everything*. She had snubbed me to the max. Fuck-you dialled to 11, and all with the request (the demand? the test of loyalty?) that I stop making money hand over pungent fist and chase after her.

My breakfast consisted of two eggs and the admission that my hopping in the car was a question of when, not if. But going after her meant stalling a Saturday night drop. Kate's offence was its own defence, as much her plan as mine. Every inch of the 401 I covered had me digging myself deeper into holes I never wanted to be in. For a start, Trevor Reynolds's rented storage shed now held a damnable amount of reeking weed. Precisely because of what I did—delivering, not growing—that weed belonged to two criminals, not just one. Both buyer and seller suddenly wanted to piss lava in my name. Managerially, I could have bought back a bit of the time I was wasting, but that'd look weak. A simple lie and some pulled rank temporarily spared me the hook, but that was a pass I didn't like to take. If I blogged out a coded message about the cops or the DEA, I might eventually have sources to discuss. A lie is a false wall, paper thin and ready to collapse. I could collar my own crew, but ground those jockeys too many times, send them home with just their casino wage, and one of those punks was bound to start thinking he could run the show as easily as I did. None of the monkeys were ready to wire their own bags, but money solves most problems. If I had learned to make bags that could fall off a car at the touch of a button, so could someone else. I was angering criminals, tempting some more and making myself into one with a locker full of pungent icky, all so I could run to Kate's whistle.

Weaving through highway traffic, I tried to just breathe, to let one breath pull in the next. Rage is a fuel, but an erratic one. I wasn't pounding the steering wheel, didn't throw a finger at every other driver, but I was still incandescent with rage. For the nineteenth time I thought of turning around, grabbing a phone, and restringing my deal. For the nine hundredth time I thought of her charge that I was "less observant than I once was."

Okay, yes, I'd changed a little with our living together. I'd laughed, pleaded guilty, and adored her a few weeks earlier when she'd asked me, "Do you remember eating with me without getting food on your face?" So we weren't on a first date anymore. We lived together, cooked together, no longer had to finish all our sentences. Before her boozeless August, come five o'clock I could offer her a glass of wine with nothing more than a raised eyebrow and a nod towards our rack of glasses. True, we didn't seduce each other anymore so much as take off our own pants, but she too reached for her belt, not mine.

Inhale. Exhale. Make your case. To her and to you. I had to decide what the relationship needed to be if I was to stay in it. That resolve didn't last past her mother's front door. I had been to Gail's at Christmas. She'd been down to Windsor for a few suppers, and we forced our chats on the phone before the star took the line. Gail and I were emotional colleagues, not friends—keen to like something about each other and palpably relieved not to dislike too much. But whatever Kate had told Gail in the last day had dissolved our affected civility. I got the full hoodlum greeting at the front door. Curtain swept back for a look-see, muffled voices conferring behind an engaged deadbolt. Finally an orchestra of locks was thrown open, although Gail kept the door chained (oh please). A hot August night and my relationship fell down around me.

"She here?"

In the narrow crack of the open door, Kate whisper-argued with her mom before she suddenly stepped out and shut the door behind her. Her eyes were black elastics: not firm, but far from breaking.

I started. "Do not insult me, further, by asking what I'm doing here."

"No, no insults. I promise."

"Well then listen—"

"Can we get out of here? Go to High Park? Just give me a sec to get ready."

"Whatever she wants."

"You really want to talk here?" She gestured around at her mom's front step.

"Quickly."

On her return, Gail waited until Kate swung the door open to say, "Take your cell." Kate didn't, nor wallet either. Just shoes and a half-dead look. ·

I was ready to treat Gail's final shutting of the door as the starting bell. Kate wasn't. "Not a word, please, Antony, until we get to the park. Okay?"

"Right, you leave, you fly off without—"

"Ant, look at me. I'm asking here. Please just wait."

And wait I did, wait I would. Am still.

I managed to keep up a kind of silence, if you discount my breathing. Kate endured my hammerfist gear shifts and side-kick lane changes without complaint. When we arrived to the park, she wearily said, "There's a huge tree in the centre. We'll talk there. Promise."

Maybe you would have been communicative or a good listener or dug your heels in for immediate vengeance. I seethed but followed her. She guided me through the dark winding paths towards an enormous oak I was too furious to appreciate. I barely noticed the few stars persisting against the city light or any of the branches waving hello and goodbye in the moonlit breeze.

"This is it," she said, sitting herself atop a picnic table.

I spewed. "All right, listen. This may be your manipulative way of ending things, but don't think for a second you're walking away without hearing what a selfish little bitch you've been."

"Ant, look at me. Really look at me." She sat with her feet shoulder width apart on the bench of the picnic table. Her spine, normally a flagpole of confidence, wasn't quite stretched to its full height. Uncharacteristically, her chin kept wanting to tuck in a little. "No, not *fight me with your eyes*. Not *pretend you don't and have never cared*. About me. About us. Look at who I am. Look at who you love." Her mouth and chin started quivering. She shook her head back and forth. I didn't want to be, but I was her mirror. When her eyes filled with tears, so did mine, wet for I don't know why.

"I'm pregnant," she said, quietly but firmly. No whispers. No looking away. With that, she got her spine back, raised her cheeks in the scattered moonlight. "We're pregnant."

II. Across

26. Three Short Days

HIS FIRST REAL CRIME WAS stealing a gun. Stealing a gun during a war: the man had to keep things whole.

Legally, Grandpa Bill had bullets for all of three days. Half a day, tops, within fifty kilometres of a German. The only soldiers the modern English Army has exempted from basic training were the Great War tunnellers. Bill and the other moles went from Major Norton-Griffiths's Manchester office to the front in just three days, and at several times a normal soldier's pay grade. As a private contractor, Norton-Griffiths (aka "Empire Jack") had laid off most of these same men, Bill included, when he abandoned a Manchester sewer contract to try to create his new army unit of tunnellers. A War Office handshake had made their major, and a few lies about age and experience made his former sewer diggers into the 170th Tunnelling Company. Drive a truck in a twentieth-century army and you still had to go through basic. March. Salute. Get insulted and drenched in spittle. Compete with the guy beside you, help the guy beside you. If you so much as typed at the Front, you first learned how to bayonet. Load and fire. Hurry up and wait. Carriage return. Not Bill.

Up top, the opposing trenches were often just one hundred metres apart, close enough they could smell each other's cooking. Belle Isle and many an abandoned Detroit parking lot were six times that distance, and I could hit them with a trebuchet as a teenager. No way the untrained were to be given kill sticks that close to the enemy. A muddy sergeant greeted each newly arrived mole with a callused hand outstretched to relieve him of his bullets. No worries: Bill wouldn't have gone rogue with his Lee-Enfield. My bet is he didn't hate the Germans. Underground, sure, he'd have killed a man coming at him, but not with the infantryman's hell-furnace hate. How can I know a man I never met? Scraps. History. Possible genes. A library of phrases handed down from Gran. Second-hand war stories are still war stories. (If you've read this far, you might agree.) Long before history books did, she told me that the rifle and bullets Bill was required to carry when boarding a troop train out of Chatham was reduced to just a rifle upon arrival in France. Rifles, not bullets, are visible from a distance. Bill wasn't to think he was lethally armed, but the Germans were. His rifle was my Detroit skyline: only impressive from a distance. The diggers weren't over a week before they'd dubbed their obligatory but idle rifles "walking sticks" or "Kitchener's walking stick." Where's my bloody Kitchener? The small-mouthed, spear-like grafting shovels and push-picks were their weapons. Birthright, vocation and curse. Gran: "For nearly four years, he held that shovel in his hands like a second spine."

A shovel, his legs and his ears. Lungs that could take it damp and dirty. Like the less safe half of Windsor's Safe Sisters, Bill earned his above-average wages on his back. The blast tunnels for Messines were just three feet high and two feet wide. The moles' speed came, simply, from shovelling with the legs more than the arms. An angled wooden frame, "the cross," allowed them to drive with the legs all shift long. This plank cross was a low, wooden beach chair crossbred with an ab-cruncher of the future. Fold and unfold your legs. Stronger than Jerry's arms, that.

In the tunnels, everything was sound. They had to knock their support timbers together by hand lest a hammer blow summon the German *mineures.* Tunnels of sound and touch. Underground, they devolved. Crawled more than they walked, heard more than they saw. For the rest of his (short) life, Bill whispered when very upset. Whisper-screamed. Whisper-swore. Theirs was a war of listening. To maintain silence, they communicated more with gestures than words. Mom and I trained Voodoo with as many hand cues as verbal commands, while Bill and the lads had to use gestures to stay alive. *Stop. Softer. Check the* [air-quality] *mouse. Shutter the lantern. Flooding ahead.* That last one crossed the Atlantic with him. In Windsor, when he or Gran were in mixed company and wanted to let the other know that some windbag was about to flood the conversation and room with bullshit they'd worm one hand and wrist up and down to mime waves then point forward. Eventually, that became family code for *rowing to Cuba.* Here's someone who's going to need to row out of his own flood of bullshit. More than sixty years after the war, Gloria the progressive parent taught baby-me some sign language before I could speak. Tap the fingers of both hands together if you want more. Show Mommy what kind of animal you see. Three fingers pressed to the cheek for a cat. She taught me to speak with my hands before I could with my mouth. Twelve years later, Gran taught a version of those same hands to swear with that worming tunnellers' wave. Phrases, gestures, the values embedded in a joke: family lingers. Look at your fingers scrolling through this and think of how many different templates they're built from.

Crime can be vicious or greedy or wonked through some bad fucking psychology, but it can also make perfect sense. Army rules said Bill wasn't allowed bullets, let alone a pistol, but every step he took in France occurred because rules were being bent from Kitchener's office on down. The moles were a Windsor rowing club if ever there were one. Untrained, well paid, and drenched in rum. When I finally had Detroit's Earthly Paradise Café up and running and went travelling, I once spent days in London's Imperial War Museum sifting through archival photos. Many of the initial volunteers for the first tunnelling company were over fifty. Army regs shunned any man over forty. The same day these laid-off sewer diggers successfully haggled a self-made millionaire for high pay, they smiled for a group photo. Nearly to a man, they smile with their lips closed. In 1915, almost all the moles who signed on as thirty-four-year-olds were actually old enough to have already lost most of their teeth. Only one man in the 170th, the youngest, shows any pearl. No archivist's pencil labels him William Williams. The photo was catalogued by company and general, but the men have been lost to dust. Still, I elected Mr. Pearl as Bill. Why not? Even if the one blazing smile is his, I'll never know if he was really my great-grandfather. The genes are a mystery, but the emotions aren't. With you, the opposite might be true. Here (maybe) is smiling Bill.

All families row a little, plenty a lot. As for armies, well, Churchill wasn't wrong. The first casualty of war is indeed the truth. Bill wanted a pistol for life underground, and he had to lie, cheat, and barter to get it. In the cramped tunnels, the obligatory rifles were more hindrance than protection. To a man, the 170th transferred their bayonets to shortened shovel handles. By the end of the war, special knives were being forged for tunnellers. Evolutionary biologists argue that an animal is a model of its environment. No trench or tunnel soldier would disagree. The wet, pestilent infantrymen who lived in the trenches were a modelled response to the new environment of the land-sweeping machine gun. Gran described knives I'd later see in photographs and sketches at the library: a studded finger guard and pointed butt turned every available end and surface into a point of attack for fighting in the cramped tunnels. Even still, only officers or special patrols were allowed pistols. The tunnellers were one big special patrol. Trench soldiers weren't allowed to hide in the tunnel entrances during shelling but could be conscripted at any time to carry sandbags, dump spoils, or ply the bellows of manual pumps. Still the tunnellers were, officially at least, denied small arms.

Even a couple is an economy. Every meeting with someone else is a bit of a bazaar. My desires, your stock. And vice versa. (Ask Windsor, city of vice.) Bill's demand for a pistol occurred within a very healthy supply. The trenchies lived around every gun manufacturers were making. To be without their rifle was an offence punishable by a dock in pay, a beating, or, when stakes and/or officer whim were high enough, a pistol shot through the head at dawn. Hierarchy was a key reason the tunnellers were denied pistols. Infantrymen shat with their rifles across their knees, while officers had batmen oil their (costlier and privately owned) sidearms. Military law didn't want a pistol in Bill's hands, but he had chaos on his side. In WW I, the leash on the dogs of war kept getting severed by machine gun fire. A raiding party or night patrol out on a recce might go out with four pistols but leave three corpses in the Nome. When everything is wet, muddy death, when your days at the front divide into wet and wetter, shelled and shelled harder, some can still keep their wits about them long enough to hide a verboten pistol in one of a dozen olive pockets. What could be worth an officer's beating or a week of latrine duty? Rum.

Canada's brief dalliance with (alcohol) prohibition only happened while Bill was underground. Like so much that matters in this ragtag country, it happened provincially, not federally. Quebec can also *se souvient* its unthreatened thirst, while Ontario prohibition was sold as "war austerity." The fight-and-fuck juice suddenly became unworthy when our farm boys were drowning in the blood-soaked mud and introducing the world to the maple leaf. Thing is, those boys were paid, in part, with rum. England conquered the world with technology, discipline, racism, and rum. Centuries of English sailors got their daily tot and so too did the trench lads. In the race to tunnel and blow up someone who was racing to blow him up, each tunneller was allotted more rum than the other soldiers. As always, scarcity=value. One clay-kicker couldn't drink all his daily rum and wound up washing his feet with it (a surprisingly smart move in a war that had more foot disease than bullet injuries).

No man is a criminal island. Bill had never held a firearm until Kitchener's Lee-Enfield was thrust into his hands for the midnight crossing to Calais. He wasn't on the ground an hour in France before this firearms virgin wanted a pistol for close quarters. He couldn't get a pistol alone or hide it from the bagging partner literally breathing over his shoulder. Their digging race usually had them stripped down to just pants. Fine then, two birds with one bullet. Pool the rum, save our hides.

The tunnellers never lacked for containers. The vertical access shafts, forward-marching tunnels, and the narrower arteries of listening posts or mines couldn't have existed without canvas sacks to carry out the spoils or, come game day, pack in the Ammonal. Water jugs were hauled in and, eyes averted, urine cans hauled out. In the early, crude days before geophones and listening posts, soldiers in January 1915 would dunk their already freezing ears into decapitated, water-filled petrol tanks embedded in the trench floors. Is that Jerry digging through or just the pounding of your own terrified heart?

Prisons have economies. Ships have economies. Go into space, and you'd swap tubes of puréed ham for tubes of puréed squash. The trenchmen traded all the time. Cigarettes were the daily hello. Much more expensive, French postcards had curves that weren't barbed wire. Until the tunnellers floated along on their higher rum rations, every non-abstemious soldier thought all day long of how to get more rum out of the quartermaster. In a life of constant fear, deprivation, and discomfort, a rum diet was, Bill gambled, the second-last proposal the 170th wanted to hear. Surrender the drug that soothes your fear of death. Brothers, let us forego our amber succour. But take the fear of death straight up for a week, and we can better fight death. Together, our rum can buy us odds. Fuck death.

You've heard of white noise. Even my little stint underground made me nearly forget that noise could be anything but threatening. Underground, the noise is red, ochre, shadowy. The tunnels were woolly with the breath of the diggers yet saw-toothed with the constancy of their kick-shovelling. All that work with the constant threats of a cave-in or counter-explosion made them thirsty. For all my green money, I'd rather be drunk than high in a tiny, multiply lethal tunnel. Thanks to Bill's other international tunnel, I too eventually learned that there's paranoia enough underground.

I've read many of the names of his war dead, but I'll never know the name of the guy who snatched him a warm Luger that first winter. Bill's war was international lunacy, and few wars are anything but officially excused mass murder. Still, I have helpless respect for the room in Parliament with a list of Canada's fallen. Every day, a state employee in white cotton gloves turns over an enormous page in our ledger of the dead. Show the record. Front the names. What, though, of private history? Without this message in a world-wide-Web bottle, this story—mine and maybe even some of yours—wouldn't exist. Your name alone keeps plenty alive.

Click here and you'll see Sun Tzu's *The Art of War* and its early claim, "all war is based on deception." True for the war on (some) drugs and true for Bill underground. The canvas sacks they filled with spoils hardly came out clean, yet their mud scars were often a little darker than the trench mud. Lucky infantrymen got to "wash" the surfacing bags in the nearest puddle. Other than the mud provenance, the moles had no trouble hiding the fruit of their excavation. The trenches were constantly collapsing from artillery fire or wet, insistent gravity. Sandbag here, sandbag there. For prison tunnellers, hiding the spoils can require as much labour as digging them. Then again, they tunnel to escape, not to kill.

Imperial War Museum folders, their edges softened with wear, still hold neatly labelled schematics for fake digging equipment. Pickaxes were mounted on axels and frames so some temporary conscript could sit in the tunnel entrance tugging a cord tied to the pick handle. Other pulleys and cords knocked dummy timbers together. Hear this, Jerry, while we actually tunnel two metres below you. Digging to Cuba. Across my river, Barry Gordy had his Motown musicians rehearse and record in a room dubbed the Snake Pit. Bill's decoy tunnels were much more lethal.

How, in all that, was he to accept not being allowed a pistol? The war was all guns all day long, but not this one, not here. Not you. Laws are borders, and some of us slip them. A week of co-operatively pooled rum stored in tin water canisters bought them a foraged Luger off a thirsty Welshman. More than eighty years later I would creep along a damp, international tunnel thinking of that bartered Luger. Would I find it rattling in a skeleton's hand? Was Windsorite Bill killed defending himself or killed with his own gun? Fresh muscle would still distinguish if he'd been shot in the back or the front, but a desiccated skeleton wouldn't. Had Bill dug his own grave with his tunnel to Detroit, or someone else's?

27. Initial Solutions

PREGNANCY, YOU THINK OF WHERE you're going but also where you've been. A puck in the net. Finally turning on that oven. The garden and its singular, tremendous fruit.

Ever the outsider. For all that words had formerly helped us into each other, levers and keys into body and mind, the words *I'm pregnant* banished me. Initially, I was without words. Terror. Disbelief. Wonder. She had quickly reached for that polite fiction and added—*We're pregnant*—but no amount of Cuban fully dissolves a border. And Kate was on the other side of language now. Words were paltry and slipshod compared to her new argot of sensations: soreness, stirrings, revolts.

Awe. Incredulity. Confusion (but the pill?). Then the internal debate about where, when, and how I could say *abortion*. We were twenty-fucking-five. She'd wanted to be a lawyer for half her life and here she was in pod before her final year of law school.

Abortion. A lifeline. For her, for me, for we. Abortion. A red warning light flashing on our console. A button I needed to press. Abortion. The dog you've raised to now let off its chain. And, above all, mercy.

I'm pregnant. Hear that and there's already distance between the two of you. *I'm pregnant.* She was, and I was left behind, the salaried NASA scientist watching the ship and its expensive payload power off into inner space. The word was the thin edge of a swelling wedge tapped between us. Maybe if I just shifted to the side a little, that wedge would lose its purchase and clatter to the ground. Thing is, tai sabaki only works in advance, not retroactively.

I hadn't suspected for a second. *You're less observant than you once were* had referred to my not noticing a missed period, the swellings and retreats, the red cave she backed into then emerged out of. Of course as soon as she said it, I recognized that our carnal routine had been a while without its change and that, yes, I'd been too busy slinging green to notice. I thought she'd stopped drinking because of the Windsor heat.

Then wonder. Unfocussed, inarticulate, probably costly wonder. This is the strangest, most unique thing to ever happen to you. Simultaneously you think you have just won the weirdness lottery, and yet nothing is more natural. You even question fate: did that rogue pill malfunction, or allow? To some, *genetic fate* is a contradiction; to others, it's redundant. At times, who doesn't believe (want to believe?) that we're also genetically drawn to our partners, not just rationally and emotionally compelled, that cells and genes are incomplete without the other? Love isn't, can't be, all policy and debate. Rude biology will have its rut. The scent of him or her, the sweat you make together then mingle. These genetic compulsions are easier to see once the words *I'm pregnant* eject you from the plane.

Sitting with her under an enormous tree in the half-light of High Park (!), a four-minute father, I felt a little like rain. Not a single drop but one of many. We could still hear traffic and street noise. Passing headlights slopped light through the canopy of leaves above our heads. Car doors woofed shut. A streetcar clanged by. All those noises, each activity, the city itself—everything had originated in the grunts of sex. Like it or not, Kate and I were suddenly members of a club, a tribe. Or maybe not full members yet. Applicants. Reluctant applicants, I hoped. I got a little of my head back. All that noise and bustle didn't simply begin in sex. However unfairly, it all began with male ejaculation. All these genetic contracts signed by male pleasure. Both the species and the world would be so different if human conception also required female orgasm. In training Voodoo, I'd learned one slogan more important than all the rest: You get what you reward.

No, I didn't immediately leap to hold Mother Kate. I hope that's to my credit. I wanted to think, even a little, not cling. Either she wanted the same or disapproved of my initial few minutes hanging off. When I did finally lean in for a hug, her slack arms and firm spine made me feel farther away, not closer. An unreciprocated hug is failure mimed. I said the second-most honest thing I could. "Oh, Kate." Writing now, I admit that doesn't sound anything like *abortion*.

Yes, my first question was rehearsed. My "Have you seen a doctor?" could have been caring, could have been responsible. It was also, of course, my way of saying, *Are you sure?*

"I've seen one pee-stick plus sign after another is what I've seen. Five tests, three different brands. I've seen no period and darkening areolae. And my boobs hurt like hell."

Already her face had a new way of looking off. Get pregnant and the thousand-yard stare just comes.

"Still though, you should—"

"*Still though* what? Still a drug smuggler, though?" She turned away and even slid herself a little along the picnic table.

"Not yet, okay, Kate? Not yet. Keep talking to me. Any idea what happened?"

"Let's see…Wasn't there one time when you fell on top of me with your dick hard? We fucked is what happened."

"I mean with the pill."

"The pill doesn't always work. Welcome to Club 3 Percent."

"But you took it like usual!"

"Like always."

Even in the half-light I could see her glare.

"What do you think? Last month I decided that having a baby with a criminal would jump-start my legal career? This isn't my fucking fault."

"I'm not saying it's your fault." There, we had said *fault*. Time to start talking solutions. *Pregnancy* not *baby*. Never say *baby*. "Kate, I love you. I want you to be healthy and happy. I—"

Shit, we were kissing. She was all python, pulling me in, wrapping me up. Our tongues alone were suddenly more intimate and more daring than we had been in days. Wet, Greco-Roman wrestling one minute, slow pink signatures the next.

"Come on, in here," she said, guiding us toward a darker path into the woods. Once you break the in-case-of-emergency glass, you might as well reach on through.

28. Medea, Medea

MY MOTHER INTRODUCED ME TO infanticide. Even without her Chicago *Medea*, I learned that we single children of single mothers often barely survive. I wanted Kate to endure the sound of a vacuum Gloria had chosen not to hear. She must have been tempted, even before Trevor lit out. They were vagabond actors, unstable financially if not emotionally. Legally, he was an exile. By the time he packed his bags again, did she want me or was it simply too late to hit undo? Before Kate was up the pole, she told me that 95 percent of Canadian abortions are performed by week twelve, the sticking week. (Another little gem she picked up in that knowledge sandwich between law school and Safe Sisters.) Trevor left his note of *un*s, and nothing else save some genes, shortly after three months.

Gloria: tough love and tasteful earrings. The week she signed a permanent contract at her school, she hung up a copy of the title page of Thomas Bowdler's nineteenth-century *Family Shakespeare* on her classroom wall. This expurgated edition of Shakespeare's plays "endeavoured to remove every thing that could give just offence to the religious and virtuous mind." This single sheet of framed paper was another of Gloria's tests, a little gateway to separate the B students from the A's, those who thought she approved and those who learned she didn't.

The Family Shakespeare. As if families shouldn't know how they begin, where and how their lifeblood first ran. Billy S. knew how we keep things whole. There was no innuendo he wouldn't reach for. Or stoop to. *Bearded* this and *staff* that. Rings and hoops and coins. Purses, gloves, flowers, and everything pink—all played for smutty laughs. Locks get picked in the night. Warm winds part velvet curtains. In Shakespeare's garden, some nights the plum tree is easier to climb than others. This was

Gloria's specialty. She too smuggled contraband past her enemy. To her, Bowdler "drove a Cadillac."

You've seen the (trademarked) hood ornament of Detroit's pride, the Cadillac car. Has anyone else told you it was stolen and is another local counterfeit? Around 1604, Antoine Laumet Cadillac started his lying in Nova Scotia and Quebec before he went professional and founded Detroit. Another entertainer honing his skills in Canada before chasing the bigger American audience. He was barely off the ship in Port Royal, Nova Scotia, before he started calling himself Antoine de La Mothe, appropriating the name Lamothe from a nobleman back home. He also stole Lamothe's coat of arms, a symbol that would eventually grace the hood of every Cadillac car and serve as the company logo. He was Gatsby before Gatsby. As soon as he was put in charge of Fort Detroit he quintupled the price of a jug of brandy. Another local fortune founded on a buzz.

Mom showed me what she thought of liars and cheats long before I started selling my pre-rolleds. At seventeen, I assured myself she couldn't have known about my street slinging. She was away in Chicago most of that year. But look what she showed me as co-author and star of a rewrite of Euripides's tragedy *Medea*.

An actor for a parent. Strange and not so strange. The actor is a soul in a situation, a body, voice, and mind throwing or catching someone else's ball. So too the parent, always aiming for a moving target. Perpetual jazz. You only get to teach the lessons you have occasion to teach, not those you want to teach. Once when we drove past a playground, Mom announced, "Every child is a mimic." Little did I know.

When I was in the monkey years myself, three, four, five years old, she used to terrify me, to indulge me by terrifying me. Our cat and mouse game might start with some reading on the couch, though crucially this would be hours before bed. Daytime couch reading became horror reading. No book in the world will ever hold me like *Treasure Island* once did. We must have read some scenes two dozen times, and still I froze every time Israel Hands began climbing the mast after young Hawkins. Mom's voice was pure menace, her tone as steely as any dagger she was describing. Watch out for her lips. Snarls of derision. Mercilessness in a slit. Pouts of entreaty. And then the chase would be on. When a character she was reading about leapt for someone else, she would toss the book aside and leap for me. It wasn't until I watched her *Medea* more than a decade later that I realized she had lunged with an actor's timing, not a predator's. The arms she reached out for me were intended to cue my sprint from the couch, not to catch me. One action created a space for the next.

Learn even a bit about the Greek myths and you see that character=action. Oedipus stabbing out his eyes. Penelope undoing her daily weaving. Medea and her spiteful infanticide. She kills her sons to spite her husband Jason, her cheating, scheming husband. Medea=infanticidal spite, not just infanticide. Mom, not Kate, introduced me to this scorched gene policy.

When Gran and I flew to Chicago to see Mom as Medea, that famous mother and anti-mother, I'd never been more proud. All love involves pride. The heart wants to own, not rent. That was my mother on stage getting ready to off her children, and I was respect from head to toe. But of course Gran, not I, had actually lost a homeland and a child to war, male vanity and nationalism. She was closer to Medea than I'd ever be.

Obviously the play was for strangers, strangers in another country even, not me or Gran. I didn't take it personally, but given Mom's spin on the funky cold Medea, I couldn't help but take it professionally. Whereas Euripides's *Medea* is set in ancient Corinth, a coastal Greek kingdom, Mom's was set in Canada's Cornwall in the late 1960s. Corinth was a narrow isthmus connecting the Peloponnesus to mainland Greece and frequently had ships hauled over it on sledges. Cornwall straddles the Canada/US border, is near the national rail line that ferried cargo from the Atlantic to the Pacific, and sits equidistant to Toronto, Montreal, and

Ottawa, a busy hub in the draft-dodging wheel. More important, more lasting yet more timely, was the story of young, love-sick criminals on the run. Euripides had Medea running from country to country with Jason to get away with the golden fleece, a kind of super wool/magic cloak they stole from Medea's dad. Bonny and Clyde in a trim, fast ship. In the rewrite Mom did with her director, Medea and Jason were American hippies trying to smuggle a strain of pot, the golden fleece, into Canada so they could profitably turn on, tune in, and drop out. Quite specifically, they needed to drop out of the Vietnam War, Jason having burnt his draft card in the US before he would burn Medea's hopes and heart in Canada.

The whole year she'd been away, I'd thought my handshake of nations work with street weed flew below the Mom radar. How could she have known I sold? She might've suspected I smoked pot—what teen doesn't?—but selling it? She went off to Chicago with my first trebuchets collecting dust in her crawl space. How could she have known they'd been put to fresh use while she was away? Watching her play unfold, I lost confidence that my green lantern had been visible to only a select few. Inseparable from her skill, a calibre of acting I'd never seen from her before, was her accusation, a retracing of the homeland borders.

You don't need me to convince you that a family member is the worst enemy you could ever possibly have. Similar brains similarly clicking away. Even worse, when we fight family we're likely to half-hesitate on the killing blow (but only half-hesitate). Her *Medea* hit me with one thought more insistent than the others: Trevor Reynolds, Trevor Reynolds, Trevor Reynolds. She was using him to get at my green.

In life and love, why don't we pay attention? Again and again we confuse optimism with amnesia. Jason, you found yourself quite an ally in Medea, a woman willing to betray and rob her father to aid you, the accomplice without whom you couldn't get the fleece, let alone escape with it. As you fled her father, the stern of your boat just metres from the bow of his, she murdered her brother, hacking him to pieces and scattering his body so Papa would slow down to collect the remains. Was Medea a determined and resourceful ally? Absolutely. A loyal lover? Unquestionably. Anyone you should dare to cross? Noooooooo!!!!!!!!!!

In Mom's version, the murders became political. With Jason a Vietnam draft dodger, Medea's brother would also be subject to the draft, conscripted by yesterday's veterans for today's very different war. In the original, Medea laboriously dismembers her brother and tosses him to the winds. Mom's Medea gave up her absconding brother's location to the local draft board to similarly distract and delay her vengeful father while she and Jason made off with the seeds and clones of his pot strain.

With all that on stage, Mom had me doing the cost-benefit analysis of feminization long before Kate ever did. Medea robs her father, flees her home, and murders her brother while Jason watches. When Jason and Medea arrive to Corinth/Cornwall with the golden fleece, Jason barely pulls their boat ashore before he begins his bid for Glauce, the local king's daughter. Worldly ambition, that Macbeth drug often shared by couples, is his rationalization to the spurned Medea. "What need have you of more children?" he asks her. "But it makes sense / For me to gain advantages for those we already have / By means of those to come." Darling, bigamy with a princess isn't really bigamy. Careerist bigamy. Estate-planning bigamy. C'mon, think of the children.

Who was royalty to a draft-dodging, counter-cultural American hippy? A farmer near a border. In the exodus of Vietnam War resisters, many decided to keep resisting once they got here, and that meant growing their own food, not supporting Big Agri. While urban Toronto had its American ghetto, where Trevor Reynolds sometimes skulked around Baldwin Street with Kansans, Texans, and Georgians his Yankee ass never would have met in Michigan or New York, others felt that if they were already checking out of family and the military-industrial complex, dodging both consumerism and careerism, then they would truly check out. Back to the land they went. In the late 60s, just as Canada shifted irrevocably from growing food to importing it, up boiled the hippies. Most of the history you can find on this exodus fails to note that more American women came to Canada than men, and more stayed. These resisting, nomadic women knew where to take the seeds.

In Gloria's *Medea*, King Creon had a Cornwall farm with a few isolated, neglected acres none of his own children wanted. Up came Jason with a pocketful of seeds. He could dodge the draft and have a nice little grow-op. The easiest way for him to overgrow Government A was to marry into Government B.

Creon was nervous to see Medea walking around after Jason had cast her off for Glauce. (Weed does have its paranoid side.) He prepared to send Medea into exile, permitting her just one last day to bid farewell to her sons. Secretly, he planned to expose her to Canadian immigration in hopes they'd deport her. Enter Aegeus, King of Athens/a border-crossing New York congressman. Hearing Medea's plight but not yet knowing her plan, Aegeus agreed to shelter her provided she could make it to New York and use her herbal powers to help his wife conceive the child they hadn't yet been able to have. (There we grow again: add pregnancy, have story.)

Of course Medea never intended to slip off quietly. Jason dared to rob her so thoroughly then abandoned her publicly. Ultimate humiliation. What could Medea/Mom strike that would hurt him in his new life? The piece of the old he was still trying to cling to: their sons. Infanticidal news stories surface every year. A single mother caught in the avalanche of post-partum depression or a berserk, woman-eating sire, some self-proclaimed victim turning victimizer on his genetic audience. At least in art, only ideas and feelings get hurt.

Gloria knew we had to understand Medea emotionally, had to say *maybe* if not *yes*. In Euripides's day the violence was offstage. He had his chorus *tell* the audience that Medea takes a cleaver to her brother and poisons her children. In the original, the poisoned robe she has her sons take as a gift to their new stepmother is carted off, and its consequences come back as overheard screams and reactions. Today we're eyeball deep in sex and violence. We demand a show, and show Mom did. We sat in an American theatre during its first war with Iraq watching a play set during its war with Vietnam. Rather than killing child actors on stage, Mom took the old device of poisoned clothing and turned it into a contemporary symbol of child-killing: the military uniform. How could Mom's war-resisting, regime-renouncing, pot-growing Medea kill her sons with poisoned clothing? By sending them back home to the US and its brain-dissolving, class-gobbling, profit-churning military. Stranded in Canada and spurned by a draft dodger, Mom's Medea didn't immediately kill her children. Instead, she took them home vowing to raise them as war-loving, father-hating patriots keen to enlist. In the closing scenes, the American audience watched images from Gulf War I projected onto Medea and her sons. Burning oil fields, sweeping helicopters, camouflaged khaki, and convoys bisecting deserts—all made liquid by a digital projection poured over the entire stage while Medea's uniformed sons looked back at us through military-issue night-vision goggles, half mask and half eye of the technological tiger. In her closing tirade to her husband, Mom/Medea stood so firmly I could feel her quads burning, her heels bolted to the stage. Eyebrows, cheekbones, and jaw—all raised with searing contempt for anything foreign, anything not her own, poison from her mother's breast. Medea, Medea, a mother to the last drop.

29. This Bird Has Flown

NO SURPRISE THAT I THOUGHT of Mom and Medea while I waited to start talking abortion with Kate. In a relationship, the word is a submarine, and it surfaces rarely. In the beginning, a man can tell himself it would be presumptuous to talk consequences before consummation. Carts before horses. Once the chemical decision is made, the pharmacological constitution of the land drafted, pill or no pill, how often does the actual word come up? Three times? Four? Maybe one of you is brazen enough in those early, talky dates to ask, What's your stand on abortion? (My stand? Right on the little fetus's head.) More likely you lay the birth-control ground rules then retreat into separate, silent camps. Our discussion about the new scarlet letter—*This adult life brought to you by the letter A*—involved an early declaration of Kate's and then her later calling me on some bullshit I'd been carrying around. Very early, before she recognized how I really made my cash, she told me, "Of course I'm pro-choice, but you should know I'd have a hard time aborting my own child." Who wouldn't? And when she said that, was it really true of the moment or was she stretching her life forward a little and already thinking of herself as a salaried lawyer, not an incomeless law student? About two months later I naively trotted out some stat I'd read about lawyers having more abortions than any other profession. Kate demolished that prejudice without even exhaling.

"Do we actually have more abortions or just admit to them? Obviously your stat is just based on a survey of women. Would the Sisters answer that survey honestly? Would the secretary who feels judged and ridiculed every workday state that for the record? We're more honest, Ant, not more murderous."

Clutching each other in High Park, we were clearly about to
sail into honesty country, yet nothing in a relationship is treated as
euphemistically as abortion. When a family member dies you'll hear
lose, pass, and *go,* even if you yourself say *die, death,* and *dead.* Only if
they're close, though. Husbands and wives don't pass; they die. But great-
grandmothers? In Gran's perpetual decline, I slid around phrases like
when Gran's gone or just *after.* Mom was the more irreverent, once saying,
"When the old bird has finally flown." Speaking of the bird, with Kate
preggers, I started thinking more and more of Gran in her lean years of
loss. Neither husband nor son was ever even a corpse to her. The Williams
men and our vanishing acts.

Porn is everywhere, but abortion is still a secret. *Abortion.* Even in
a couple's home, the word itself is rarely used. *End. Terminate. Options.*
Third-wave feminism (aka blowjob feminism), that wave crested
and fell with not just the pornification of the world, but the *amateur*
pornification of the world. When tens of thousands of young women post
naked pictures and video of themselves for strangers, has feminism won
or died? YouTu•be or Not Tu•be, that is the feminist question.

We don't want to hear about abortion or see it, but we lack Oedipus's
severity and would never put out our own eyes. Like Odysseus, we too
could tie ourselves to the mast if we really wanted to hear that siren song.
Remember that Kate waited until night to disclose. Waited until night and
took us to a dark park. Maybe she didn't want to see too much of my eyes.
Or maybe she wanted a better view of that warning light going off in my
head. *Abort. Abort. Abort.* And then we were busy.

Usually the intensity of the make-up sex is directly proportional to the
severity of the fight. Threat and vitriol become fuel. I'll show you what
you almost lost/gave up. You won't get exactly this with anyone else. (So
we want to tell ourselves.)

Make-up sex plus pregnancy sex. No one fucks with the abandon of a
woman in her first pregnancy. All her sexual life she's worried this could

happen, that this deep switch could be thrown. Now that the engine was finally burning, Kate took us into overdrive. In a darkened recess of a wooded park, we tried to hold each other in the after. Her half-naked back was pressed against the rough bark of a maple, but she made no effort to move away. Distraction? Hair shirt? As for me, I surrendered to the physical. "Sleep with me. I want to hold you, sleep with you."

Motherhood, tragic motherhood. I learned about tragedy from my mother (and grandmother). On the news, bus accidents and illnesses are inaccurately labelled "tragic." Tragic=pitiable. And *hero* now generally means victim. Little Timmy fell down the well, so he's a hero. Gloria taught me motherwise. Tragedy is chosen. The whole point of tragedy is that the suffering is self-inflicted. What I do to become king makes me a terrible king (or queen, as Mom's *Macbeth* would soon show us). Motherhood is tragic. To be so needed, so wanted, so central—but only for a while. If you do your job well, your child will outgrow you. What a recipe for unhappiness.

Witness Kate's mother. What had Gail been through in the last twenty-four hours? A phone call from her only child, perhaps a teary phone call, asking if she could, in that delusional and propagandistic phrase, *come home*. Who would have first used the H-word, Kate or Gail? If it had been Kate, had that been strategy or honesty? Oh the mom-flattery of the word, especially from an adult child. I have scholarships. I'm almost finished law school, live with someone else, and yet we'll all pretend your home is still my home. If I had a Trent Reznor poster on that wall when I was fifteen, surely the room is mine forever. A phone call from a glum Kate, then Gail's fretful, hopeful afternoon before the mom money started flowing. Plans for dinner out. Pick up a little cake on the way home. Maybe some flowers. But judging all the while. And how much news had Gail received? Did she get to hear *pregnant* before I did? Gail was a Chinese immigrant who had fought her way past a limited education and managerial sexism into a lucrative real-estate career. In her day she had to quit her job to have Kate, so she knew all the stepping stones: killer LSAT score, law school, internships, bar ads, and then the slave years making money she wouldn't have time to spend. For a young lawyer, a baby doesn't officially threaten her job, but every woman who steps aside for a baby lets another strident one barge up the middle. Those corner offices come at a high price.

What did Gail know? What did she suspect? Maybe *abortion* wasn't the only word Kate and I were keeping silent. This park sex we'd just had, was it pro-body or just anti-word?

"Sleep with me. I want to hold you. A hotel, your mom's, wherever."

We drove to Gail's to sleep, but didn't sleep much. Kate went up to her mom's room and did whatever quick diplomacy was necessary to get me back in the house. She returned downstairs with an armload of bedding and nodded towards the basement. At a maximum distance from the matriarch, we were terrible. Every piece of cast-off basement furniture was put to use. (Wicker: how it pinches.) We snuck upstairs to make pasta at 2:30 in the morning, though Kate didn't reach for a bottle of wine. Near 5:00, I was awakened in the best way possible. At the end of that round, dawn spilling into the basement's small, high windows, I finally saw what was happening. We weren't being biologically close or turning the force of a fight into sex or drawing together in adversity. Nor were we simply buying the vase we had already broken. The little I saw of Kate's eyes and the extra-dirty things she said and wanted to hear finally revealed the sex for the drug it was. She couldn't sleep for worry, could not or would not drink or smoke, so there I was, a flesh drug, hiding her and letting her be hidden. Definitely not the time to say *abortion*.

30. *The Sugar Deal*

ABOUT THE OTHER PREGNANCY. FATHERS aren't the only mystery here. You must wonder about Gloria's mother. Don't we all.

Truth be typed, the abortion wasn't the only mercy killing I'd been contemplating that August. By the time Kate was dividing and sub-dividing, Gran was 103 years old. A century with small feet. A war-torn century. She had crossed the Atlantic three times, once after each world war, though the second was a return trip. In her day, many people were defined by one crossing, the Atlantic their second birth canal. Generation after generation of immigrants. An army of war brides coming in after a nation of farm boys went out. Gran went back again to keep herself whole. Herself and/or all of us.

After her first war, Gran had sailed with her man beside her, promise and their hearts flung at unknown shores. Peg and Bill, the moll and her mole. Peace may have been declared between nations, but between people she knew it still needed to be coaxed. Bill spent his war in cramped tunnels, had survived by using his ears and his hands. Six months after the guns went quiet he and Gran were at the ship rail staring at the most expansive horizon on the planet (staring, in fact, *at* the planet, its great blue curve).

When Gran crossed back again in 1946, her skin no longer smooth, she'd have sailed through a longitudinal ghost line, felt the tug of those two younger souls passing through her, young souls unable or unwilling to read the French summons now tucked into her handbag. In 1946, a smile a stranger to her lips, she clung to the foremost railing every day, burnished her skin with the cold salt air. For the first few days, she reread the letter that had brought her on board and had launched a thousand hopes. Quickly enough the thin paper was no longer necessary. The orphanage director's words had already burnt into her before she booked passage. But the photo he sent was rarely out of sight.

If this were another boring Canadian farm novel (excuse the redundancy) or mill-town saga, I'd reach now to shake a hatbox archive. The hatbox, originally purchased by a broken-hearted and/ or consumptive great aunt at SomeExEuropeanBody's Mercantile in downtown Empirillia, would wow you with pickling and preserve recipes and letters recounting the boxed lunch socials. The crown jewel would be not just a birth certificate, but an *English* birth certificate, a meat-inspector's stamp from some distant, better Away. To douse Gran in this saccharine crap, our multiply subsidized hallucination, I'd speak reverently of the dusty military telegram, its paper softened with age but its words still as hard as bullets. *WE REGRET TO INFORM YOU...*

I'll spare you the Cuban.

Grandpa Vic caught his nugget in April of '45. Historically, that's a hard pill to swallow, getting popped just weeks before the peace. According to some, he was at least able to leave a little something behind.

April '45, Victor-Conrad dies and Gran's thrown into a hell few of us can imagine. Her last link broken. What's the point? What's a country without children? Then in May, Victory in Europe. Salt in the old girl's wound. In January '46, her life changed with a single letter. No, not just her life; every life mentioned here. A French orphanage worker/con man threw a letter across the pond, and we are the ripples radiating from its splash.

Look up the phrase *French letter*. Pretty much the exact opposite of the letter Gran got. If you believe Wikipedia, when young Victorian gents set out on their grand tours of Europe, chasing old art and young hookers, their passage to Rome took them through southwestern France and introduced them to the ingenious gut work of the French shepherds around the town of Condom. A little sheep intestine over the pole and *voilà*, no pregnancy diluting the family line (i.e., coffers) and no syphilis going home to the English ladies. Back in London, the brothel-going gents eagerly awaited the arrival by post of more domers from France. These French letters eventually went on to climb the social ladder in London and ultimately greeted the visiting gentlemen of France when they were over shopping for a little crumpet.

Always this mud we sling at borders. During the Renaissance, Italian anatomist Gabriello Fallopio ('discoverer' of the Fallopian tube, this story's best supporting actress), started working on modern, effective condoms to prevent syphilis. His work anonymously won a convert from his busy countryman Casanova. Casanova's racy *History of My Life* repeatedly refers to his trusty "English raincoat," which had in fact been designed, tested, and advocated by a fellow Italian. Perhaps in homage to the Venetian Casanova, the French Marquis de Sade wrote affectionately of his use of "Venetian skins." The French wanted *les redingotes d'Angleterre* and the English wanted French letters. Made here but marketed from there. Shagging to Cuba. Pre-World War I, the French gentlemen couldn't learn directly from French peasants, *mon dieu*. If the milords and seigneurs were going to learn from the plebs, if high were to stoop to low, they needed a border and some water to wash themselves clean. Condom was the Windsor of France. We always need to smuggle vice through some Away, claim it's the custom of some foreign, unknowable other. Jungle boogie. Ontario hydro sold as BC Bud. When Gran got her French letter just after the war, the vice in question was still very, very far away.

Dear Mademoiselle Williams,

Please allow me to introduce myself before I deliver news of the days of your heroic son here in Calais. I am Monsieur Belliveau, of the orphanage of St. blah blah…I know my good French people, who are ravaged by war… yadda zut alors yadda…There is this one darling farm girl who was so grateful to the sacrifices of our liberators. She recognized your son Victor-Conrad for the gentleman he was. In a moment of gratitude she suspended her virginal honour. Now, moon die, here is a child of sacrifice, a baby girl, born to a fallen Canadian soldier and, alas, a young woman lost in childbirth. With the depravations of war, your granddaughter would face a miserable, no doubt short, life of malnutrition and exploitation. The tiny orphanage babies of France are dying every day. My duty compels me to relay this news of sadness to you there in prosperous Canada.

That's a version of the story Gran received. She'd been translating from the Cuban for years and knew it really said: *Your son knocked up a prostitute. How much are you willing to pay for the baby?*

Plenty.

In time, cost, and labour, Gran's baby odyssey was much more challenging and expensive than that of a contemporary North American woman booking time off from the firm and cancelling her pedicures to fly to Vietnam or China with a bank draft and a baby carrier. In March 1946, Gran took a train from Windsor to Halifax, a train she knew would be coming back out of Halifax still full of demobilizing soldiers, her son not among them. Then the week-long crossing by ship to England. The prodigaless wore a silver fox stole on her return to an England of crowded trains, piles of rubble, and hotels without soap. She visited busy offices, typewriters clacking, phones ringing, and made inquiries with her British passport, her northern accent, and her new world money. Handed out quarter-pound bags of sugar and coffee as a Williams knows how. One afternoon a busy English major would have been surprised to see Gran sitting before his desk for an unscheduled meeting. If he was observant, he'd have noticed new nylons on his secretary the next day. Gran greased palms with butter and American dollars, trying to learn what she could about Belliveau. Windsor's daily groceries were gold bullion in pasty-faced England and diamond-studded platinum in horsemeat France.

Spontaneous criminals are an insult to us professionals—whimsical, emotional, narcissistic. Not for my tribe. Preparation. Preparation. Preparation. Gran dug in to enable her success. She did all the homework she could to get the drop on Monsieur Orphanage, a man audacious enough to ransom her possible grandchild. She tried offices in London and Paris hoping to determine whether he was a legitimate official or just another grifter with a stained collar and a half-loaded pistol in a threadbare pocket. But in 1946, there weren't any more legitimate officials. "Mademoiselle, where are records in all of this rubble? There are bodies we cannot find, let alone records." Another pack of cigarettes wasted.

With rail service still decimated in France, she hired a car, paying the highest gas prices the world had ever seen. Calais was sick of foreigners, and she couldn't find a proper interpreter for hire. Oh well, she was there for the body anyway. Walking around, the silver fox stole now hidden in her luggage, on the cusp of raising a daughter who would go on to study and practice mime and all manner of experimental acting, Gran surprised all but one thing she knew about herself in order to get what she wanted. Approaching women in the village, she'd flash a goodie or two and attempt to convey her point through gestures. Half a dozen times a day she'd hold up a photograph of Victor-Conrad in uniform then rock an imaginary baby in her arms. She'd point at herself, cradle her arms again, then point back to the photo before miming VC's death. This could have meant, as it did in Mom's stage version of this scene, that her fingers were bullets against her own chest. Of her beseeching mime, Gran told me, "Your vanity prevents you from being understood. Death wipes away vanity."

Stories get new layers with each generation, but each layer adds distance from the source. My images of Gran in war-torn France don't just come from Gran herself. They also come from Mom or Gran telling me about Mom performing a version of Gran's story as part of some early 70s theatre. *The Sugar Deal* played to a warehouse audience of ten to forty people willing to check out "a theatrical experience," aka screaming under minimal lights, aka therapy with an audience. In an evening of mixed theatre, Glore did her bits with a suitcase and photographs, ending with a bundle in her triumphant arms. Decent theatre, I'm sure, but she followed an act that consisted entirely of adults riding tricycles while blowing kazoos and just before a leotarded orgy of seven groaning, barking, whimpering "actors." Mom is the first to confess that her one-act play, with its actual characters, conflicts, emotions, and social commentary, was a complete flop. "In the early seventies, that wasn't the war people wanted to hear about." Trevor Reynolds had played the orphanage man.

However intimate *The Sugar Deal* was, Gloria chose to end it with the Gran character getting the baby, not with how she later dealt with the letter. This is pretty much the only time I know of that Mom has checked her disapproval. (She should remount the show now that she has the money.)

Picture Gran (or Mom doing Gran) as she tried to get the lowdown on Monsieur Belliveau. She'd approach village women with her dead soldier-boy mime and her bag of goodies. Finally she'd point to the curate's letter, to his name, and raise an eyebrow. Legit? *Un peu.*

A suitcase full of butter, sugar, coffee, nylons, and cigarettes. A handbag full of money. Those bags were my grandparents. By the time she finally went to the orphanage, Gran had already acclimatized to not speaking, had grown perhaps even to prefer it. Silence the mother tongue for a mother who'd lost husband and child. She hadn't forgotten that Belliveau had written to her in English; she'd ceased to care. Her baby's baby might have been within walking distance of her. She was frantic to inhale, to touch, to feel with her lips. She used the minimum number of words possible to get to Belliveau. When he greeted her, she interrupted him to say, "Show me," and held a hand up to silence his pitch about local depravations.

What matters as much as where we are born? Drinkable water utterly refutes the idea of karmic reincarnation. How can anyone cling to a belief in fate or destiny when half the hospital beds on the planet are filled because of water-borne diseases? Geography determines aristocracy. Then there's the roulette wheel of genetics.

Crucial nursery-room fact: babies don't always look like a little squalling version of just one parent. Spin the genetic wheel and you could get one of four grandparents or unseen great-grandparents. A nose will form, but its template is completely unpredictable. And a baby's face can change.

Gran's house has a mantel lined with framed photographs, never a speck of dust on them when she was alive. Bill grinning in uniform (the one he stripped off when tunnelling). A wedding photo of Gran and Bill. Victor-Conrad in uniform, taunting his bullet. Gloria's headshot as a young actor. My high school graduation. And, much earlier, the two of them, Gran and Glore, caught in a London portrait studio. Well dressed but neither of them smiling. The faces of victory.

In photos, baby Gloria only looks plausibly like ol' Vic. True, Gran held her, smelled her, traded stares with those little blue eyes. No doubt she could calibrate bone and body in ways I can't just staring at a small photograph. Adult Gloria, okay, plenty of Victor-Conrad across her eyebrows and in that blade of a jaw. But baby Gloria? We have to wonder if Gran wasn't just seeing what she wanted to see. Was it perception or preconception that had her turn back to Monsieur Belliveau ready to haggle? Is the propaganda true? Do women somehow just know?

You can probably tell I've done some reading about born-again fathers, those bio-dads who, for whatever reason, don't meet their children until the children are already some version of adults themselves. One emotional wanderer writes of getting tracked down more than a decade after a brief fling. He was presented with photos of a tween girl. No. Yes. His soul-searching included a talk with his own mother. When he asked her opinion on whether or not he should go ahead and arrange DNA tests, she took one look at the photos and said, "Don't waste your money." Still, I can feel Gran's gamble.

The French were finally getting bread again, but they hadn't tasted butter in half a decade. The next day, when Gran summoned the grifter to her rooms, she left her beefy chauffeur outside her door and was sure to be buttering bread when Belliveau arrived. Money does have a smell, mostly of the filth it has absorbed. That little tang is associative to a degree (trust me), but the literal smell of money will never turn as many keys in a hungry man's brain as the smell of food. "Café, monsieur?" she asked, pouring another rare smell into her warm room.

Gran described this scene to me as the last threshold of her life. "I had already changed more than I ever thought possible. First with the war. Then moving, Canada. And the Windsor business—ooh, la, la. Then death. One, two, nearly my own. I knew that baby was my life again, was all the goodness I had left. But I also knew Frenchy was trying to squeeze me. Well, his grip wasn't anything compared to Death's."

"Café, monsieur? Please, sit. Sugar?"

Once he sat, she began. "I don't know that this baby is my grandchild. How could I? But I do know that she is in need, that you are all in need." Here she must have opened a suitcase. "Five pounds of butter. Ten pounds of coffee. Five pounds of sugar. And two hundred American dollars."

His reply was part spittle, part venom. "Missus Williams, you insult me. You insult my country. You insult your granddaughter." He rose to leave. "And the memory of your son."

There was Gran, not a scrap of post-secondary education, no corporate experience, no job shadowing, yet snarling like the best of them. Where was the meeting? Her turf. The fact that it was unscheduled, that *monsieur* was summoned and had answered her summons showed them both how hungry he was. What did she do first? Offered him some of the fruits of her power *(Café, Monsieur?).* Then she gave him a (polite) command. *(Please, sit.)* Carrot and stick. Carrot and stick. *(Sugar?)* And when he tried to snarl, she snarled back.

"*Monsieur*," she answered without rising, "we both know that the world is now an insult. Money lives beyond insult. It doesn't see or remember. It has no pride. And if you don't want my money, others will surely do much more for much less." Her mime and nylon work with the local women had already unearthed his home address. "The butter alone could get plenty accomplished at 51 rue Delambre."

When Gran told me this she paused to ask, "What was he going to do, hit me? No man could hit me harder than life already had. He just breathed heavily for a minute before giving me a little shit-sucking smile."

"English in voice, American in spirit," he concluded.

"He asked for four hundred. I got him at three. I would have paid five times that. More. Everything. I couldn't stand any second I wasn't with her. But we weren't going to start life as a pair of doormats."

Another life change for a fistful of dollars. Baby Gloria spent the night bawling in the backseat of the car as Gran pressed the driver to move on. "Do not stop. I will pour you more coffee in half an hour. Drive. Drive."

She didn't pause to see extended family in England. "I knew I'd never see them again, but that was somehow the deal. The old or the new, not both. I held the future to my chest and wouldn't let it go."

Gloria would grow up to understand and agree with all but one of Gran's acquisitive gestures. Yes, you have to spend to get what you want. Live prudently, then spend when opportunity and fortune coalesce. And it's good for your character, not just your wallet, to fight for better terms. Gloria would also have shunned the uncles and aunts in Manchester, would have spared them a ruddy-cheeked intrusion in their lean years, would have dodged all questions about the bundle in her arms and the holes in her heart. But Gloria disagreed profoundly with Gran's disposal of Belliveau's letter.

On the return crossing, a second sail to Canada she never thought she'd make, Gran made her way to the rearmost deck, tore the letter apart and tossed it into the salty wind. "Why cling to a lie?" she said for decades of her wiping that French slate clean. Gloria was told the story at twelve, hated it by fifteen, then simmered with quiet resentment for the rest of her life. Over the years she would tell me, "That letter was the only link I had to my mother."

If she'd been honest, Gran would have replied, "Exactly."

31. Homeschooling

PREGNANCY, THE INNER SHADOW. YOU'RE never not pregnant.
Here a zygote, there a zygote. We were pregnant as we packed to leave
Gail's and we'd be pregnant when we got back to Windsor. Before we left
Toronto, I took us CD shopping for the drive home, each of us glad for
mutual consultations and headphone auditions. We wanted anything save
the admission we were nervous of a four-hour drive with nothing to do
but talk. On the highway, new music only rescued us for a while. During
the first CD Kate reached over to turn down the stereo. "I just don't know,
okay. I don't know, and I don't know when I'll know."

"The jury's still out?"

I got the first of many looks for that. Fine by me. I'd take a few weeks
of sharp looks and huffy sighs to get us out of a lifetime of disappointed
looks and frustrated groans.

"That it is." She raised the volume again.

Several songs and dozens of kilometres later I tried an entirely
rational (if scheming) line. "You need to see a doctor. That's the first step.
We still don't even know for sure."

She patted my thigh. "*You* don't know. I do, but not you. This time
you're rowing in *de Nile*."

Well it *was* hard to believe. I'm a lapsed engineer, not a lapsed
"pure" scientist, in part because seeing so easily equals believing, seeing
and touching. In ways, *pregnant* was still just a word. And hopefully a
temporary one.

Admittedly I'm telling you things about Kate I never knew about
my mother. Well, generations accelerate. Now that fourteen is old for a

girl to never have given (but not received) oral sex, probably at school (maybe even on a school bus), what's inappropriate on a controlled-access blog?

With the pregnancy, I was always going to be on the margin. The only question was how far out. Soon enough, Kate would be the glowing, growing centre. In my frustration I later yelled, "What do you mean the pill 'didn't work'? You think I can sell drugs that don't work?" Agreed— tremendous asshole. Tremendously lost too.

Along with Kate's breakfast, the pregnancy brought up another of Mom's lessons. Gloria began each year of acting classes by having students stand and be silent. "Raise your hand as if you were going to pat yourself on the head. Raise it a few more inches. Now slowly lower your flat hand in front of your face." The adolescent shoving and joking would evaporate by the time their hands passed their foreheads. "Keep going. Pass your eyebrows. Pass your nose. Below your chin." Uncomfortable and uncertain, they'd always move their hands in unison with hers. After she had passed her collarbone, she'd say, "There. Most of you have already disconnected. Once your hand passed your throat, maybe even your eye sockets, your mind wandered, didn't it? When you moved away from your head, you thought you'd moved away from you. Not in this class." (Oh, Mom, another artist sacrificed on the altar of a dental plan—and for me.)

With the pregnancy, I had to hope Kate was still in the first day of class. Stay head, please. Be your brain. Whatever you do, don't start to feel from the bottom up.

Pregnancies begin so privately. However divisive, unwelcome, and corrosive our pregnancy was, it was ours. Kate hadn't told Gail, and in August at least she hadn't told any friends. Hopefully this was more than just nervousness over a miscarriage. Safe Sister Melissa told me that as many as one-third of Canadian pregnancies end in miscarriage. Trust an escort to know how many pregnancies stick. (And trust Kate to double-check the stat.) I've now seen, read, and heard that some women announce later and later, hoping to outlast those first, uncertain months, while others announce earlier and earlier, claiming they want to destigmatize miscarriage. That or they want to elbow their way into expectancy's limelight ASAP. Kate would have kept quiet, even in better circumstances. She'd have treated a miscarriage like her body had fired her from a job. She also liked her privacy. Or so I thought until Safaa left an invitation on our answering machine.

Kay, Ant, listen: Bryan's parents are going to a wedding over Labour Day! We can have the cottage to ourselves! Call me before he gets itchy to invite anyone else.

We were invited out of the city to breathable air, had a chance to walk on earth or pine needles, not vomit-stained concrete, yet suddenly Ms. Prior Proper Planning was non-committal about going.

Notice how the word *apartment* begins with *apart*. You might be distant emotionally, but in an apartment it's hard to constantly separate yourselves physically. An apartment is a boxing ring, each wall a set of ropes you can bounce off and come back swinging. In our swelling yelling I began to suspect that houses have multiple storeys just to give couples room to separate during a fight. As I'd pack my casino uniform into a bag and prepare to bike to work, she'd yell or mutter or say to my face, "Business to take care of?"

"Like we don't need money here, either way."

If you think an invitation to a northern Ontario cottage couldn't possibly offset that kind of nastiness, you've never been in Windsor in the summer. Night after night with temperatures in the 30s, a daily humidex pushing 45, all of it ripping straight out of Satan's ass. The pollution cooked the air and the air cooked the pollution. Dare to try to escape the ankle-nipping fakeness or the eco-costs of air conditioning and your open windows could find you awakened by the stink of Zug Island and the other refineries when the wind shifted. Please, bathe me in lake water.

For better or worse, Kate and I were all each other had for the pregnancy. We'd snarl then lick, hurt but heal.

Invited to a cottage for Labour Day. *Labour* Day, hah! At any other time, this was the grand prize of the cottage invite raffle. Labour Day weekend, the holiday of the working class, has become the perfect weekend for the affluent to head to the cottage. Slow to warm but equally slow to cool, lake water is at its warmest. The days are hot but the nights no longer slow roast you in a tongue-and-groove sauna. Most of the bugs are dead. That Bryan's parents were unable to go due to some anti-cottager's inconsiderate wedding was a once-in-a-decade occurrence. If we had all been twenty, not twenty-five, Bryan might've invited a dozen so-called friends. (In a lifetime, how many genuine, life-enriching friends do we have? Six?) Instead, we'd be just two couples. A long weekend at a cottage with only the 4.1 of us.

The invitation was a shadow ninja leaping around our apartment. When Kate wouldn't give me a straight answer as to whether she was going alone or we were going, I countered with "Does Saf know yet?" Yes, yes, I twisted the knife on *yet*. Once again Kate turned her shoulders and marched out of the room. The next day she'd refer to being away but avoided using clarifying words like *we* or *us*.

Pregnant. Betrayed by a greedy battle within my own genes. Most of my genes said yes to my trade, said if I didn't live as an individual first I could never truly be me and therefore never really part of a couple. Really, though, there were coups and mutinies afoot even there, selfishly blind genes delighted to copy and paste with/in Kate. Without this unplanned swelling, Gran and ol' Bill would be unto dust. Victor-Conrad and his unknown mate would be mere points, not points on (intersecting) lines. Glore's wisdom would all be finite. Abort, and I'd say a kind of yes to Trevor Reynolds having said no.

Pregnant. The fight was like a brush fire: we put it out in one place then it started again somewhere else, often, it seemed, as a result of our smothering the first blaze.

"Saf's your friend. Doesn't she deserve to know when or if we plan to arrive?"

"Sure."

"Sure what, Kate? Sure you've talked to her? Sure there are *any* plans?"

"Commitment can be nice, can't it?"

Out the door for a double shift after that one. *That special glow,* my ass. She had an inexhaustible supply of moral trump. Same fight the next day.

"So, what, I'd be a better person if I just left Saf and Bry dangling in the wind?" I asked.

"Strangers, strangers you like. Strangers you think of."

"Safaa's a stranger now, is she?"

There again was a hard stare from the face I was trying to love. "Right now *everyone*'s a stranger."

Yet when she was tired later that night she crumpled into my arms. "How could we go to a cottage and not drink? It would be so obvious."

Did I really want a cottage weekend of this? Could I endure others? Could I endure not being with others? If anything, I gambled on funshine. Let her remember pleasure, feel it. My abortion campaign had been all wrong. I'd concentrated on our inadequacy as parents and our derailed love and careers. Maybe I just needed to let her climb into a bikini again and self-interest would rear its smooth midriff. A woman who owned three bikinis couldn't want twenty years of drudgery followed by forty more of nostalgia for drudgery. C'mon, Kate, stay Kate. She, not I, had previously coined the term *lobotomommy.*

"We'll just say we're not drinking," I proposed. "A month off to kick-start your seriousness for final year. Or detox." *Detox*—the word batted about in our charged air. *He*tox. *She*tox.

"Yeah right," Kate muttered, her banished grin returning just briefly, "you at a cottage without a drink. Have you ever been on a dock without a joint?"

"Sure I have." Finally I was able to stroke her neck again, smell her cinnamony hair. "Sometimes I bring a pipe."

"All right, then, let's go swimming."

So off we went, two more Canadians hoping that the temporary north would be beautiful, and able to go there precisely because of the money we made in the ugly, industrial south. All that beauty with a gas pedal.

Early in a relationship, a car is a bubble of affection, a floating, private island. Let's play each other music. One of you might read a short story aloud. Hands are not constrained by seatbelts. Then somehow the months transform the car interior into a food processor, a sealed, cornerless space of whirring blades. Four, five, seven hours together, maybe eight inches between you, and nothing but talk. Couples do one thing really well for each other, and it doesn't happen easily while driving. The hours stretch out and each of you begins to see formerly invisible dashboard gauges marking time and ire. Blitzkrieg invasions and departures on the CD player. Snappy lane changes. Cletus, meet your parents.

In Windsor, we had piled into the car with hope and bulging knapsacks, with road food and a shared need for fresh air and a deep lake. I had proposed we take back roads, burn another hour but at least see something. But back roads—didn't I realize?—meant fewer reliable places to pee. There was the start of parenting, two compromised individuals compromising inside a small hot space, a resentful piss the only hope of her shorts coming down. Parenthood, a highway life. We headed back to the 401, baby still on board.

If you're surprised or alarmed to read that I didn't know more about what we were doing or what was ahead of us, welcome to a relationship on life-support. Each night we slept in the same bed was a surprise, but so was each moment one of us stormed away from the other. That we were headed north, that she hadn't cancelled or asked me to stay behind, that we might soon be swimming, our chests rubbing together in a wet, treading hug—I clung to hope. Driving for five hours in the concrete chute of North America's busiest highway showed me how naïve and pathetic my half-plan was. We had been silent for nearly a hundred kilometres.

"Has anything changed with Saf, you know, *knowing*?"

"Don't worry. I haven't told her that we're proud parents."

"We're not parents, so that's good. Anything about the drinking?"

"I said we've been fighting a lot and probably wouldn't be drinking much."

"*Fighting a lot*, great. She's gonna think I fucked around. We'll get the eggshell treatment, and I'll get the cold shoulder."

"What was I supposed to say, 'I got a bun in the oven and the baker wants to yank it out'?"

"It's still just batter, not a bun." I shot her that driver's look, part distraction, part proprietor. "Couldn't you have told her something a little more conclusive? Like we're going drug-free for a month or we're going to do a cleanse or we've bet each other—"

"You mean *lie*. Couldn't I *lie* to my best friend?"

"Yeah and lie effectively. Saying we're fighting a lot and probably won't be drinking much is a lie. Or two. Or three. They're just not good lies."

"Well you're the expert there, aren't you?"

Huffy silence tightened over us like a jar lid. Save bickering a little over directions or implying derision for each other's music, we were oppressively mute for the last hour. Only the final turn onto a tree-lined country lane allowed us any pretence of affection. My hand suddenly found hers as we passed beneath a canopy of kissing maples and steered towards summer's evening sun. "You're my darling. I love you." I brought her warm hand to my lips. She let us (me?) have the moment, enjoy it, smile in the thick, hot light of early September.

Arriving to the cottage itself, stepping from the cramped car into warm breezes, was anything but easy. A parking area and garage sat at the top end of a long, rectangular lot that sloped down to a sparkling lake. Beneath it, down a flight of cinder-block stairs, rose a two-storey log cottage that blocked most of the twinkling lake behind it. Indigenous music greeted us in the sound of a screen door creaking open then snapping shut. Safaa stepped out onto a long porch holding a drink. She wore a bikini top and a sarong, was barefoot. "They're here," she called back before rushing to meet us.

The rank humidity of our home life was suddenly washed away by clean lake breezes. Immediately my shoulders rolled back and the top of my skull rose an inch or two. And I was fully aware of the flesh coming toward me. "Saf. Great to see you." I completed the hug she offered. Would you rather I pretend my fingers didn't notice the absence of anything beneath her sarong?

Bryan, shirtless in a pair of cargo shorts, greeted me with, "Ant, beer?" while holding out a cold bottle. Oh heavens.

"Bryan, thanks for having us up. Actually I'd love a dip before anything. I'm hotter than hell."

"Why do you think we have a dock?" He tilted the bottle neck my way a second time. "The cottage wet bar."

"Just a swim for now, thanks."

Kate and I exchanged another pair of pinched looks as we hauled our luggage out of the trunk. Foolishly I reached for her heaviest bag. "I'll get that."

"Not when I've already got it you won't."

A cottage on Labour Day weekend was indeed the worst scenario possible to try life without drink. An increased exposure to nature minus work minus Windsor pollution equals drinking time. My industry runs on one slogan: You can always feel better than you do. By the time we had been for a swim and unpacked a little, we had a cocktail to refuse for the cottage tour. Soon after that we were declining a sun-downing gin while supper was grilled. When a salad bowl and a platter of steaks were passed around, we had to fight off some chilled rosé.

"Didn't Kate tell you we're Mormons now?" Once again I tried to dodge a bottle and a pair of eyebrows titled my way. "Actually, we thought we'd start a little cleansing program up here. Clean air, clean blood. But pour away for yourselves. And here's a little thank-you present for later." The sack of weed I handed Bryan could have liquefied their skeletons and spilled their lungs out onto the floor like newborn puppies. "We couldn't arrive without a gift."

Kate's failure to engage in conversation with anyone gave me hope. Perhaps that summer meal was just the temptation she needed. Was she ready for years without booze? Was she going to pack away our Riedel glasses and decanter to reach instead for sippy cups? Her LSAT score was in the nineties. Could she even bring herself to say *sippy cup*? How could she go from scheduling Brazilian waxes to scheduling play dates? Suddenly King Midas became our sommelier, muttering *Be careful what you wish for* as he poured. I wanted Kate to be Kate until she suddenly accepted a glass of wine.

"All right, just a taste," she said as Bryan tilted his sweat-beaded bottle once again.

"Triumph!" Bryan half-yelled, splashing more than a taste into my beloved's glass. "Antony?"

"I'll just share with Kate. No sense dirtying a second glass."

"Suit yourself," he replied, smiling to the ladies on either side of him.

Kate didn't meet my eye.

Okay, sure, a few sips of wine wouldn't really 'tard a fetus. An entire glass of wine was nothing compared to the total deletion I claimed to advocate, but this public bait and switch was the ugliest thing I had ever seen Kate do. There, just once, I got religion and saw the wine for blood. As the Spanish say, only those we love can break our hearts.

Without drugs or love (excuse the redundancy), I suddenly couldn't stand the fake lawyer chat about hypothetical travel and dream homes of the future, all in a cottage paid for by Mommy and Daddy. When Kate took her second sip of wine I excused myself by saying I'd prefer a cup of the stars and headed to the lake.

Supine on the dock, dark water lapped steadily beyond my feet and weathered boards supported my back. A starry northern sky above—all that ragged, stellar dust hanging there whether I wanted it or not. Finally the inky lake water read me a list of options.

1. Leave now. Take the slap you were oh so purposefully delivered, hop in your car, and abandon the bitch to the company she has clearly chosen. Here was the one time I could squeal off without worrying about whether her pills were still in a bag in the car. I could have moved out of our apartment over the rest of the weekend while she tramped her way back with her boozy pals.

2. Smile and encourage her to drink and smoke with abandon. Get the party on and drown Cletus the fetus in shiraz for all I cared.

3. Walk back into the cottage and guzzle wine. Be a dragon of smoke. What's good for the goose…

4. Cry into her hair.

Every star above me was a taunt. Romeo and Juliet, the "star-crossed lovers." No single fight or bout of loneliness can instantly make a privileged Westerner believe in fate, in a path pre-written for you in the stars, but on *Labour Day* weekend the stars can do one hell of a job showing you what's beyond your control when your chick's up the pole. Imagine the resentment of every atrocity-fucked African when they stare up at the stars. What put the rich, not them, in the land of free education and drinking water? Even the dock beneath my back reminded me of how powerless I was. My long, straight body lay out on the long, straight dock, yet these brief lines couldn't survive four seasons of the water's ebb and flow. Lying in the dark, it was easy to picture myself from above, see myself as some kind of public sculpture.

At the shoreline, a tasteful little placard would announce my title: *Brief Imposition (aka Fatherhood)*.

Sadly, foolishly, I did nothing that night save wait. Waiting can be the cancer of relationships. You hope that more time will improve your situation; not worsen it. Really, though, you'd be better to attack your problems with the knife and/or chemo. Cut it out. Carpet-bomb. Take no prisoners. And if you're going to do chemo, best have some of Canada's finest on hand to soothe the bod and restore the appetites.

To my surprise, when I finally returned to the cottage it was already quiet. No braying laughter or slurred conversation greeted me. No music thumped in the dark night. The only lights were a fluorescent stove light in the kitchen and a single candle burning on one enclosed porch. I was just another dumb moth to a candle.

Kate sat in the corner of a couch with her legs curled up. Even in the smudged candlelight I knew exactly what each side of her ribs would feel like, the closer side scrunched down a little, the farther reaching up. She did look at me.

"So what's going on?" I asked.

"They found us so fascinating they went to bed early."

"And us?" I held out my hand.

"Okay."

Was that love or had we slipped into the lethal relationship stage of being each other's sleeping pill? Did she want me or just a warm body and strong arms?

As I bent to blow out the candle, I saw her wine glass beside it. She'd either barely touched what Bryan had poured her or had other glasses and drank this one down to a comparable level. My delay there at the candle meant I was behind her as we climbed the stairs. Only I grinned as we overheard the rhythmic creak of Bryan and Safaa's bed. In our bed, crisis or no crisis, there was the cant of her hips, that harp I couldn't see or feel without my memory playing its music, without familiar plucks and dives already trembling in my hands. Her warm back against my chest. The smooth backs of her firm legs.

"Don't."

Seconds after I let out my sexless sigh, that father's deflating hiss, we both heard small feet padding lightly down the hall—Safaa's second, telltale trip to the bathroom. This overheard mark of sex in a northern bedroom unavoidably took chaste Kate and me back to a story of hers from when she was seventeen. We heard Safaa's movements and thought of a younger Kate's whether we wanted to or not. So deep and pure was our dysfunctional silence that we even heard Saf lowering the toilet seat after the bathroom door had swung closed.

Kate, not I, had previously trained us in the kind of forensic urological listening we then couldn't help but do. Informed, assertive Kate had been on the pill since she was sixteen. "Don't let me fall asleep," she had told me during one of our early post-coital dazes, later explaining that to avoid urinary tract infection every woman should, as the doctors say, "void" after intercourse to rinse unsterile ejaculate out with sterile urine. In the trajectory of a relationship, that early clarification later became a mild complaint. "I wish I could be the one to come then snore for a change," she'd say, rising in our dark then marching down the hall. On early dates, when we were all wandering hands, a bottle, a jay, and some good music prompted her to tell me a story which aroused as much as it surprised.

"The summer I turned seventeen my friend Emma and I were dating these guys in a band."

"A *band*? You mean a get-laid team."

"Generations of screaming women can't be wrong about the six-stringed dick." She flashed me her hundred-dime smile before continuing. "Our guys worked at one of the Orillia resorts for the summer."

"Oh no."

"Oh yes. We'd drive up on a weekend night. One of her parents' cars or my mom's, even her grandma's a couple of times."

"Something tells me more than just cars are going to get pooled here."

"Chris and Matt had a third roommate, Dan, and soon we were going up with his girl too, Becca. They worked nights, so there wasn't a whole lot of time with the drive back. We'd get there, have a little smoke, spin some music, and get busy. But this was an employee's bunkhouse. When I say roommates, I mean *room*mates, not housemates. The first time it was just Emma and me, two couples at two ends of a long messy room, plenty to hear and some action you could see if you wanted to. But when Beck started coming up, that made three busy beds.

"It never did become full-blown group sex. Those single beds were like rafts, and no one swam across. If we'd been older, someone might've. I might've. But then again, if we'd been older we would never have started off in the same room like that.

"The real orgy was sound. They were all musicians. Only work, movies, or fucking could keep a guitar or drumsticks out of their hands for two hours. Played with each other and against each other. At night, we got it in both ears. If you heard one spank, you'd soon hear a second, then feel a third. Call and pink answer. Gender expectations had never been so clear. They wanted us to moan, scream, whinny. The sex wasn't really raunchier, just more showy. Every BJ required a mane of tossed hair. It could seem guy-driven, but the more they got the room going, the more likely each of them was to drop out of the race."

"Ah, seventeen."

"Exactly. We heard who came, who was left unfinished, who had trouble—"

"Making the caged bird sing?"

"Or so it seemed. We heard the big decisions, but not all the little ones. Who was willing to bust his or her knees on the bare wooden floor, who got nasty near the end, who preferred—or at least got—commands, not invitations. But you could also hear what you weren't hearing. You'd catch the end of a whisper or hear frustration in the groans. Have you ever been in a group? It's not so much different as there's just more of it. Like driving a bigger car.

"All that sound—yours, his, hers, theirs—then just the scurry of a whisper. Later of course there would be laughs, jokes between beds. But what was being whispered in that shared dark? Eventually Em or I would have to break the darkness to head off to the can. Without a word, one night was all that was necessary to clarify who was on the pill and who wasn't. At least Dan the rubber man lasted the longest.

"Those car rides up and back, they were also their own little room. What we hadn't seen or heard in the bunkroom came out later in the car."

"Post-game analysis?"

"Endless. TSN turning points. Locker-room interviews. If one of us got a finger in the bonus tunnel one night, then next week the other two would. But the dirtiest talk was on the way up, not back, the gals thinking, not just recounting. This was before porn was everywhere. Driving in the dark, our itchy knees all angled in the same direction, we said everything without ever saying that the girl talk was becoming the real sex. All of that goading, prying, magnetic talk. Each of us learning what we wanted, what we were getting, and what we weren't. The guys thought they were getting it delivered, sex as easy as pizza. Really they were just finishing what we had already started in the car, putting what we'd made into the communal oven.

"There were three beds, one at each end and one in the middle of a long wall. That bed in the middle was the limelight. You got watched from both ends. Tit city. Again, would this have been possible at any age but seventeen? Originally the middle was Emma's bed. We rarely saw her on her back. Watching her one night, I whispered into Matt's ear that I wanted us to have that bed next week. Make it happen. On the drive back, I told the girls we should start rotating beds, that each couple should take a turn in the centre. Throughout all of this, Emma and I would always have to march off to pee, one of us walking down the hall, knowing the other heard us, felt us. The sopping sorority."

Kate had driven me crazy first telling me all of this, good crazy. That story had been part of the sex in my apartment which had led to the love in my apartment then the everything in our apartment. Kate then and then and suddenly a chaste northern cottage. Silent and unable to sleep, each of us knew what Safaa was doing down the hall on her second trip to the bathroom. Kate cleared my hand off her hip. She wanted a warm chest zipped into her back but a eunuch's hips below. With a little curl and an abdominal shrug she let me know she didn't want my arm touching anything more sexual than her own. I was needed but not wanted—fatherhood.

You leave a relationship in stages. When the sex started to leave, at least one of us was bound to follow.

32. The Uns

BACK THEN, YES, I WANTED to undo the pregnancy. CTRL-Z that late pill or progesterone-immune sperm. Undo. Undo. Undo. A pregnancy most unplanned. Kate's indecision left us with the undead unborn. Gloria—and Trevor—had already schooled me in *uns*.

As Kate despondently started her last year of law school, cells and student debt accumulating, I did think of my paternal infection, of me trying to avoid a little usurper just like Trevor had. My elementary school drama with pea plants and photographed eyes wasn't going to let any of us forget the human-no-papa-going virus I carried in my genes. I still claim my motivations and methods were different from Trevor's, but of course an unplanned pregnancy is a binary. You're for or against, on the team or not. As our weary exhales burdened days then weeks, hugs were either squirmed out of or locked together with desperation. She cried so regularly during sex it became our new thing, another spill or taste. But she also resumed shutting the bathroom door to pee.

These are his eyes, aren't they? When my science fair question had hit its mark, Gloria took some time to calm down then asked for a few days of ceasefire. "I can show you one thing, Ant, one more thing about him, and that's all I have for the rest of your life. But you should know you probably won't like what you see. Wait until Saturday, then this last piece is yours for the asking."

She was right, it was indeed a *thing* she had to show me, a prop she had kept in the wings for more than a decade. Saturday was to be the opposite of Father's Day. You can have a thousand educated thoughts about gender, then in actual parenting, messy and constant parenting, you're repeatedly backed into one of a few messy corners.

Will my daughter be another victim or, if not, pathologically selfish and manipulative? Will my son be another asshole taker or, equally unwelcome, a coward?

Wait until Saturday. I'd learned by then that there was no point trying to whine or bargain once Mom had set rules, nothing to gain and dignity to be lost if I tried, so I sat it out. Concentrated at school. Kicked some (gr)ass on the soccer field. After school each day I was flagrantly good, but from a distance. Did homework quietly in my room. Proposed a meal rather than ask what was for supper. Single children of single moms, you've got to learn silence, its opportunities, its rewards, its respect. Silence is your coin.

Come Saturday morning she greeted me with four words, one of them as bright as these Web links. "Eat your breakfast first." *First.*

Breakfast dishes cleared from the kitchen table, she tried one last stall. She lifted a large manila envelope from off the top of the fridge and did her gentle but direct look into my eyes. "Antony, you've asked for information, however impolitely. I agree you deserve to know. But look outside. It's a sunny, spring day out there. This envelope is now yours and yours alone. Its contents will almost certainly upset you, and there's absolutely no reason why you have to open it now."

She laid the envelope in the centre of the table. "I'll be around the house all day. Nothing you say will be wrong."

I was twelve and had waited six or seven years for this. I wasn't about to go for a bike ride instead of opening that envelope. As soon as she was out of immediate earshot I shook out the meagre contents. Two photocopies slid free. The first was a copy of a smaller piece of paper. The copied edges of the notepaper were faint but uniform compared to the brief, scratchy handwriting it contained. Here, take a look.

The unwilling
led by the unqualified

doing the unnecessary
for the ungrateful.

No salutation. No date. No signature. And not Mom's handwriting in any way.

The second sheet was a photocopied article from an early 70s issue of *Time* magazine. Two photographs pinned down the columns of text. A master shot showed military caskets being loaded onto a giant jet in Vietnam. A detail shot showed a chalk inscription on the wooden lid of one casket. Some anonymous American soldier had scrawled this same indictment of *uns*, this litany of negation, on the casket of a fallen comrade. *The unwilling led by the unqualified doing the unnecessary for the ungrateful.* The Vietnam War in a sentence.

Boy-sponge, I absorbed every word. I had never read more quickly or with better retention. Antony, branded. In the beginning was the Word, and the Word was with Dad, and the Word was Dad. I was immediately incapable of forgetting all those *uns*. And yet the copied article, not the note, kept bringing me back. The note was from Trevor, the article from Mom. She distracted me with history, allowed me to fixate on the context, not the kiss-off. This soldier's mantra of *uns* had been engraved on Zippo lighters and written out on helmets, ammunition cases, even rifle butts. No doubt some Saigon engraver's stall did a steady trade switching between one grunt's paean to freedom (*Death before dishonour*) and these *un*doings. You can still find these engraved Zippos for sale online, or at least you can find intentionally scuffed and faux-aged counterfeits. Oh, weBay.

Again, you wouldn't believe this in a novel. One night at the casino, smoky work a welcome distraction from September's should-it-stay-or-should-it-go debate with Kate, I saw this same slogan of uns printed on the T-shirts of half a dozen buzzcut American soldiers over for some post-Iraq whoop-up. Thirty years after soldiers wrote this little anti-poem against their government's war in Vietnam, the same government was now printing it *for* soldiers on tax-funded T-shirts. Government-funded, anti-government swag, the keeping-things-whole fashion line.

I'm running now like I was running there in Mom's kitchen, observing not confessing. Yes, my stomach went squirmy and my ears rang as I read Trevor's note. Alongside that sticky heat was a spreading thaw that pulled me out of myself. I could see my own neck, my skinny arms raising and lowering one page then the other, the back of my head twisting left then right. With the article, Mom had sewn me a net of history, knowing it would slow my fall but not prevent it. She'd also spared me going to her with questions and playing parental catch-up. I stood alone, obsessively rereading a copy of the note with which half my genes had tossed me aside while calling Gloria unqualified. And me ungrateful. At least this note of mine took months to write, not two seconds.

With a first, unplanned pregnancy, sure, a young Gloria would have started out unqualified. But she was a learner and a doer, Medea offstage long before she was Medea onstage. For a hippie who'd been in one protest march after another—US troops out! No nukes! Pro-choice NOW!!—raising another resource-consuming North American baby was/is certainly unnecessary. Ironic that most mothers would condemn me for putting what I want ahead of what a baby might want. Look at the selfishness of North American mothers putting what they want ahead of everything else. Go on, have two kids, have three. You love your kids, and love can't be bad, can it? Malthus, Schmalthus, right? There is no argument. There is only *I want*, so stop pretending we're any different. Gran, Gloria, Melissa and her sisters, me, Kate—we all said be honest about what you want.

The unwilling led by the unqualified doing the unnecessary for the ungrateful. Family life in a sentence. If Gloria was the unqualified, that made me the ungrateful. Well, T-bone, we're all waiting to see about that.

How was I supposed to go to school on Monday after reading Trevor's rejection letter on Saturday? Do exponent homework? Watch cartoons? A man who had fled his homeland to avoid fighting in Vietnam had been as unwilling to raise children as he was to kill them. No half-assed poetry lesson in school would ever stick language to me like absent Trevor's note had. It took me years to fully appreciate that the one poem I'll never forget has an anonymous author, no fame sought or bestowed. From the start, Mom showed me it wasn't Trevor's phrase, just something else he borrowed. Then again, when the man was mostly just words to me, it was hard not to confuse *father* and *author*. That's another family curse I haven't stopped.

A kitchen table is as good a place as any to admit that half your genes come from an asshole. (Though with a laptop, you're probably not reading this at a kitchen table.) Mom didn't hear any shattering glass or slamming doors. No screaming. No crying. Eventually she came back with her own line ready. "That's the note the man who called himself Trevor Reynolds left me one afternoon after we'd discovered I was pregnant with you. Abortion was still quite daunting then, legally, and it certainly wasn't an option for me emotionally. I wanted you even when you were a possibility, even when he left, even when I realized who he was and wasn't."

It was hard to look her in the eye, but for several reasons I didn't want to be looking down.

She pressed on. "You know the phrase *nature versus nurture*. Always remember that nature and nurture are like length and width: you can't have one without the other. There's no nature to see without some nurturing, and nothing to nurture without nature. Yes, you have his eyes, his cheekbones, probably his shoulders. But you're you, not him. You are becoming you—by choice, by experience, through education. Both your nature and your nurture are very, very different from his."

I didn't last the weekend before I tore up that copy of Trevor's note and scattered the pieces into the Detroit River. But of course Gloria had expected that. (Encouraged it?) The photocopy showed the edges of an original note I hadn't yet seen. Eventually, I got it too.

FYI, manila envelopes are still called manila envelopes even though most of them are no longer made in Manila. How did they earn a global reputation for strong paper? By making it from hemp.

33. A French Inhale

BACK THEN, YES, I TRIED to prevent more life coming into my world: guilty as never directly charged. United I stood, divided I would fall. When a different life started shutting down, I tried to focus on Gran's high score, not her end.

The length of Gran's life changed the shape of mine. If she'd passed before my time, if her smuggling and war stories hadn't come from her directly but had only been filtered through Gloria, if she'd been a photograph, not a retired smuggler on the other side of the room, would I have strolled downtown selling joints out of my teenaged pockets? Once I'd started, sure, slinging got its green thrill into me, but part of what first took me downtown were the countless hours I'd spent beside an old woman whose legs had once carried bottles over to the other side. And when it came time for her to cross the River Styx, I had comforts to offer. Tea from the tillerman.

Over the years, plenty of moms (especially mine) and a few dads have tried to tell me how much I could learn from the dependency of infants. Sure, but what about the dependency of the very old? What, we can only learn from smooth skin, not wrinkles? Your love list has a cut-off age? Try saying that in divorce court.

Gran broke her ankle during Mom's MFA year and needed Elevator Antony for two months. We grew even closer. By the time Kate and I were waiting and weighting, Mom and I discovered that an even older Gran was spending nights on her couch rather than mounting the stairs. Even though her body was failing, at 103 her mind was still good. She had no trouble learning to use the cordless phones I'd begun sprinkling around her rooms. When I first proposed getting her a MedicAlert pendant, she'd said, "I'm no prize racehorse." On Attempt No. 2, it was, "Big Brother's not going to have the eye on me." When she finally relented I was half-tempted to tell her I'd be paying for her transponder by sending off electro-magnetized bags of weed. The electronic bad met the electronic good. Robin Hood with shorter, whiter arrows in his quiver. But technology can only do so much for an ailing body, and eventually I had a bigger plan than just the pendant. I was lying to both of us by putting a phone in her hands if I wouldn't be available at the other end. In the summer, Mom and I, even solo Kate, had been able to juggle regular visits. But when school resumed for Kate and Mom, we needed to change the game.

Gran had never asked anyone's permission to start smuggling, hadn't asked anyone else's advice whether or not she should have sailed to France, should have gambled on baby G. Did I ask a non-asker if she'd consent to my moving her bedroom of nearly eight decades down into her wainscoted and unused dining room so she wouldn't die on the stairs? She who lives by direct action dies by direct action. But I needed Gloria's help for the switcheroo. One evening when I was sick of bickering with Kate, I swung by Mom's. She made us tea.

As always, I thought I was being reasonable. "Look, this business with Gran and the stairs, it's dangerous, it exhausts all of us, and it's never, ever going to improve."

"If you're proposing putting her in a home, it'll be over two dead bodies. At least one of us won't go down without a fight."

"Jesus, Mother. A *home*? What do you take me for?" I shook my head. "I want to move her down into the dining room. Clear out the table. Make that her bedroom."

"What's this, dying on the instalment plan?"

"The next time she's got a doctor's appointment or goes for her hair, you take her. I'll handle the furniture."

She poured more tea. "Careful with that table of hers. It's worth more than your truck."

"When did *you* work in the trades? I'll wrap it in blankets. I'll slide. I'll lift."

She nodded.

"And that's not everything. I'd also like to hire a careworker. I can swing it or maybe you want to contribute."

"Why, oh why, couldn't you have stayed in school and gone without money for a few more years like a proper young person? You've been working for half a decade, I've been working for three, and you tell me I *may* contribute? A money bully's still a bully." She shook her head for a little pause then found something else to lob at me. "And what makes you think she'll accept strangers into her home?"

Incentives, Mother, the right incentives. Dog Management Lesson No. 3: influence doesn't consist of convincing another to do what you want. Influence involves showing another that the two of you share mutual interests, that in fact they want what you want.

The following week Mom took Gran to the hairdresser's while Reese and I flew in to move the furniture. He didn't make a single joke about old lady smells and spared me much eye contact. After our years together, he knew how to earn a tip.

Gloria plotted Gran's return, suggesting the old girl might take it harder if both of us witnessed her first seeing her bed in her dining room, that prototype of a coffin. Mom had invented an excuse so I would be the one to pick Gran back up. I knew she'd be tired, which was both good and bad. The Gran I met at the hairdresser's wasn't so much Gran as a five-foot-two-inch need for a nap.

"We'll get you home to bed."

Beyond the closed dining-room doors, I'd left Voodoo in her back garden so she'd have something to look at other than her relocated bedroom furniture. So intent was she on a nap that she made no comment on the dining room's closed pocket doors and simply headed to the stairs.

"Actually, Gran, I've moved your bed down here." I slid open the doors. "Your garden's beautiful from in here. Take a look."

She remained immobile at the foot of the stairs, her eyes a little more rheumy but her jaw still as hard-edged as a tombstone.

"Look, Voodoo's out there."

All animals have flight distances. (You've read this far but are still keeping a wide flight distance by not hitting <u>Send</u>.) Species and individual determine how far an animal will tear off from a startling noise before glancing back at the possible threat. Surprise a fox, and you'll see its face glancing back in seconds. Make a loud noise near a rabbit, and it will be a cannonball of blind fur until it reaches the next field. I stood there asking Gran to admit that her flight distance had shrunk from the Atlantic Ocean to straddling countries in the New World to just a few yards on one storey of a gorgeous house she'd no longer see two-thirds of. Her upstairs was becoming a ghost town. A cheval mirror and a sewing table forsaken unto dust. A balcony door unopened in years. The house's best river view abandoned. To her I was the nursing home ambassador, the man come to shrink her whole life down to one closet, an undertaker with a tape measure up his sleeve. But she'd already abandoned most of those upstairs things anyway.

Being right in theory did little for the reproach of her doing and saying nothing. (Pattern. Pattern.) She stood there, affront perched on one shoulder, desperation on the other. On to Plan B then. "I also brought you some organic marijuana. In the little medical research that gets done, it's the wonder drug. Arthritis, any pain, anxiety, muscle relaxation."

Wait, sorry, are you on the Big Pharma boat to Cuba? Maybe you're not pulling the oars, just enjoying the profiteering, lobotomizing ride. Fact: minimally processed plants still provide one-quarter of Western medicine. Fact: Westerners constitute 20 percent of the world's population yet consume 80 percent of the world's pain medication.

The nineteenth-century English and American opium wars didn't end, they just switched from soldiers to pharmaceutical reps. Given global demographics (i.e., the West's fucking baby boomers), the World Health Organization details a looming global "pain crisis." Demand for pain medication will far outstrip supply, fuel costs will be exponentially higher, and, sheep to the American shepherd that we are, weed will still be illegal. When a palliative plant comes from away, we call it medicine. When we grow one in our own backyard, it's a crime.

Gran remained mute with indignation and reproach. Through the window, Vood gave me the head-tilting idiot stare. I crossed to Gran's walnut bedside table to remove a pipe and matches. "This is some very pleasant weed, like a quilt of hugs. Top drawer here whenever you want it."

Finally she shuffled to the bed and sat. Every moment she hadn't spoken increased my fear that she'd rebuke me with something like, "That stuff's for riff-raff." Instead she held out her hand for the pipe and nodded at me to light her up. Before leaning towards the bowl she finally spoke. "So this is your deal, is it?"

My blue-green genie slid into another contested room.

"Just try it down here," I coaxed. "Try it down here for a week."

By the time I was ready to leave I thought she was already asleep until she opened her eyes and stopped grinning to speak. "For God's sake, roll me some. If I'm going to smoke on my way out, I want a cigarette in my hand again. I haven't smoked in half a century."

Turns out this one-time recipient of a French letter could French-inhale like an Old World hooker. Normally I don't sample during work hours, but the first time I handed Gran a pinner I had to follow her into the greenshine. Private, observable fact: the shit works. Her shoulders would visibly relax. Her appetite revived. For the first time in years, she'd ask me to put on records. Blossom Dearie. Sarah Vaughn. And she got chattier. "Next time, bring that girl of yours. She might as well have my cheval mirror."

I still maintain that my care, not my wares, earned me the royal favour (and curse) she bestowed a few weeks later.

34. Speered

THERE'S THAT LINE IN *RAGING BULL*, the obsession mantra.
"Weight, weight, weight, weight." When he was boxing, it was all anyone
ever asked about, all he thought about, the focus of his days. For me
it was risk. Risk, risk, risk, risk, risk. The cops. Kate. Gloria. Other
criminals. For civilians, the police offer more than protection. They
also subcontract your risk, shoulder some of your worries. Sure, you
generally don't fret about how many times you can tase an airplane
traveller before he dies, but you know what I mean. Cops get to speed on
duty and off, and civilians don't have to fight very much. On my side, we
don't get these scapegoats, the fall guys in blue, the cannon fodder with
nightsticks.

Most criminals are greedy bullies. Greedy bullies or, just as bad, greedy
little followers who try to impress someone, maybe even themselves, by
being more bullying. They rob, abuse, and exploit their families before
they set to work on strangers. Once they've robbed and hit their way out
of one family, they usually go looking for another.

In Canada, everyone in my trade, *everyone*, is far more worried about
gangs than cops. The 'Namese in Vansterdam. Jamaicans in Toronto.
Bikers anywhere outside a city and anywhere east of Toronto. And we're
all bankrolling them. Weed should be the easiest drug to keep out of gang
hands: it's grown not manufactured, can be grown in every province, and
seeds can be obtained through the mail and/or transferred from one crop
to the next. One advantage of weed being illegal is that the plant has been
spared any of the suicide genes Big Agri is trying to build into every crop.
Sixteen-year-olds can and do grow totally serviceable pot, but Canadian
smokers are still Canadian. The majority don't grow their own food or

smoke. As a grower grows, his ears are always cocked for the sound of an approaching Harley.

At the casino I swam in fast currents of worry. Working with crews, all that was necessary to send hurt my way was for someone to want a little extra money and not mind selling me out to get it. Businesses, governments, schools, parents, criminals—we're all fighting short-term accounting. If a friend of a friend of a loose-lipped employee knew a friend who knew a biker, blabbing about my operation could earn the blabber a shot of cash. When two bikers made a point of speaking to me one night at the casino, I had to take it as more than coincidence.

They might have been there looking for their own chisel on the casino, though if so they shouldn't have arrived dressed as bikers, all whiskers, gut, and leather. They could even have been another pair of money-throwing gamblers. That is, if they hadn't made such a point of talking to me. Repeatedly. And after they roared.

Given this blog and a pile I started with a trebuchet, one of my guilty pleasures is obviously gear. From trebuchets to this website, the tech snares me. Hummers and tanks, no. An ingenious tool, yes. I'd never handwrite an 80,000-word apology/hello. But really, a Harley? A Harley Davidson is *designed* to be noisy, to roar on demand. A $15,000 fart joke. Or a purchased growl.

Normally at the casino we didn't see too many bikers. Given the short lifespan of "gaming" workers mowed down by second-hand cancer, I doubt there's one alive who remembers casinos before electronic surveillance. Even bikers can recognize that they'd be spotted if they so much as walked along the casino sidewalk in full regalia. Of course they could always try disguises. Shave. Sport a tweed sheep-fucking cap, not a bandana. Prefer a Hawaiian shirt to a leather vest. But then they'd be reduced to size alone for intimidation. Cops, soldiers, bikers—they all want their uniforms and their teams. Boys with boy packs. Peters fucking Pan.

The night I saw a hulking pair of bikers roll around the garishly lit casino drive for a second time, I could suddenly feel my thighbones, knew how far my elbows were from my ribs and felt the outline of my cell in my back pocket.

The casino's circular driveway was designed as if gamblers were bees and we needed to be the brightest flower on the glowing Windsor waterfront. Crossbreed Walt Disney with Albert Speer (Hitler's "architect of light"), give the spawn truckloads of rainbow-coloured lights, get him drunk on local rye, and you might recreate our multicoloured cave entrance. Despite the bubbling and chugging of the fountains and the trickle of horrible music, the entrance was more flower for the eye than mating call for the ear. When the bikers roared up the first time, my crew and I (as well as everyone else who wasn't deaf) definitely noticed. On their second pass, when they stopped to sit and idle behind the unloading Lexuses, I could tell myself and anyone else who asked I was doing my legitimate job as I radioed security before striding over to meet them.

"Evening gentleman. None of us is licensed to park a bike, so if you just head down the street to—"

"You don't talk very loud," said Thug One.

"Not a lot of *force* in the voice," added his partner.

Each of them was at least 275 pounds and six-foot-something. A lot of fat, sure, but no doubt plenty of experience with pain.

"You want to talk—" I pointed at the bike's keys and mimed turning them off. "You want to game," I nodded my head down the road, "head to one of our lots. I'm asking you to move. The cops won't be so polite."

For the next fifteen seconds, each of them pretended their eyes were actually emitting the mechanical roar. "You won't phone the police." No. 1 finally said before he then his partner cracked the air and roared off.

As soon as they were out of sight I was dialling Kate and rushing back inside. Their departing bikes filled one ear and her ringing phone the other. C'mon. C'mon. Shit, voicemail. "Listen carefully. Lock the doors then turn on the balcony lights. Keep a phone *in your hand*. Do this now. No debates." I scrawled a note about my absence then tried her again as I ran to my bike.

The worried sound of her voice scraped me. I interrupted her to say, "Lock the front door. Move now."

"Ant, what is—"

"Get it locked, NOW."

"Slow down. For a start, I've been locking a door behind me since residence. Secondly—"

"And the lights. Get the outside lights on but then move away from the windows."

Uncharacteristically, she paused. At least I could hear her moving around the apartment.

"You wouldn't scare me without a reason. What am I looking for?"

"Probably nothing."

She waited.

"But maybe two bikers. Big ones. I'm on my way now."

"Listen to yourself."

"Don't hesitate for a second to phone the police."

I got there ridiculously quickly, which mattered and didn't. The casino uniform I tried not to wear much in front of her looked even worse pasted to my back with sweat. Slipping across the lawn, tiptoeing up the stairs, ears pricked, eyes roaming—I'd never felt more connected to the pregnancy than when I thought she was in danger. I know, I know: asshole as charged, and all unnecessarily. There was never any sign again of those bikers, not at home or the casino. Pregnancy can rewire even coincidence. It's like a colour filter changing everything you see.

I unlocked our door as quietly as possible to the sight of Kate holding my baseball bat to her shoulder. Each of us said all we needed to say with a look. You have no right to do this to me. Agreed.

After two largely silent hours of fewer and fewer glances out the window I wound up uttering yet another cliché I shouldn't have. "I panicked over nothing, nothing but coincidence. Better safe than sorry."

"This is hardly safe, and we're already sorry."

Her back was a wall I slept against.

35. *Mombeth*

THE GREEK MYTHS HAD THEIR meddling gods. We have our cellphones and answering machines. As another crucial September week ticked past with the batter still in the oven, I came home in relationship limbo to two more significant phone messages.

First, from Glore.

Hey, kids, great news. With my new backer I got the Capitol Theatre! Kate, don't you think Antony should wear a suit for a change instead of that valet uniform? Let's celebrate. Love vous, Mom.

The second message plucked the hairs on the back of my neck.

Hey, Kate, it's Melissa returning your call. I can meet you Thursday or Friday.

Was it good or bad that my pregnant lover had called up her sex worker acquaintance? Melissa's team definitely knew birth control. And its alternatives. Then again, why would Kate have given Melissa our number, not her cell? The plot thickened along with the zygote.

Another thing about actors: they don't get mad; they get even. In public. *Theatre of war* isn't an accidental phrase. All wars require planning and drama. With my secret backing, Gloria had chosen to direct *Macbeth* that fall long before Kate and I had stepped so far into our own river of blood. Given her months of preparation, Gloria couldn't have set out to include our homegrown content, but she was also never one to miss a creative opportunity on the fly.

With her *Medea*, I'd been utterly impressed. And proud. Best of all was the layered surprise of admitting there was more to her than I knew, and that the unknown bits were admirable. Wicked eyes brighter than diamonds, shoulders and thighs flared with strength. With her child-killing *Medea*, I'd thought about her and my street dealing. With her *Macbeth*, the murderous couple, she demanded I think about Kate and me. She turned *Macbeth* into *Mombeth*.

Macbeth is Shakespeare's shortest tragedy. Where Hamlet ponders, Macbeth does. The thinker and the doer, reason and instinct, opportunity found or made. Here again Billy Shakes coaxed history into the familiar tragic arc of a self-propelled rise and a self-generated fall. This time, though, he did it with a couple. Not just the human heart in conflict with itself, but the human heart in conflict with itself and another heart it loves. Conflict, paired.

By the time Gloria got the Capitol Theatre, we were secretly in the family way. (Excuse the redundancy: families aren't families without secrets.) As Mom moved from design sketches and working concepts to casting and the exploratory first read-through, Kate and I ineluctably moved day by day to parenthood. Gloria used money she didn't know was mine to sign a theatre-rental contract during Kate's sixth week. The show would go up at Thanksgiving, the end of our eleventh week. I prayed for peace in the eleventh hour and was prepared to do plenty to give thanks.

The first month of a pregnancy usually flies below the radar. Best to go for the A-vacuum ASAP. How could you miss what you barely knew you had? The count starts with the last period, not the moment when the white agent provocateur swims on through, so you've already lost a couple of weeks from the get-go. Behind the clock. Under the gun.

You'd think that two atheists with bounders for fathers would be immune to any saccharine delusions about families and Thanksgiving, but tell that to hope and/or hormones. I gambled that the October long weekend would be good for my cause, that a well-fed and traditionally wine-soaked weekend at the one-quarter mark of Kate's final year of law school might remind her how close she was to the time limit on this decision. I could also hope that spending time with her mother and mine, each with their holiday cocktails of judgement, misperception, and arrogance, their *hors d'oeuvres* of manipulation and their entrées of disapproval, would send Kate running for her tallest boots and a cocktail shaker, not mat wear. If you're wondering how I could hold on so long thinking that on Day 48 she'd tell me of an appointment she wasn't willing to make on Day 47, remember that she wasn't just young and pregnant. She was young, pregnant, and surrounded by women her age who were all about to become lawyers.

At the end of August, the calendar had been my enemy. Kate was still isolated, cut off from others and, crucially, out of competition. Anyone on a second university degree has learned to play the whole season, not just the single game or tournament. In summer, Kate might have thought of her, or Cletus, or us. In the fall, she'd have other women to think about, other, striving women.

Generally she hated that law school was yet another girl aquarium, the bright fish illuminated for all to see. But the future contract makers were already involved in a dozen contracts, some of them hard. Each of them knew they could still get great jobs with a B+ average, whereas only a monastic amount of studying would earn them A's. Three years of bags under the eyes and no friends to earn a GPA some firms would find frankly off-putting or three years of some studying, but also movies, books, dinner parties, and weekends away? For the B+ crowd (i.e., anyone who wasn't hoping to work in The Hague), law school was yet another fashion show. The aspiring legal ladies still wanted to be bar girls on Friday nights but now suddenly office tramps as well. The crisp shirts. Oh, the high boots and short skirts. A new tote bag each term.

While the majority of law school may have been another fashion show, Kate had also pointed out its diehard cell, women with chewed fingernails who could give you the daily body count in Iraq. The men with dark stubble, slim cellphones, and zero body fat who had compendious knowledge of Israel and the UN. Blond experts on Kosovo wore combat boots to mandatory classes in real-estate law and tried not to go insane.

I don't hide for a second my hope that Kate's competitiveness or envy or fear of rumour at school would tip the abortion scales she wouldn't tip just thinking about us. Was this hope healthy? Mature? Admirable? No. No. No. Whatever got the job done.

Turn over the rock of many social problems and, yes, you'll find the footprints of a departing father. Bullying. Arson. Illiteracy. All those pleas for attention even if it's negative, all those fuck-yous to the self and the world. Too true, but my preference was to be a non-father, not an absentee father. Also, I did have a Plan B. Nature, gorgeous women, and the insurance industry abhor a vacuum. If I didn't stick around to pay bills, take out the garbage, and run errands, someone else surely would.

Throughout Mom's rehearsal period, Kate and I continued to have our fights, thaws, and freezes, while my shill at Cronus Holdings doled the cash out to Glore. Twice I agreed with her gamble to run Shakespeare and a tragedy during Thanksgiving weekend. I encouraged her both as her son and, secretly, as her backer. Thanksgiving, a long weekend in which southern Ontarians no longer need to flee the climate and polluted landscape in which they make their money. And of course families get together on holidays. What's a family without blood, betrayal, and tragedy?

Originally we planned to see the show twice, on opening and closing nights. Two different dresses and suits, a slightly different show. But that was before we saw what Mom did with and to *Macbeth*. She started with children then got worse.

Act I, Sc. i. Thunder and lightning. Enter three WITCHES.
In Gloria's case, that was enter three girls. We're talking nine or ten years old. All Asian, dressed in rags. Black hair matted and clumped. They wiped runny noses on torn sleeves. Flashes of lightning revealed sores

on their lips, dirt-smeared cheeks, and filthy hands. Push a broom down a Calcutta alley and you'd collect these girls. This was the face of global poverty, each of them starving, illiterate, and capable of fleecing your pockets in a second. When Macbeth first saw the witches, this medieval Scottish nobleman's opening question could have been asked by any North American tourist to New Delhi. Macbeth carries a sword, we carry a fanny pack, but each of us asks: "What are these / so wither'd and so wild in their attire, / That look not like th' inhabitants o' th' earth / And yet are on't?" Here were the global poor, of my species yet not, deserving my guilt yet too alien to matter.

When Macbeth continued, "Live you? or are you aught / That man may question?" I heard the first private knife sharpening in the rented theatre. Indisputably, there had been a little emphasis on *man*. "Live you? or are you aught / That *man* may question?" Kate and I kept looking at the stage, not each other. At Macbeth's line, "You should be women—" the little witches drew the backs of their grimy hands to their dirty cheeks. With their elbows pointing high above their shoulders and the backs of their wrists pressed to their blackened cheeks, they wiggled their fingers in front of their mouths to suggest the "beards" Macbeth puzzles over: "You should be women, / And yet your beards forbid me to interpret / That you are so." Ten minutes into the play and Mom was talking crotch. *You should be women* and elbows raised in the air like knees in metal stirrups. Fingers as beards at a hairy mouth. And young, Asian girls. Give Gloria some production money and look what she does.

Part of me was still able to admire the risks she was taking. No male director on the continent could do what she'd just done with child actors. But that beard joke was like a road sign pointing exactly my way. Even worse, I felt like a mom in thinking so. Aside from Gloria, dozens of people worked in her cast, crew, and production team to bring a four-hundred-year-old play to life for up to five-hundred spectators across a six-night run, and I thought it was all about me. But how not to? A man on the illegal make who's murderously afraid of children.

You may not want to hear this (but you have thought about it). Sitting in front of this trio of girls (Asian girls: Web porn and gendered abortion) raising their arms/legs to wriggle pubic hair in front of them—well, all this beside my Kate. Those girls on stage inverting age with their raised legs, that was life, not the polite lies we slop around it. Go to a wedding and nothing about the manicured event suggests that two crotches are being joined. No rented chair, centrepiece, rustle of silk, nor (toxic) salmon fillet acknowledges that first and foremost this is a union of genitals. Surely the relevant question is, Do you take his sex and you hers? How can you keep things whole in a rented tux and a dress that never gets worn again?

In a darkened theatre, Mom's darkened theatre, I saw in a flash what I was about to lose with Kate, that patch of private grass, lawn of refuge, picnic, and play. No one else had so captivated me, challenged me, or vexed me, and nowhere was Kate more half-Chinese than between the knees. Every day we saw race in the knitting, my tight curls to her wiry hair. All of this and more was coming at me in the first ten minutes of *Mombeth*.

I was watching witches and thinking of mothers. Both are terrifying in isolation and in packs. Gloria pulling puppet strings in front of me and Kate reorbiting beside me, all with Shakespeare's taunting lines. "Live you? or are you aught / That man may question?" Well, there was every thought I had about what was quickening inside Kate.

Art is a staircase, Mom told me more than once. Learn where it maintains ground and where it rises or falls. I heard that phrase echoed dozens of times when I had carried Gran up and down the narrow staircase of her house, my feet feeling out the risers and treads I couldn't see for the thin body in my arms. In the theatre, Gloria climbed a step in Lady Macbeth's first scene as she read a letter from her travelling hubby. He describes his meeting with "these weird sisters," the non-father Macbeth claiming the witches as family. *Sisters*, not *witches, women,* or *girls*. Gloria extended the stage convention of having an actor read a letter aloud by having a pre-recorded voice track by the Lady Macbeth actor double the recitation. At times the recorded version lagged behind the live, portent echoing portent. At other times, the two versions were layered in stereo, the recording thickening the live and vice versa. When Lady M. lowered the note after she read it, Mom hit us again with a recorded "This have I thought good to deliver thee." At this echo, Lady M. crumpled the note in front of her hips. Macbeth's words but Lady Macbeth's voice. And body. *Deliver thee* was said directly in front of her hips. Pride, fear, and wonder bit into me.

As Lady M's speech ended with that letter crumpled in front of her hips, I tried a little theatre Morse, pressing my leg against the side of Kate's. She didn't press back.

36. *Mombeth II*

FAMILY, IT'LL MAKE YOU BLIND and it'll make you see. Without Mom's production, I'd have gone on misremembering Lady Macbeth's famous line as "unsex me now." How could I do that, living here in polluted Windsor? We've got one of the highest cancer rates in Canada. We tip the scales for Hodgkins lymphoma and babies born missing chunks of their brains. Our MS rate matches that of third-world toxic dumping grounds. Wind-sore Windsor. The nearby Aamjiwnaang Nation has one of the highest rates of female births in the world, two girls for every boy. And in the hooker capital of Canada, the line is definitely unsex me *here*.

Gloria refracted Lady M's unsex me soliloquy by sending out the three child actors again, this time clean-faced and dressed not as witches but identically to Lady Macbeth. "Come you spirits," the lady called, and out came these three little Lady M surrogates to mime behind a translucent scrim. "Come you spirits / That tend on mortal thoughts, unsex me here." Each of the three mini-Ms mimed the presence of breasts, breasts each child actor clearly did not have, then ripped them away. One minute the miniature trio moved together, three parts of the same whole, then suddenly they were independent. Two girls stood behind the third and moved their hands and arms across hers. This accompanying mime emphasized already memorable lines in a speech that needed no emphasis for Kate or me.

Did Mom know all of the arrows she was firing into us? Could she count the ways? *Unsex me*. The most obvious interpretation, Change my gender. Stop me from being a woman. Whether that means turn me into a man (*sativus*) or neuter me (*sativum*) is a director's choice, and Mom made hers quite clearly. Anything but *sativa*. *Unsex me here* could also simply mean undo the sex I have had. Turn the clock back before that forgotten pill or the night of the vodka bareback. This undoing became more and more apparent each time Lady M uttered that double-agent of a word, "come." Each child dancer had been cruising about in a slow and exaggerated shuffle, a low-to-the-ground labouring of flung feet, angled knees, and long transfers of weight. At the single word "come," they simultaneously jolted upright as if shocked.

Their work together was taunting enough. Apart, they were murder. They scattered from their first shocking "come" into separate roles. The middle ex-witch/child/mini-M slid to the ground to recline on her back, knees raised and breath chuffing like a birthing mother. The second knelt behind her head to mop her brow and coach her breath. The third lay between the patient's knees as their madam made her hard bargain: "unsex me here, / And fill me from the crown"—grunts from the birthing child/mother—"to the toe topful / Of direst cruelty!" At the butcher's lines, "Make thick my blood, / Stop up th' access and passage to remorse," the child physician and her child patient suddenly had a very different gynaecological procedure on their hands.

For all my terror, helplessness, and rage, I was still impressed. Once again we watched a woman subordinate her life and career to her husband's and/or her uterus. All that for an audience of mostly women who earned substantially less than men, were promoted less often, were rarely chief executives. Even more undiscussed were the abortions. In a crowd of two hundred adults, how many of the women had responded to pregnancy by saying *not now*?

What balance. Glore never ignored a scene's journey for its destination. Witness her gall. Start to finish, the whole play was one big relationship scrap. She's more impressive; no, he's more impressive. He's nasty; she's nastier. The switching, swinging Macbeths. Notice that the one Shakespearean female with multiple memorable lines is the dominatrix.

In Act II, Mom sent her Lady out in a leather corset, all kink and riding crop. You might know a line of Juliet's and a phrase of Ophelia's, but it's Lady Leather we all remember. *Unsex me here. Out damned spot.* If you've got another of her lines, I'll wager it's *take my milk for gall.* "Come to my woman's breasts," Mom's Lady called as her surrogates cupped air in front of their small chests to latch even smaller, invisible heads onto their imaginary breasts, heads which they suddenly flung aside as the line continued: "Come to my woman's breasts, / And take my milk for gall." The next few lines had the weird sisters up and dancing together again briefly before two resumed their work against one. Shifting gears on the third and final call to "Come," two of the dancers slipped behind the third, one working low on her body and the other, well, high. As their lady called, "Come, thick night, / And pall thee in the dunnest smoke of hell," the upper-body dancer worked behind her standing sister to roll and pass her a mimed joint. Below her, the crouching third put something into one of her hands before reaching across to extract something from the other, the classic green handshake. Then for a second time, two of the sisters again attended to the north and south poles of the third, the upper patting a brow and smoothing back hair one second then seizing her arms while her lower co-worker kneeled to yield a shining scalpel. We knew where and how the blade struck as Lady M concluded, "That my keen knife see not the wound it makes, / Nor heaven peep through the blanket of the dark / To cry 'Hold, hold!'"

An abortion production of *Macbeth* from my mother, beside the woman I didn't want to see become a mother. When the house lights came up at halftime, the audience applauding already, I turned to Kate. "You told her."

If you've heard this from Kate, you'll have heard that I had been the one sitting closer to the aisle and that in waiting for an answer I had blocked not only her exit but also that of the dozen well-dressed people waiting down the row. All true, but listen to her reply.

"Will you let me by?" she asked instead of answering my question. And when that didn't work. "Us?"

Maybe she meant everyone down the row. Maybe.

37. The Zug Exhale

INTERMISSION. THE PLAY WAS SUSPENDED for fifteen minutes.
Kate and I had been suspended for nearly as many weeks.

Will you let me by?...Us?

If you want by, go.

But the crowded theatre wouldn't let either of us by. The half-shocked,
half-impressed audience kept us shackled together with small steps in
the busy aisle then down a crowded staircase. Strangers in dry clean-only
clothes were never more than six inches away, often less. At the doorway,
I let Kate pass in front of me. Was she already picking her steps a little
more carefully? Walking to shield?

"Are you thirsty?" I asked the back of her head.

"A pee first."

"There'll be a lineup. If you're thirsty, I should get in line now."

"Okay."

"Okay what? Water or Perrier?"

"Perrier. Thanks."

One of the least heard words in the language was flitting about the
crowded lobby. *Abortion*—a bird flown in from the dark outdoors, beating
its circuit of panic. Even more frequent, the bright, single syllable *she*.
She, most of the actors. *She*, my mother. Lady She. The women who had,
who hadn't, who might have. Normally the A-word is *the* secret. Gloria
once told me that women in book clubs often confess to their affairs and/
or those of their husbands. Semi-strangers mention miscarriages while
eating little sweets off little napkins. Nearly 30 percent of them will have
had abortions, but none of them say so. Suddenly I was hearing it all over
the lobby. Imagine what Kate was getting in the ladies' room.

I stepped out of line quickly, one movement shy of leaping and ripping my hair out. She'd told Gloria, and I'd been standing in line to buy bottled water. She told her. She told her. She told her. For Kate to have said "I'm pregnant" to Gloria was a cowardly way to deliver her verdict on the pregnancy to me. What, she was going to tell Gloria and still get herself taken care of? Look what Mom had to say about that.

I moved between the bar lineup and the women's room door. This second spat beside the Detroit River would be my call, not hers. When Kate emerged, I stepped forward and pointed to the exit. "Some air."

Fittingly, we had to pass through smokers to get any privacy outside. The Zug winds were up, so we only stepped from one stink to another.

"You had no right to tell her when we still haven't made our decision."

"*Our decision? Rights?* I puke enough in the morning. Yes, Antony, I shouldn't have told your mother. And I should have let you know as soon as I decided, but *decide* is a tricky word here. This isn't like booking a trip or choosing a major. As for you, the second thing I know is that I wish I could have this baby with you. A version of you."

Apart from her, I was incandescent with rage. In front of her, I felt less enraged than irrelevant, and that feeling had been growing for two months. Fatherhood, my feelings—big deal.

"You talk as if humiliating me in there means nothing. The pregnancy—"

"The *baby*, Antony. Our *baby*. Not a pregnancy, a baby."

"The pregnancy is one thing. Shutting me out and telling Gloria is quite another. Look at what she's doing to us in there."

She reached for my arm. "I am sorry about that. I had to tell someone, a woman. Safaa's too much of a witness. Melissa—not right either. I thought this would be better than telling my mom. You get pregnant and you need to tell another woman. You just do."

I shook free of her arm.

"'Need to tell.' Aren't you the lawyer? You mean *want* to tell."

That lit her eyes up. "Don't you get it? I'm no longer a law student with great prospects. This is bigger than that, all of that. Your rights. My rights. Neither of them make a fuck of a difference to the little tadpole heart inside me."

I'd never before seen someone look stronger by crying. Her eyes welled with tears and threatened to unbalance her forehead, but she swung her jaw out to right her skull and stare back at me. "I know what my body wants."

"So do pedophiles. So do rapists."

She flashed me an *asshole* look. I flashed back: *an asshole who's right.*

"Listen to me. I go to sleep pregnant. I wake up pregnant. My blood is pregnant. Remember Orwell writing about being unable to shoot a man while he takes a shit? That's how I feel. It doesn't matter anymore how the rifle got into my hands. It's there, and some poor fucker's got his pants down."

"I'm not thinking *how* either. I'm thinking *when*. If we can't be good parents, why be parents at all?"

"*Can't* or *won't?*"

"You tell me. You cannot work seventy hours a week and be a good parent. Period. Choose your moment, darling. Six or seven years from now you could be set and I could retire, get a hobby job. Teach taek. Finish school. Become a green builder. Remember Enron? Most of the pirates stayed on the sinking ship until it took them down with it. But a few got out as rich as princes."

"Yeah, the stripper guy."

"The *smart* guy. Just being a parent doesn't make somebody a good parent. Most parents are shoppers and wipers. At best, they round that out with chauffeuring. But you have to want to drive to soccer practice. I don't, and I don't think you do either. Fear of blood on our hands is never going to make you more patient with shrill cartoons and plastic junk everywhere. Parenting may be affectionate or meaningful, but it isn't intellectual. You're the smartest woman I've ever met. This isn't the right time, in your life or mine, for wiping and yelling."

"That doesn't make it the right time for killing, either. Do I wish I weren't pregnant, that for me a big decision was still whether to buy or lease a car, a Windsor firm or Toronto? Yes. Am I going to kill to get it? No."

The theatre lights flashed us back to our seats.

"I'm going," she announced, then did, hailing a curbside taxi. After a few steps she turned back to say, "Tell her I had to pee too often to stay." No mention of the expensive shoulder sweater she'd leave me to collect from her seat or simply abandon. But she needn't have said anything. Her striding away alone was the highest compliment she could have paid Gloria's *Macbeth*. Mother Kate was beginning to gel, a woman looking after her own or at least armed with the perfect excuse to do what she and she alone wanted to do. Why stick around for the second half of the play? She knew how it would end.

38. Cronus Productions Ltd.

YOU CAN GUESS WHAT GLORIA made of Lady M's "Out damned spot" line. The blood of careerist murder on manicured hands. Convenience blood. Sure, Mom, point taken. But remember that her career was possible after five years of university, not eight, and that she hails from the last generation of lifetime careers and constant employment. Eat the boomers.

I bristled through the second half. She did Banquo's ghost as an aborted child come to life. Once again one of the child actors was dressed to mirror, in flagrant miniature, another character. For Glore, Banquo's ghost was unborn. Later, towards the bloody climax, Macduff saying he "was from his mother's womb untimely ripp'd" somehow made him both aborted but also born of a caesarean, a fetus-man with a score to settle. Watching indictment after indictment, piecing together this variation on tragedy's grand message—you reap what you sow—I was forced to admit I was doing more than awaiting my word with Glore. Surely part of me was also sitting there, in public, passive and quiet, to staunch Kate's wound. Cold comfort, though, hearing Macbeth's "I am in blood / Stepp'd in so far" speech as his vote for abortion when the Kate parliament had just voted otherwise.

Wherever Mom was in the theatre, biting her lip in the wings or watching like a hawk from the control booth, she wouldn't have liked the mathematical image I saw so clearly amidst all the hot oranges and cool blues of the stage lights. Alongside the estranged Macbeths I could also see back to an old textbook and its photograph of a Venn diagram set into a commemorative stained-glass window. Watching Mom's play through the stained glass of rage, I saw every relationship as a Venn diagram of bodies and minds moving together or apart, hugging or slugging, admiring then exiting. Two lovers start out with the hope of aligning their planets, shifting their borders, sliding me into you and vice versa. Then, for some, a child, a third circle, a waxing and waning solar system of infants fixated on and imitative of parents they'll eventually hold in contempt before maybe, maybe consenting to the pity visits and guilt calls. Across the water from the theatre, nearly one-third of American children were being raised by single mothers. For everyone in this story born after Peg and Bill, our Venn diagrams with our fathers had the briefest of intersections, a mere genetic download. That single touch then so much work to keep things whole.

Staunching my wound, seething, collecting my thoughts—whatever I was doing in that theatre had a predictable curtain call. By slipping out of my seat as soon as the final (roaring) applause started I was able to avoid the crush of bodies which had slowed us at intermission. Here, finally, spiky rage shot through me. Everyone rising around me seemed so politely refreshed for having watched a fake tragedy with good lighting, to have been momentarily shaken in their nice clothes.

My asking for backstage admission and going down to the green room was a descent into Gloria's lair, but what else to do? If you call the duel, your opponent gets to set the location. Laughter and a whirlwind of smells thickened as I descended worn stairs. The fatty smells of cosmetics, an acrid wave of hairspray, the crowbar of sweat. Rounding a corner, I saw the green room full of the half-undressed cast and the black-garbed crew. They hugged so frequently they created a communal, rotational dance, hug to the left, spin, now hug to the right. As someone in a dressing gown hinged one way then back I saw two seated queens, Gloria and her Lady M, drinking bubbly out of coffee mugs. Just before I reached them, I nearly collided with the child actor who had played Banquo's ghost.

"Arlene," Gloria said, "this is my son, Antony."

"An excellent performance," I told her. "Congratulations."

"Thank you. I'm sure you've developed an eye." Turning to Mom, Arlene said, "Well, darling, I really should get this shit off." She rolled her eyes around to indicate the thick mask of makeup on her face. "Nice to meet you, Antony."

Gloria glanced behind me. "You're alone down here?"

"Alone now period, looks like. You can imagine how I might like a word."

"This way."

Shortly after a play, the stage is one of the few empty spaces available in a theatre. Gloria led me up a series of tiny backstage staircases. Watch your head here, and again here. Props sat ready on a side table in the wings: envelopes, swords, a leather-bound book. Once we hit centre-stage, I could see and sense her rooting her feet to the deck boards and squaring her shoulders. As of opening night, a director's job is finished, and she walked the boards with palpable envy for her actors.

"I thought you should know as soon as possible that with a child coming I'm going to have to consolidate my finances. I can no longer splurge on indulgences like this," I tapped the painted, plywood backdrop.

"What are you talking about?"

"Don't worry. You seem to have a hit on your hands. I'm sure you'll find another backer."

"Antony, I understand if you want to talk about the play or the pregnancy, but my show and its sponsors are not your concern."

"I am your sponsor, Mother." I smiled. "I am Cronus Holdings. This," I swept my hand from temporary backdrop to rented seats, "is all *family money*." In the Williams' lexicon, that meant smuggling money.

"I don't know what you think you're doing," she sputtered. "I'll phone Gordon Clarke on Monday. If I have to have him show you receipts, I will."

"Gord already sends me receipts. His company is my company. Cronus Holdings is publicly registered, registered to me. Gordon's just a subcontractor. You could have looked me up in an hour. But of course you didn't. Not when you were busy getting what you wanted."

"Get out."

"You played that card long ago. This time you'll hear me out before I leave. Even now, I'll acknowledge your strength. You deserved the money, used it well if not fairly. Yes, you've landed some hits here, made a big point, but it also happens to be all for you. Don't for a second say this play was for Kate. You're always single because other people are too imperfect for you. Again, your choice to make. But that doesn't give you the right to hand out report cards, not to me and certainly not to Kate."

"Love *is* a report card," she replied. "No grades, no love."

"Well then yours needs other criteria than whether or not I'm you. Or Kate should become you. You're more right than you know sending out those little girls to look like Mommy. Vanity and motherhood onstage together at last."

I did a little half-stroll before continuing, arced about on the thrust of the stage. "We may not speak again, so let me say two more things. I've given Kate more respect than I've ever given anyone, more than I knew I had to give. And yes, in part that means giving her a hard time. I learned this from you, *admiringly*. Respect cannot go untested. And that's precisely why I'm willing, as you so charmingly put it"—I gestured at the set around us—"to dip my hands in blood. Because I know Kate can do better. That you have meddled in this so deeply is un-fucking-thinkable given why you're doing it. You want a grandchild for an audience. Sure, you'll gain a life here, but you're taking one too. Kate's. Here goes her career. And the best years of her brain."

She stepped towards me, the stun worn off. "You naïve little shit. You don't have any idea what she'll want in a few years."

"But I know what she'll lose. And so do you. Motherhood fills your arms for a decade. Romantic love can do it for a lifetime."

She gave me some chin. "You're just disappointed because now she might actually slip off your money leash. You say you love what she can do with her mind, so long as that doesn't mean independence from you. You want her to have a big brain but an empty wallet so she'll cling to yours."

"You of all people have lost the right to condemn my money." I turned and tried to make that my exit line.

"I could turn you in," she said to my back, "make you grow up one way or another."

I turned to face her again. "We both know you're not about to do that to your grandchild's father." I stretched my eyes open. In the suddenly still air all we did was stare, both of us knowing whose eyes looked back at her. When her silence became her answer, I walked downstage and climbed into the aisle, passing row after row of empty seats as I left. Halfway to the exit I did the tunneller's worm with my hand then pointed my thumb back at her. *Flood behind.*

39. Ambassador

I WALKED OUT OF THE theatre and surrendered once again to my lifelong pull down to the river. The reflected lights of two cities, two countries, looked greasy on the rippling surface of the dark water. A plague on both your houses. How sad to walk alone when Voodoo lay somewhere beside Kate in our apartment. Once again the bridge turned on its magnet for me, pulled me towards its leaping metal. Another metre, another ten. I walked towards Gran's house counting my ifs.

I would never have written all these posts if Franz Ferdinand's driver hadn't taken a wrong turn in Sarajevo or if Gavrilo Princip hadn't shot Franz Ferdinand. If war and travel hadn't shifted from muscle to machine. If division didn't lead to conquer. If assembly lines didn't have appetites. If Gran had lived in a time and place where an illegal career wasn't the best one open to her. If Bill, Trevor, and I didn't fall for women who run in the rain. If Canada hadn't been ruled by an England which bankrolled its empire forcing Indians to grow opium it forced on the Chinese. If WW I hadn't allowed Bill to quintuple his pay without ever learning to salute. If the US prohibition on alcohol hadn't preceded a second world war which gave them the clout to prohibit marijuana elsewhere. If nations of sheep didn't beget governments of wolves. If Henry Ford had been a mechanically gifted boy in Georgia, not Michigan. If Antoine de la Mothe Cadillac hadn't recognized that the Atlantic gave him a licence to lie. If Michigan strippers could take it all off. If an Ontario government hadn't put half a billion dollars into a Windsor casino owned by an American company. If slavery, unilingualism, mechanization, genocide, and a temperate climate hadn't made the US an economic superpower. If Gran hadn't lived so long and Victor-Conrad so briefly. If a hundred ifs hadn't made the war in Vietnam. If my mother had killed her heart one man sooner. If I'd been born a girl. If Mom hadn't discovered the half-lies of theatre. If the grass wasn't greener on the other side of the border. If citizens governed government. If the pill was perfect, not close to perfect. If the global kajillions spent hunting sub-atomic particles hadn't produced the Internet of the late 60s and the Web of the mid-90s. If Kate's father had been from, and absconded back to, Barrie, not Scotland. If the world preferred beauty to guns, reason to rule, love to greed.

What fraction of the Italian marble and cedar framing in Gran's house would have existed without the wars? Without Prohibition? Someone is always getting squeezed, one class or race done by another. Walking in the October night, I could see the big patterns but not where I was going to spend the night.

Physically, I could have slipped into Gran's and slept there. I've had a key to her house ever since I had a key ring (we're an escape route family). But what, I was going to risk scaring or waking a woman who was over a hundred and explain myself to her sleepy homecare worker? Two of my doors were closed to me, and I was reluctant to use my third. Maybe I'd just peek in the window.

I crept silently onto Gran's porch to stare into one home as I was losing another. Of course the house I had in mind didn't have all the plastic trays and pharmaceutical boxes I actually saw through her windows. The doors to her new bedroom were closed, yet still I could see white health-care boxes, tubs of lotion, and vessels for various unwelcome liquids riding the antique tables in her parlour. I was fleeing diapers at one end of life only to meet them at the other.

This is life, not art: no neat symmetries here. While leaving Kate and Mom, I didn't peer through Gran's windows and suddenly see her twiggy arm fall out of bed at an awkward angle. I didn't rush in to hear a deathbed confession, didn't tearfully say, "Go now," or "I'll miss you." Still, she drew her final breath sometime that night. It would be a rare centenarian who gets an autopsy (cause of death: being old), so I can concentrate on the night of Gran's passing, not its hour, and say that she left her life the same night I left our apartment.

Where to go? What difference, if any, would it have made if I'd surrendered to temptation or spite and called Melissa? We'd chatted a little at Safe Sisters events, had been in the same room enough to read the man/woman barometer. I'd occasionally needed to track Kate down at her place. Surely the jury can't help but notice that I'd kept a hooker's number in my phone. Truth be typed, I should've called. I spent the same amount of money on a hotel room, and I didn't make it laugh even once. Hurt, alone, and unable to sleep amidst all the brass lamps and bland prints of a hotel, I couldn't stop going over and over two competing yet extremely unwelcome thoughts. One: everyone thought me an asshole for being who I wanted to be. Two: nice guys do indeed finish last.

Have a taxi-meter brain and you never lose sight of the fact that in life you have to pay for what you want. If Gloria and I had tried to care for Gran ourselves (not that she'd have let us), one of us would have had to hold back our post-*Macbeth* nastiness in the morning to call the other with news of the old girl's passing. Hire a private health-care worker, and you can just tell them to try two phone numbers in case of emergency.

When you pay someone to care for a 103-year-old relative and they phone you at 7:00 in the morning, you call back thinking, *Dead or dying?* Then, inevitably, you circle up the family wagons. I phoned Kate while driving to Gloria's.

(Great-)grandparents, those ambassadors of death. Gran's death was imminent as long as I could remember. She was history in a housedress. How could skin that dry even stay on a body? Now that she'd made her century and died in her sleep, I was suddenly more sad for the losses in her life, not the end of it. Her decades of mourning for two men she lost but couldn't even bury. The indignation of her shrinking, leaking body. Glad to see her go before she worsened.

That was my attitude as I approached Mom's driveway. Apparently Gran's flight was harder on Glore. For a start, she hugged me as soon as she saw me, hugged me then held me at arm's length. "You fucking Williams men," she said between sobs (and rationalizations).

I can recognize forgiveness and need when I hear them. Forgiveness, need, loss, and complete denial of the fact that I still hadn't forgiven her. But here too was another of my women in an empty nest. She'd lost her grandmother, her father, and her mother all in one go. I led her back inside and set two mugs of coffee onto the kitchen table (that drug for the heart of the house). Funeral home A, B, or C? "I'll call."

I was worried about my uncharacteristically rag-doll mother until she got us with a joke. "I can't help it. I close my eyes and think of England."

Gran had spent nearly eight of her eleven decades in Canada, yet you can't bury an immigrant without thinking of the old country. Their ledger has an extra row at the top.

Mom's next comment wasn't so funny. Like a toddler's, her laughs suddenly tripped over themselves and became tears. She nodded at the phone. "Get your girl. If you still can."

"She's coming."

"Lucky you."

Luck or work?

The funereal paperwork was provincial. The thoughts were both international and personal. The funeral itself was social. Only Gran's will was private. And it, not her death, was the surprise.

The smaller the family, the more likely you are to inherit swag. I'd already inherited the gene for making money, so over the years I'd thought more about making my own than being handed any of Gran's. While I certainly admired her house and its riverside lot, I'd spent the last decade keeping my green fingers off of Windsor real estate. Home ownership is coveted in civilian life but a problem in drug crime, easy proof that you're involved. But Gran's house was the only sacred ground

I/we knew. For a start, it had always felt like our house, a house each of the three of us had a claim to, a haven in, and a use for. That's why Mom had been mad when I was hired to paint it as a teenager, my getting equal billing.

Mom didn't object, even welcomed, Kate joining us for the reading of the will. Given that Gran wouldn't have dreamt of hiring a female lawyer, I'm sure Mom wanted to even off the gender sides. The 3.4 of us sat across from Lawyer Don and listened as Mom was given the cash, all of it, then I was awarded the house. Ol' Bill had left Gran substantial savings and no mortgage, and she had started drawing a national pension before the world knew of Pierre Trudeau. The cash wasn't negligible. But it also didn't have a sweet view of the river. When the lawyer announced my getting the house, Glore did some very audible huffing and some very visible looking away.

I'd thought Kate was swimming with the team until she, not Gloria, asked when the will had been drafted.

The lawyer replied, "Does it matter?"

"We'll decide that, thanks," replied Kate.

"Well?" Gloria echoed.

"This is a recent will, but an accurate one, a very, very solid one. Margaret wanted this will respected."

'Twas indeed the time of birth-certificate names. Gran's will had been drawn up in September.

The house was one blow, the timing another. Gran couldn't have known about Kate. She'd recently been smoking more weed than Snoop Dogg. What, on the way out the old girl could *smell* pregnancy?

"Let's remember what we all know about houses," the lawyer continued. "Antony may now own it, but it's possible for everyone to use it."

For her response, Gloria walked out. In the parking lot, she barely glanced at us, muttering, "I need to be alone," before she drove off.

On the other hand, Kate was fun and business both. "Let's go."

Gran, how could you?

Driving over we were one more vehicle funnelling down to Riverside Drive. I assumed the viewing would be banal, tedious, domestic. I'd simply stare at all the cleaning that needed to be done, the plastic things to be discarded, count the walls thirsty for a coat of paint. The smells of urine and mothballs would repulse and embarrass. But arriving there with Kate once again at my side, the feeling of ownership swamped me instantly. Imperfect, isolating, and fictitiously elating ownership. At least until we got separated on different floors. She gravitated to the upstairs and its riverside view. I headed down to the basement.

Only a fool would take his pregnant, exish lover who runs in the rain to view a riverside house with a forest of hardwood floors, acres of tile, antique pocket doors, a perpetually rising value, and a gorgeous view. Whatever you do, don't do that.

III. Up

40. Width, Height

WHILE KATE WANDERED AROUND UPSTAIRS, I went down into the basement, the one place in the house I had always been discouraged from going. I could hear Kate pulling out drawers while I finally got to thoroughly examine Bill's crypt.

Down there. What a self-effacing euphemism. Notice there's no *my* in *down there.* I simply can't imagine referring to my tackle without calling it mine. Also, crucially, *down there* isn't *here. Down* becomes *away* even though it's down a woman's own body. As Kate sought me out in Gran's basement, we both saw that I had no confusion over whether or not *down there* was mine.

I'd been pacing the basement, half-ascending the stairs for multiple views of the riverside wall. Even in my suit I stroked it repeatedly, traced one or both hands over the cool cement, trying to press against or cradle all that terror and wonder. What fucking balls on ol' Bill. What lethal fucking balls. After three days of funeral-home clothes and government forms in triplicate and old lady kisses, my hands were itching for a sledgehammer. I loosened my tie and took another look at the width of the staircase, the height of the windows.

Generally I agreed with the math of Kate's classmates about an LLB vs. DIY. When you're about to earn $200/hr copying obscure words onto long paper, why balk at paying a plumber or mechanic $90? But generationally, hold on. Ol' Bill had tunnelled under the German trenches when he was the same age as an Antony unable to tunnel under one university degree. He built most of the house, both in the beginning then with additions and renos in fits and starts. Deepened the basement. Expanded the second storey. Added a garage. Why could most twentysomethings in the 1920s build a version of a house when today they can barely build a fire? Kate's classmates were great managers of their music collections, yes. Great survivalists? Won't we all see.

Granted, Bill's training and experience were extreme and nothing to be envied. World War I was hell in cold mud. But the man could get things done, either by himself or with a few borrowed hands. Deepening a basement was par for the local course. Tunnelling into another nation to smuggle booze was extreme, but forget the act for a second and remember the location and the man. He'd tunnelled through generations and history then sailed across the deep water to wind up looking at just a kilometre of mud between him and a fortune. Why work the line when he could dig his own and found a dynasty? His big prong into the yanks. His grave. All from the family basement, a wife and child above him. The Detroit River was his Rubicon. Staying in the house after her man crawled in and never came out—that was Gran's. She too had defined her adulthood with the wind at her back, the literal and the legal. When Bill died she could have packed up again, returned to England with the money for a new life or pressed west, headed to Vancouver or Victoria, the end of the white world. But she held out and held on, lived life in a mausoleum.

The basement Gran had all but forbidden me to enter had a doubled riverside wall. She'd waited some time after Bill crawled out without returning—a month, maybe twelve—then had a second wall laid over the top of the first and what must have been his tunnel entrance. Bill had masons instead of pallbearers, local hands who had received favours from him or were paid by Gran or remembered the Battle of Messines. Immigrants who could keep their mouths shut (or veterans that were proud to) had sealed him in. They'd have known they were sealing off a goldmine, but imagine the wailing above them.

The slightly younger mortar of the riverside wall had fewer cracks than the other walls. The dusty top of the second cement wall hung in front of the wooden sill, not just below it. Four inches thick. Hard, but not impossible. Mentally, I was already working on *To Do* and *To Get* lists when Kate finally came down the stairs. I could afford to be a little honest. "We bury her, yet I think about him out there. His second No Man's Land."

"I hope you're not thinking of joining him. Come back up. You inherited a house, not just a basement."

Back in the living room she had already perfected an unfolding/ enfolding new posture that could switch from displaying her belly to shielding it. Unfolded, she glanced out a window at the river then looked back at me. "When do we move in?"

It was my turn to say, "I don't know yet, and I don't know when I'll know."

41. Or Another

MY CAREER HAD STARTED WITH a truck full of tools, not a pinging inbox. I hadn't forgotten that making often starts with breaking. Two days after I inherited Gran's house I raced down the basement stairs in my work boots to swing a sledgehammer at that doubled riverside wall. Nothing is mine until I've fucked with it. At minimum, I need to see how something works. I'd heard about Bill's tunnel and grave all my life. Kate, Gloria, even me, we all half-knew that sometimes we choose to see while at other times seeing is forced upon us. With the basement, I chose to see. With Kate, well.

The real force is in the hips, not the arms. I raised the sledge to my shoulder and took a Babe Ruth stance. I tried to concentrate on my breath and my aim—not on that Orion's Belt of distant bodies, that line of me, Bill, and Trevor somewhere in the distance—as I whipped my hips and arms forward. When the sledge hit I was just me, me, me.

A sledgehammer blow falls like a cannon shot, woofs deeper than thunder. When you've absolutely got to smash your way out or in, accept no substitute. At first the wall appeared to hold up. Castle-wall pride spat back the sledge (along with a few cement teeth). But I had felt the hammer's sweet, deep punch. After another blow and another I went in with the masonry chisel and crowbar. Working just inches from the wall I noticed old, trowelled seams in the cement, signatures from the anonymous dead. Nothing makes you more attentive to something than your laborious, careful and planned destruction of it.

The first blows were just recon, a dusty assessment. Aside from my safety gear, I made my exploratory hole in the outer wall with tools no different from what Bill or even his grandfather would have used, just steel focussing muscle. When Bill dug for King George, he did so alongside officers licensed and armed to shoot him dead whenever they wanted. Eventually, though, every manjack among them, officer and tunneller alike, was invited to propose new tools for the epic dig, from stronger spoil bags to spear shovels to better waterproofing for the explosives. Both Tommy and Jerry went into the war hung up on class. Underground, there was no class, just the quiet, terrifying race to blow up someone who was working day and night to blow you up.

Underground, ingenuity prospered, and not just with steel and cloth. Pumps, rescue breathing apparatuses, underground geophones—everything perpetually refined for the push. In my basement digging, I often wondered if part of the violence of that war was a consequence of the armies being so close but unable to see each other. The smell of their sizzling supper. Singing in a language they could hear but not understand. The murder of proximity. Kate called me a jukebox of war stories, but we don't always get to choose what we'll understand, what keeps us whole.

I could feel the traces of Bill's handmade work but knew early on that I wasn't going to continue my work unplugged. I sat on the basement steps to compose *To Get* and *To Do* lists. Kate would be writing radically new versions of these same lists weekly for the next decade as Momma chained herself to pharmacy and grocery store. I tried to ignore all that by renting a diamond saw, a power saw so sharp it could cut through your sarcophagus, your coffin, and your bones without so much as a whine. The saw. Heavy-duty tubs. A conveyor belt. Screw jacks. Building permit. (To explain the sound of my digging, I whined to the condolence-offering neighbours about a neglected foundation in desperate need of repair.) Even more important was a lock for the basement door.

If this were a bookstore book, not a pixelated snowdrift of family history only one or two people in the world care about, I'd throw in exotic words for theories of camouflage. Something Japanese for *same-*

hiding-same. A mouthful from Renaissance Europe would describe the art of drawing the eye away. Mother Russia would advocate grandiose distraction. In Windsor, toxic, sinning Windsor, I only had morning coffee and an industrial supply store every three kilometres to help me trick the eye. Here was the smuggler's nearly spiritual question: how flagrant should I be about the fact that I was hiding something? Neither Kate nor Glore had many incentives to go into Gran's basement. Simply gambling that they wouldn't go down might be best. A new padlock hanging off the basement door would dangle more conspicuously than a mistress's earring. Throwing a new deadbolt would be like turning on a *look over here* sign. Yet one stray trip into the basement by either of them—Kate assessing the storage space, Mom surveying the contested land—and my game'd be up.

I made a second door frame at the top of the basement stairs. Gran's door swung out into the kitchen. Beyond it my new second door swung back over the basement stairs. Were two opposing doors awkward? Yes. Up to code? No. As I finished installing the second door I finally unpacked a nagging sense of déjà vu. I had seen a dozen similarly naked door frames good on just one side in Mom's theatres over the years. Blond, unpainted two-by-fours temporarily angled down onto the staircase runners. Kate, Gloria, me, Gran, maybe you—we all discovered that *good one side* is true for lumber, theatre sets, and family members. No sooner had I triple-checked the lock than Basement Threat No. 1 knocked on the front door.

By this point in our lives—spared cancer, not yet guilty of affairs—only death or pregnancy could dwarf everything else in life, wash away mistreatment, overshadow my AWOL night and Kate's theatre of cruelty. Spreading out her hands, thrusting her face forward a little, still on the porch, she said, "I'm a simpleton."

Mea culpa, a diagnosis, and a sales pitch all in one.

She stepped in. "The more complex this is, the simpler it is. I'm finally binary: yes or no, on or off. I can't pull the trigger, Ant. I won't. I'm the lobotomommy now."

Keeping a baby was definitely a decision someone made more than once. For her at least, *yes* had become daily.

"Every single second I'm part of this baby, a baby that's made from us. Baby, body, us—there's no difference anymore. I can't even remember the me who would have been embarrassed to show in school. This is our baby."

She started crying again as she stepped inside, but it was just a mild leak. No abdominal heaves, no quivering chin. The tears were no longer a surprise nor, really, was the hand she reached out to brush dust off my forearm, nor the circle of her fingers that lingered around my arm. Why question the way she grabbed my warm T-shirt and pulled me into her? Crying? That's just one more coaxing of the inside out, another wet spill from the body. Besides, she was entering the hey-sailor trimester. More than just skin brought us together. Our chromosomes undressed us. We were ruled by the double-helix and briefly became one on Gran's couch, upside-down, right-side up. Pregnancy: you've got to take it one shag at a time.

Despite that new glue, I used the basement work as an excuse to half-move out of our apartment. We were probably just in another lull between storms, so I attacked my foundation wall morning, noon, and night. Kate was hot and cold for me, and the house was near campus. She started stopping by for, well, brief, non-studious visits. Upstairs, we worked our way through the rooms, owning them in the canine, pungent way. Her future was clear, and ours was "don't ask, don't tell." I did neither. One tunnel or another, all sweat, work, and hope.

42. Blow Your Mine

THE KATE I WANTED WAS eclipsed, displaced more and more each day. Some nights I'd spend with her in our apartment, others in the work house breaking large rocks into smaller ones. We were together for the first few nights after she announced her decision, part need, part going-away party. Quickly enough, where I spent Wednesday night had little influence on Thursday night. She wanted me then she didn't. Re-opening the tunnel access I'd work into dangerous exhaustion one night, dragging my body from basement to shower to bed. The next night I'd date my probably-lost, exish partner. For better or worse, humour resurfaced.

"Prenatal classes," she'd say. "More like pre-nuptial classes."

Or, "I've always been an early achiever. Look at this, I'm a single mom before I'm even a mom." Other nights there were tears, some silent, some not. We had breakup sex without fully breaking up.

Not yet. Not now. Most will think I should have crumbled, signed on, sublimated my life to the errands and chores of parenting. How could I treat a woman pregnant by my, er, hand, with anything less than slavish worship? She was expanding the tribe, was finally becoming a woman. Hello? The tribe doesn't need expanding. (In fact, our tribe is killing all the others.) And doesn't anyone else, maybe even a few women, think it's reductive, offensive, and just plain sad to believe that a woman only comes into her own by caring for someone other than herself? In taek studios over the years I'd catch glimpses of the weekend self-defence industry, those pony-tailed instructors who briefly coach paying women by repeating, "Defend yourself like you're defending your child." Self-effacement for a fee.

Not yet. Not now. We'd have been driving to soccer practice on our thirtieth birthdays, would be just another pair of North American shoppers with a gas tank and plastic everywhere, the planet be damned. Banquo, how could we stoop for sippy cups when we hadn't yet reached for ball gags? And, now more than ever, we'd be walking away from a fortune, life-changing money.

In Gran's basement, I wasn't quite digging to America. Technically, legally, and logistically, that would have been nearly impossible. Publicly accessible government documents, not conspiracy theories, alerted me to microphones and sensors in the ground along the US border. The International Boundary Commission was a long way from Bill's war underground. Then, tunnellers were often required to lie in a tunnel's side chamber while holding a stick in their mouths in the hope they'd feel if Jerry was at the shovel. A stick in the mouth. After the next war, in the 50s, one sacked atomic scientist used a seismograph at Berkeley to look for the successful testing of a hydrogen bomb he'd been removed from. The test explosion on the South Pacific island of Elugelab spiked a seismograph five thousand kilometres away in California. I'd tell you to look up Elugelab on Google Earth, but the American explosion destroyed the entire island. The sticks keep getting bigger and our mouths more sensitive.

I wasn't trying to dig a new hole into America, just hoping to investigate an old one. Bill dug his tunnel long before Homeland Security probes were sunk into the Detroit mud. I couldn't know what I would do with the tunnel, or its remnants, until I knew what was there. That same attitude worked for Kate and against her.

Archaeologists don't dig like builders. Not even I would have wasted all that lost casino time sifting through dirt looking for finger bones or pottery shards, but each strike with the shovel, crowbar, or masonry chisel felt like I was cutting into an anniversary cake. From all my reading about Bill's tunnels, I knew the basement wall wouldn't open like a garage door. Instead of a muddy corridor, I was sure to meet a vertical access shaft that plunged down before a tunnel could crawl across. But knowledge and observation don't always mesh. Despite digging with the precise hope of seeing a dark, vertical shaft, the first shadowy glimpse of empty blackness sent a squirt of fear down the whole length of my spine. The pneumatic hammer stopped simply cracking chunks of cement off the secondary wall and suddenly shot on through into dark, empty air (and nearly dragged my forward hand along with it). A couple more spurts and I had a pizza-sized hole. Swirling dust, hanging cobwebs, and the studs and wooden sheathing of the shaft's other wall swung in the bright cone of my flashlight. Once more into the deep.

With my arm through the hole I couldn't reach the wooden outer wall of the access shaft. Feeling every bit like the vet saying hello to the busy part of a cow, I bent at the elbow and began feeling along the inside edges of the closest wall. Just cobwebs, ropes of them, and the cement wall I was cracking off. Eventually I found one timbered corner. Tucked into it was the unmistakable, cylindrical solidity of an old cast-iron plumbing pipe. I ran my hand up and down the cool, five-inch pipe, that leg that just wouldn't quit.

Build a house today and the sewage pipes are plastic. Lightweight, easy to cut, reliably uniform, less vulnerable to corrosion (we think). Build a house when Bill dug his tunnel, and your toilet drains would have been made from cast iron. Imagine my intrigue when I opened the walls to cobwebs, stale air, and an old iron pipe that had never carried anything dirtier than Windsor-Detroit air. It had one access opening here in the basement and climbed up through the walls, probably to the roof, for an endless supply of air. For decades, the house had been breathing internationally.

Of course I expected to uncover timber framing, but I was shocked as the cement chipped off to reveal letters then whole names engraved into the ottery hide of wood that framed the adit. I stopped using the jackhammer and worked the timber facing with a masonry chisel to uncover a long crawling list of engraved names. One letter then one name followed the next in a hand-carved honour roll. *MILES • STAMPER • BANFORD*. I uncovered them slowly, my blunt chisel following Bill the Ghost's carvings of seventy years ago. *HICKING • HEPBURN • DAVIS*. Up one side, across the header and down the other. *BARKER • LARGE • STAFFORD*. Only the very centre of the header varied that march of names. *ONTARIO FARM II*. I had to set down my tools.

The Great War's Battle of Messines was *the* underground battle of the war and the world's worst pregnancy. Bill and company dug incessantly for eighteen months to place hundreds of tonnes of explosives in nineteen branches of tunnels, and then they waited. And waited. Once the canisters of Ammonal were placed, tamped, and wired, some tunnels sat unexploded for more than a year. Every second risked detection, a counter-explosion by the German miners, malfunction, collapse, or the enemy capture of the trenches that housed the tunnel entrance.

Finally, after up to a year and a half of waiting, the Battle of Messines commenced on 7 June 1917. The explosion of the nineteen mines was one of the largest explosions the world had ever known. Window panes as far away as London got rattled by the Messines blast. Combined, the explosives exceeded the blast of three million grenades. Flames shot 800 feet into the sky and cooked the air to more than 3,000°C. The biggest mining attack in the history of warfare was to precede the largest English artillery attack to date, which would precede waves of bayonet-wielding bullet catchers. Attack by man-made earthquake. One of the mined tunnels had been named Ontario Farm.

Ontario Farm. Even before Bill's engraving, the phrase had acquired multiple layers for me. As a teenager reading about the war I first thought Ontario Farm was just a label. By the time I fell for Kate, I recognized that in 1917 Ontario basically *was* a farm. Smelling my own deep, dark earth there in the basement, I could see that Ontario may have been one big hick farm back in 1917, but when the world went crazy in the Flemish mud, the steady supply of farm boys from Ontario (etc.) won the war. They had the higher ground; we had the numbers. To the English generals, Canadians were subordinates. To the Germans, we were death on two swift legs. They called Canadians "killers of Germans." Flanders Fields was a thick ledger, and *Ontario Farm* had been written in the largest, boldest letters going, all in that red farmboy ink.

It wasn't a coincidence that Bill had lived in and around the Ontario Farm tunnel in 1917 then immigrated to Ontario itself in 1919. When he and Peg chose to start life over, they already had their Mecca, their North Star. Bill and Peg, Gloria and Trevor, Medea and Jason—they all knew you can build a destination up from a phrase, from an idea in a mouthful of words, especially when the phrase belonged on the other side of some contested line. *Ontario Farm*. Password. Beacon. Curse.

Solid, liquid, gas. Dig, go beneath the surface, and you've got so much to think about with solids and liquids that you can too easily forget about gas. You can even forget about gas before carbon monoxide makes you too stupid to think about gas. Bill and the lads had a variety of medievally simple technologies for gas detection. If a candle could no longer burn, oxygen levels were too low. Caged birds helped, the proverbial canary in a coalmine, but no bird loves a war. Eventually, bred canaries had their claws trimmed so they wouldn't be able to clamp onto their perches if they died. Proper English soldiers, their feet were the property of King and country. Mice were also conscripted. Tunnel openings began in the same trenches where regular soldiers lived in daily struggle with rats: food-stealing, disease-carrying, latrine-haunting, corpse-eating rats. Down the line, tunnellers—already separated by higher pay, more rum, and less discipline—bred, housed, and fed mice. Not for me. I could buy carbon-monoxide detectors at any hardware store and look like a responsible citizen, not a criminal. I had electric monitors in the basement and several battery-powered units ready to crawl out with me.

Preparation aside, eventually you've got to dive in. The machined and reliable old vertical shit pipe illuminated by my flashlight was encouraging, but the abyssal black air of the vertical access shaft uncaged the butterflies in my stomach. Pipe and shaft dropped into rank darkness. Destined by character, I'd been driving around with ladders and work lights since I was nineteen.

The shaft was absolutely knitted with cobwebs, but the feet of my aluminium ladder hit a floor which sounded solid and dry. That may have just been the concrete I'd been dropping, but how else to find out? Work light on my head, a spare in my pocket, I hoisted a leg over and climbed down. The density of cobwebs emphasized the three-dimensionality of the air in the wood-framed shaft. The wet newspaper smell of earth, the drop in temperature, the rise in humidity, and the velvet coating of dust on Bill's wooden framing all said *hidden space*. Despite the metal ladder I'd inserted and the chunks of cement wall I'd sent down the shaft, the cobwebs were still as snug as stirrups beneath my feet. My elbows were brushed constantly. My cheeks got tickled on every rung of the ladder. For love or money.

At the base of the access shaft, beneath the bits of wall, the floorboards were spongy but not rotten. Reputedly, the air was okay. Still, a quick peek into the tunnel itself—a concrete floor with a railway(!), a frame of concrete slabs, the auxiliary air pipe now running horizontally—and I knew I wanted it to breathe a little longer before we got to know each other. I crawled in just two metres to say hello. The old fucker laid rails. Case after case of booze hauled from one side to the other, his own private international railway. And those carved names. *HICKLING • MORGAN • LOCK*. I hauled myself back up the ladder to see them again. *WELSBY • CARRINGTON • BROWN*. Like ants crawling around and around with their loads and their communal will. *PRYOR • LEATHER • MOORE*. Bill's engraving filled the outside face of each timber, while the underside of the header was still just brown wood. At least until I raced out, pious but practical, and bought an electric engraving tool. Dark international air swirled in the shaft below me as I reached up to carve *William Williams, 1896—1925* on the underside of the same section of beam that had *ONTARIO FARM II* on its face.

Climbing up and climbing down, I'd see this inscription on each of my subsequent workdays. That done, it was time to go see Kate. Eventually, you gotta blow your mine.

43. The Land of Surprises

I WAS DOWN TO MY last two relationship assumptions and about to break one of them. Now that I owned my job site, she had more reason than ever to *not* know the details. Normally, telling her what I really did might have finalized her exit visa for Splitsville. But Bill's engraved names had crawled inside me. I wanted to be understood, not simply endured.

She was still in class when I got to our/the apartment, so I had time for a long shower. After days of digging, just stepping into civilian clothing was foreplay. Cooking was proto-sex. Shredded garlic unzipped into hot olive oil. The thigh-hugging warmth of the oven felt so generously civilized. Compact and effortlessly powerful speakers sliced and diced a little Berlin leisure-techno. A tempting life, but it all had to be paid for. I heard Kate's key in the door and reached for a second wine glass. Whoops.

Voodoo was faster to greet her than I was. He nearly drilled himself into the floor turning circles as she stepped in and dropped her bags. I'd moved to the kitchen doorway so she could see me too, but Vood was beseechingly cute. She reached down to milk his ears and cup his chin. When he was finally on his back in full, tongue-lolling bliss she looked up from rubbing his belly. "Well, look what the dog dragged in. You look nice."

"And you look great. Which do I have to be to get my belly rubbed, hairier or smaller?"

I got a little jolt not knowing whether we'd kiss. You sign a lease together and—blessing and curse—the kissing's essentially a case of when not if. Kate's silent dating scheme hadn't been enough to truly give us a new first date, but a relationship-threatening pregnancy was something else altogether. What the hell, I leaned forward and tried the tongueometer. Not boiling, but certainly above the freezing point.

My hands trailed down for hers. "I'd like to finish cooking supper then show you something. Okay?"

"Ever the land of surprises."

Warm food, a nice place, no dust in the air—I wanted to luxuriate in all of it and more. After several days of shoulder-tightening, uncertain labour, I would've liked to guzzle a bottle of wine. Not the time, though. Not the time.

Meals only last so long. I reached for her hand and met her gaze. "Obviously the pregnancy has changed everything."

"Yes and no. My wanting to love you hasn't changed."

"If you're willing, I'd like to show you something in the house. It's not illegal *per se*."

"Oh do say," she replied, but with a little smile.

"Seriously, what I show you—there'll be little separation between my work and…me."

"You're right, this I'd like to see."

Voodoo perked up at the jingle of my truck keys.

Once again we drove towards the Ambassador Bridge (that other glowing border). There I finally was, baby half on board, sinning by vanity and creating a witness. I broke my vow to never do this precisely because we'd been skirting vows for weeks.

At the house, I led her in at the back. In the kitchen, I simply nodded to point her towards the doubled basement doors. Bill's engraved doorway had made my new one useless. And indicting.

"Everything's different now save how much I admire you, so I want to show you something else I admire. Like love, respect is a kind of gravity. You've got mine, and so do Gran and ol' Bill."

She pulled Gran's basement door open then shot me a disappointment-rising look at the sight of the new, second door hanging open in the basement's dim light. Two days ago I'd built that door to keep her out. Now I urged her through it. She wasn't the only one confused by pregnancy.

A two-foot-by-five-foot cement adit in a basement wall opposite America is its own billboard. I didn't have to nudge Kate towards the opened wall. I watched her stop and read the engraved names, her curious chin upturned as at the Rivera murals. I hoped those names were marching into her as they had into me. Worse than simply trying to impress her, I expected her to be impressed. Ah, love—tests and traps. If she didn't get those names marching down the beams, the dead chiselled by the surviving, an illegal invasion after a legal one, she didn't really get me. Bill's gratitude was inseparable from his gamble. Mine too, baby. When the stakes truly matter, if you don't love what I love, then we're just working, a temporary bouquet not an annual garden. Sure, the word *compromise* may be indissoluble from *relationship*, but at times that has to bore, indict, and sadden you.

Finally, I stepped towards her to shine a flashlight on the pipe. "That's for auxiliary air, so I'm still no wiser about what got him. It may not even be intact anymore, but if it is, look out, America."

"Stop." She held out her hand for the light. With its cool LED beam, she returned our attention to the wooden honour roll. "Look harder for the lesson here, Antony. Look much, much harder." She swept the light across the names.

I already knew many of them by memory. *HALL • BICKLEY • WARNOCK*. Did she mean the connection to her Scottish heritage? *MACKILLIGIN, TULLOCH,* and *MULQUEEN*? The colonialism? Gender segregation? Apparently realization did not spring into my face quickly enough.

She reached out and set my fingertips into the brittle engraving of a name. "What's the most obvious, most relevant fact about each of these names?" she asked. "Each of these men?"

My fingertips climbed up and down the crispy lettering as my time ran out. The WASPiness? The Eurocentrism? The absence of Belgians fighting in Belgium?

"They're dead, you fucking idiot. They died underground, underage, and under-sexed. You think this will *impress me*? That it *excuses* you?!"

She turned and stormed up the stairs. Halfway up she stopped to look back down at me and the edge of that black hole. "Dead men aren't the only heroes going." She raised a foot but then lowered it. "Dead people," she added, briefly placing a hand below her navel.

When the sound of my truck reversing down the drive faded I turned back to the tunnel opening and tried to ignore Voodoo's dance routine of confusion.

Again I saw those marching names, reached in to grip that cool throat of a pipe.

44. Theseus of Canadian Tire

PLAN A DIDN'T WORK, SO I poured everything into Plan B. B for *beneath America.*

History, art, and a little imagination can always help you think of someone lonelier than you. An illiterate Rwandan girl fleeing the genocidal slaughter of her family while she walks through lion- and rapist-infested bush eating the occasional grub was definitely lonelier than I was after Kate stomped off (again). Even here in privileged ConsumerLand, my loneliness was nothing compared to that of a pregnant Thai immigrant smuggled into a new country by criminals she'll pay for ten years. My rational brain could conjure the lonely, but to my heart-brain there was no loneliness like male, self-exiled loneliness. You're nothing without your code but nothing again if no one gets your code.

I tried to convince myself that this way I was taking all the pain up front. I'd swallow down that glassy hurt to spare us all my slow death as a suburban dad grinding out his resentment with a basement beer fridge, a dissatisfying career, and yardwork. Men and yardwork. Give me a break. Plumage work, what others see from the outside. Protecting the territory, pissing on its corners. That this comes with a burning engine or whirring blades couldn't make Mr. Minivan happier as he spews around exhaust/ ejaculate, driving away the children he claims to be serving. No thanks.

Take the loss head-on. Be hated. I let myself be left so we'd each have a gunshot breakup: the heat of the bullet cauterized its own wound. Guilty as charged. I couldn't stand becoming the unsexed errand boy for a mewling little usurper empowered entirely by its lack of power. Chequebook fatherhood it would be. A monthly signed confession of failure rather than a protracted, child-damaging four- or seven- or ten-year failure of weekend boozing, McEngineering, and shopping. Fourteen-year-olds know the one in two odds of a marriage not working out, but only the divorce lawyers keep an eye on gender. In life after forty, two-thirds of divorces are initiated by women. Half his pension but none of his dirty socks. Good riddance blaring hockey. Western women now survive childbirth, but their marriages don't survive childrearing.

Appropriate thoughts to take underground and underwater. Tunnelling is fundamentally about volume. More than length, more than depth, the volume matters. The amount of material you need to extract and, always unforgettable, the amount of it hanging above you. We're probably taught geometry precisely so we can *see* math, see exclusion and intersection, borders, containment, how every inside has an outside. Geometry—the porn of math. If Bill had wanted to create a tunnel tall enough for someone to walk in, he would have had to quadruple his work, risk, time, and money compared to tunnelling a shallow little railway. In our basement, Windsor got its second light industrial railway with carts designed to carry crates of hooch and/or a prone man.

For all its years of neglect, the tunnel still looked navigable, at least at the start. Slats of prefab cement kept out most of the mud. Timbered U-frames played Atlas every four feet and held the world aloft. Even more resilient than this wood was the steel of the light rails. The morning after Kate squealed off in my truck I took a cab to Canadian Tire to buy one of those padded mechanic's creepers (aka a Windsor Hide-A-Bed), then expanded its wheel base. Finally I too was another Windsor DIYer rolling close to the dirty ground and trailing my tools. I went out with a spool of cheap nylon cord to mark distance, several water bottles, a compact shovel, an air horn, a knife, a hammer for rats, a bag full of LED lights and CO monitors I could drop along my way. I carried a cellphone, lube for the rails, and a new tarp I hoped not to use.

Curious is too small a word. So is *excited*. You can read about explorers or revolutionaries or smugglers all you want, but little of it will adequately give you the heart-swatting, pelvis-tingling exhaustion/ energy of steady fear wed to steady hope. Rolling feet first into the damp cobwebs, inching along, I was my own needle on a horizontal gauge of terror and thrill. Agreed: beauty *is* terror.

I wrote all this in chunks in case you wanted to dive in anywhere. That table of contents could let you keep things whole in whatever order you'd like. Not so with the tunnel. Tunnels are undeniably, mercilessly linear. I played out my nylon cord as I rolled, though I felt more like Champlain going up the St. Lawrence for the first time than Theseus braving the labyrinth. As the Theseus myth gets retold, his duplicity is almost always omitted. Now the Theseus myth is about a clever youth outwitting an older, more powerful male monster for romantic and financial gain, another purebred noble grinding down the filthy mixie. But the spool of yarn was female Ariadne's idea, not Theseus's. As soon as they'd sprung themselves from her father's maze and were safely on the high seas he dumped her on a remote island. Once abandoned, Ariadne was "wed to Dionysus" (translation: she hit the bong for the rest of her life). Wham bam, good-bye, ma'am. The Greek myths and the barnyard will show you fathers who slay, rape, lie, and abandon. I wasn't abandoning Kate. She was abandoning us. Underground and underwater, inching towards my fate, I was as certain of this and what I did and didn't want to find.

Theoretically I'd be most likely to find the Detroit River's second shoreline down there, a section of washed-out tunnel holding Bill's corpse unseen in Davey Jones-Crockett's Locker. But if the tunnel wasn't flooded, I might have a murdered corpse on my hands. Or two. As I rolled on, playing out my cord, never more alone, I began to wonder again about a third family theory for Bill's end. Crushed by a cave-in, double-crossed and murdered, or…Gran would never have abided any suggestion that he might have one day taken his private railway to America and then hopped another train, but Gloria and I were free to wonder. On the surface, sure, Bill's absconding was highly illogical. First and foremost, why would he have quit a smuggling operation that had been very difficult to establish then brought in crates of cash every day? He disappeared with several lucrative years of Prohibition still ahead of him. If he'd kept up his game, he'd have been empire rich, not just dynasty rich. Ask the Kennedys. Or the Gurskys. And the details: he'd have been without a car or luggage and had to have abandoned a woman and son he loved. But I'm just assuming he loved them. After several years of Prohibition rail, had the tunnel bored him? Or, even more terrifying, had lawlessness been too appealing? Once he'd stepped beyond one set of rules, maybe he'd chucked the whole lot, left Peg and VC a house and plenty of cash then signed a more exclusive contract in the biggest smuggling game the world had ever known. That and/or the road called his name. The punctuated self. The floating island. Better the devil you can make yourself than the one someone else will make of you. Perhaps I was rolling out in another gene conduit, not simply a tunnel. Maybe both sides of my family, not just one, didn't like to stick around for the colicky nights. For some, filing cabinets look more like coffins than tunnels.

I'd always been told that Peg and Bill loved each other, but those stories were one-sided and from those bygone days of lifetime marriage. The nuclear family is as obsolete as the town crier, the stage coach, and the telegraph. How much of love in the past was willed, was made, not found? Gloria, Ms. Anti-Marriage, had waited until I was old enough and then started indulging in speculations about a wandering Bill trying a third country on for size. In this she may have been reaching back a few generations to pre-emptively excuse her own interest in a bounder (or two or three). I'd never found the theory of Bolting Bill very compelling until I was rolling out under the river, thinking of how secret and private so much of his life was. Take a man out of the world, out of sex, and even out of his tribe, how's he ever go back in?

Rolling out underground and under two countries, I theorized about Bill to ignore the fact that I might meet a corpse or two in that damp dark. He was a veteran of not just tunnelling, but tunnelling in war. Tunnellers carried knives, grenades, and illegal pistols strapped across their bodies in case they met Jerry. A few years ago I went over to Belgium and got down into some of those old tunnels. The brown, timbered braces still have duelling scars from stray pistol shots.

. Did Bill's possible killer also have experience fighting in cramped spaces? My valorizing assumption had been that Bill would have been the attacked, not the attacker. But the man I was following set his own rules. Did smuggler=killer? Even if he had been attacked, if he'd struck back I might have had two corpses on my hands, neither of them distinguishable as (possible) family.

The walls and air dampened as I continued to descend. The cement sidewalls turned from grey to charcoal as they became waterlogged. In places, water began dribbling through the seams. The walls, at least, cried for what I was losing.

Every metre I rolled out I told myself I'd be able to pull Bill's skeleton from the tunnel if I had to. If there had been a skeleton or two, I would have had to ferry them back out trussed across my own body on the creeper, a stack of lonely, career-dedicated men, their skeletons piled above mine on a thin tarp. Then I would also have had to dispose of two skeletons I didn't kill. Snap the lads down into hockey bags, rent a boat with cash, wait 'til nightfall, and, like Medea, scatter my brothers piece by sinking piece. So I thought until the air got wetter.

Still water and dark mud killed my great-grandfather and a few more of my delusions. All that dipping geometry was never more flagrant than in the eventual merger of the descending rails and a deepening pool of still, dark water. As far as I could tell with my lights, the water eventually filled the tunnel entirely. It could have been a leak from above or even an underground spring from below. Frankly, it didn't matter. I'd been a fool, had been playing out fantasies, not just nylon cord. Repairing a flooded tunnel would have been impossible as undetected, solo work. Fast pumps, six hundred metres of wide hose, patching gels, SCUBA suits. Not on my life.

I raised one boot off the creeper and reached it forward to dip my heel in the stagnant water. The little splash was heard by me alone, so quiet it might not even have existed.

45. Pain Is an Expanding Gas

IF I COULDN'T SUCCEED PROFESSIONALLY…Even with jangly Voodoo at my side, each step on my long walk back to our apartment tallied my losses. Time, money, and Kate. But failure can be good for the eyesight. My work clothes were dusty, yet my vision was sharp. If I wasn't going to stay with her, I had to leave her. Yet every hour I spent with her was one more before a final split.

A walking epiphany in the motor cities. Kate's decision to keep the baby had tripped us up. We knew we were falling, but it took us months to hit the ground. Parenting is early sexual retirement. Call me selfish, call me insensitive, but make sure honest is on your list too.

Yes, Kate had booked passage to sail away from us, from sex, but as the years piled up, wouldn't one of us have done that anyway? Odds are, one of us would have become another cheater who needs a bright flame in addition to a steady bed of coals. Could she have always resisted the advances of some charming associate in Austrian glasses and a bespoke suit? Everyone wants to be special. But, like the war on drugs, the war to be special never ends. Kate or I would have needed to impress somebody else. In my books she was already doing that.

Or, tethered to domesticity too early, either of us might have sabotaged our own sexuality with drink, diet, TV, or sleep. Ah yes, the affair with sleep. In the beginning I had thought that getting Kate's sleep, dropping thousands on the bed and bedding, would get her. Yes, but only for a while. Even before I started sleeping at Gran's I was another lover lonely in bed. So many big box stores are devoted to bedding because for many the first affair is with sleep.

Half of marriages end in divorce. More men cheat on their wives than don't. A recent DNA study in England found that nearly one-third of men who thought they'd been parenting their own children were not—a third! I'm quoting a feminist here, so cut me some slack. Not the fish on a bicycle one. Greer. She has written about a spiral love life (not to be confused with a spiralling vibrator). Rather than one big lifelong relationship, each of us will have a series of significant romances over a lifetime. Five years here, eight there, each of them love, absolutely. Your character, your strengths, what you chase, and what you run from. The two of you sharing power, trading experience, levering that Venn diagram to expand each other. But then, but then. Who really keeps ripping each other's clothes off as the years pile up? Ask around. You'll hear of women who forget their knees can bend and men who essentially stop dressing themselves.

Glore once told me about a book reviewer she knew (biblically, I'm sure). He was English or American, one of those countries where someone can actually make a living reviewing books and the books have sex, humour, and plot. In two decades of reviewing, he had 2.5 big conflicts. First, whether or not he had the "moral courage" to pan a friend's book. Simply ducking the review wasn't an option for him. In his late twenties (when, you'll see, you fully meet your taste) he chose his path: no friendship without honesty. He reviewed his friend's book, negatively, and lost the friend. Dilemma No 1.5, a variation on the first, whether or not he could skewer the novel of a woman he was attracted to yet still ask her out, be sniper and surgeon both. (Duh, other than money, what do you think women want? Ah, the flattery of criticism.) He could indeed ask her out, attract her, marry her. Married, she wrote better books, at least for a while. After fiveish married years, the second full-sized dilemma: *the* or *a*? Paraphrasing some midlife crisis novel, with its drift from youthful wankfest to yuppie angst test, the critic was torn between describing it as *a slide* from romance to routine or *the slide* from romance to routine. Love isn't love without hard truths. He went with *the*. Less than a year later they divorced. Her novels improved again.

Why are we so afraid of the truth? Across a lifetime, we're sure to be needed more than we're loved, endured more than we're adored. Kate repeatedly told me, "Love is a behaviour, not a feeling." True dat. What woman keeps up the porn-star head once she knows every piece of underwear you own, when you bought them, and where you leave them around the house? Can men really think a woman prefers the pounding of a man she once loved compared to that of a man she *might* love? The woman you worship with your mouth, ultimately she just feels spit, not sex. For a while, you lick ecstasy. Eventually, she starts inspecting the ceiling paint and thinking about which of her clothes need washing.

Consider The Beatles. Talented, driven, and in the right (televisable) place at the right (globalizing and baby-booming) time. Quite possibly the most exciting lives ever lived. Look up what George Harrison called his first solo album post-Beatles: *All Things Must Pass*. Bill's tunnel/crypt lasted (sort of). European farmers are still digging up ordnance from either war. Plutonium sure the fuck lasts. Things aren't fragile; emotions are, relationships. Sad but true. Does money last? You be the judge. Go make a cappuccino on a twenty-first-century machine made by a company still rolling forward from its nineteenth-century cannon fortune and wonder whether money lasts longer than emotion.

I would have lost Kate anyway—to time, more kids, or the corner office. That one-in-two failure rate for marriage can get worse. A contemporary marriage that started at twenty-five? Our odds of failure were three in four. Eventually, no matter how you start, you're just the guy who kills the spiders, takes out the garbage, and carries the heavy stuff. In memory, Kate and I are still perfect—young, beautiful, and promising. No haemorrhoids, no RRSPs, no baldness, or gravity. All things must pass.

I returned to slinging at the casino and kept limping along with Kate (thank you, second trimester). We even tried hanging out with our clothes on a little, a movie one night then some live dykey twang rock over in the D. November is vicious and ugly even if your love isn't drying up. River valleys can be wind tunnels, and we were bitten by frigid winds on both sides of the river. Over there, the steaming sewer covers showed me what a fool I'd been. If Bill's air pipe was still intact, it was all the tunnel I needed.

I explicitly tried not to keep staring out at one of Detroit's dragon-nostril sewer covers, but Kate still caught me out. That Special Glow, PI.

"What is it?"

"Nothing."

"Ant."

"Look, it's...work."

"Super-duper-doo."

Instantly, the Detroit club became tedious, not fun. The spilled beer on the floor became just spilled beer, not the holy oil of microbrewing mixed with collegiate indie rock. Well, at least the tiptoeing was over.

"We're going to need money. However this rolls, we need money."

"Please. Legitimate house painters and casino workers have kids."

"On credit and bad nutrition."

"They still get by."

"On someone else's dime, dancing to someone else's tune."

"So that's what this is all about, your need to swing your dick around?"

I could feel my lips press down into the same little rage-line Gloria makes. "Don't be reductive."

She quietly sang, "Macho-macho-man. He's got to be, a macho man."

"Thanks, we haven't had enough theatrics lately."

Now she too looked around disappointedly. She was halfway to game day, and we were sitting on ripped vinyl chairs listening to excessively loud music.

"Be *macho?* No. Be *me?* Yes."

"You still just want to have the highest score at the arcade. A-N-T, fifty-fucking-whatever-thousand."

"Doesn't everyone want that? At least everyone you'll ever love?"

She stopped the nearest waiter, not even ours, to ask for our bill. After he'd left she hit me with, "What, you wish you could just *catapult* me home?" Malice hammered her eyes into flat obsidian.

The air pipe. The air pipe. The air pipe.

46. This One

WHERE THERE'S MY KIND OF smoke, there's breath. Bill's tunnel was filled with water, but his air pipe could still have been clear. The gods punished Prometheus for stealing fire. Bill and Co. stole air and dragged it with them underground using hoses, fans, and pumps. On one side of the Atlantic, the government taught and paid him to steal air. He didn't forget when he got to the other side. He crawled under his (new) enemy with air pipes. I used fibre-optic cable.

Seeing inside my pipe was half surgery, half porn. With its stainless-steel head the size of an avocado, the fibre-optic camera was ludicrously sperm-shaped. A crown of LED lights surrounded its one eye, and a flagellar cable snaked out behind. I topped it off with a magnetized transponder and a second tail of nylon cord. Cylindricality had never been more beautiful. The pipe's interior, untouched dust was piled gold. Each cobweb was a necklace fine.

My damp recce on the rusty rails had already shown me that every six feet the pipe had a snub-nosed T-joint and a valve for air. On today's plastic pipe those joints are glued on in two minutes. Each one of Bill's cast-iron joints would have taken him twenty times as long, but he had put them in at regular intervals. In the event of a cave-in or partial flooding, they had a good shot at getting air. So what had gone wrong?

When I finally saw the grainy, grey-scale sight of the air pipe taking a right-angled bend up at around 1,200 metres, I kicked my heels with joy. My hands wanted a steering wheel, that local birthright, ASAP.

The trebuchet money had been fine, but it was still small change compared to three decades of a lawyer's salary. Then the mule bags at the casino had really started bringing it in. Not quite a bike gang's three million a week, but I still had green up to my hips. But the casino gig was noisy and parasitic. Sending the camera up the other end of the pipe, I looked at something that could be mine alone. Victimless crime, return me to your sweet, fragrant bosom.

The camera had been on double duty, giving me a view and carrying the small payload of a magnetized transponder. Following my withdrawal of the camera, the transponder and its tail of nylon cord would chime away for up to a year. If I could locate the transponder in Detroit, fish down and pull up the cord, I'd have a conduit into the largest drug market the world has ever known.

Ever since I laid the sledge to the basement wall I'd been re-grateful for the social failures of drive-by capitalism. The car is *the* thing of the twentieth century, and its birthplace is in ruins. No other Western metropolis would have allowed me to think of a tunnel into its downtown as a viable career opportunity. But you grow up looking over at a ruined city, where some of the most beautiful buildings in the world sit abandoned, you've got a very different map for commerce.

Once again I loaded Vood into the truck for a drive we shouldn't have been taking. I missed Kate like crazy when I got over to the D. Despite the last spat, we often had a little more glue on the other side. It *is* a different country. In Windsor, we'd spend all day enduring fellow Canadians, then on the other side we'd get a little warm relief to hear the voice of a fellow Canuck. In a restaurant, we'd hear someone order *paws-TUH*, not *PASTE-uh* and splash a little more wine into our glasses. Shopping for clothes, we'd reflexively throw someone a smile if they said *en-SOMME* instead of *en-somme-BULL*.

Voodoo helped me cross and that made me miss Kate all the more. Generally, he was quite the little diplomat. Occasionally an officer would squint at him and hold his vaccination card out as if it were an insultingly bad forgery, but most were delighted. He's border collie and what? A few, not always female, absolutely melted.

In our second, different downtown, I missed Kate, the old Kate, like oxygen. She'd expanded Vood's little heart, could cup both his ears and scratch him in a hairy duet of pure pleasure. Missing her washed me out with a deflating, leaking kind of sadness. I had loved her, loved her, and was now so much smaller.

I cruised the planet's strangest mixture of wealth and war looking to accelerate the beep on my transpo. Stalin must have been smiling in his butcher's grave to see how Detroit's "arsenal of democracy" had fallen to infighting: Achilles and Agamemnon off to the riots. I drove around an intermittent downtown amongst the car companies that had stolen intermittent wiper technology from its rightful inventor before getting billions in public bailouts. Expensive boutiques alternated with boarded-up storefronts down one half-inhabited block, while another was punctuated by the burnt-out shell of a 1930s office tower. Each blackened skyscraper was an exclamation mark in social failure. When designing the city's major roads, Augustus Woodward prophetically created five "spokes" for a grand wheel. Woodward, Michigan, Gratiot, Grand River, and Jefferson Avenues still radiate from the hub of Grand Circus Park. But the wheel—as a wheel—rolled on. The Motor City isn't accidentally a ghost town. *Drive-by shooting* is a redundant phrase.

The chirping transpo kept me close to the river. I passed a new brew pub opposite the site of a recent double murder and drove under an empty monorail car carrying nothing more than good intentions and lacklustre graffiti. All that ghostliness made my plan viable, but not necessarily inviting. I'd never been so keen to have what I was doing already done. Breaking and entering, Bert and Ernie as the kids call it. Barbarian work. Daytime B&Es may go undetected in the 'burbs, and it's not uncommon for someone to stroll out of a mind-blowing afternoon at the Detroit Institute of Arts to find a car window smashed and their stereo stolen, but still. One errant cop car or an onlooker with that rarest of cellphone plans—a sense of civic duty—and I'd be fucked. Still, when the transpo started chiming out its jackpot trill, excitement shot down to curl my toes and raised my skull an inch. As hoped, my signal went off outside an abandoned building, another non-storefront with plywood instead of windows and open-air former offices and apartments above.

If you're going to break in during daylight, make it official. My disguise was a white hard hat and a reflective safety vest. I concealed my cordless drill beneath a clipboard and left Vood in the truck to bark if anybody approached. All those spinning minutes with my back exposed—God bless American ruin.

Then again, if I got in easily, so could someone else. The second I stepped inside, my reflective vest would become a phosphorescent bull's eye in a nation flooded with guns. These buildings were forsaken by taxes, laws, and most of humanity, but not all. You live outside the law, and, well, you live outside the law. Before going in I returned the drill to the truck and collected Voodoo.

Immediately inside, I dropped the reflective vest (but kept the hard hat on). Any one of the dark midden heaps I saw with my flashlight in that stale, reeking dark could have been the homeless living dead, a rag man sleeping off a crack high or a Listerine drunk ready to leap up with a flashing blade. *Skels,* metro police call them. *Skeletons,* urban zombies. Vood was crucial there in the darkness, a second pair of eyes and ears and a keen nose close to the ground. With the homeless and trench soldiers, their feet start dying first. Vood would know they were coming before I did.

Darkness can declutter the mind. Sweat lodges, isolation tanks, drugs taken at night—each capitalizes on the way darkness can sweep small objects from the shelves in your head, clear the coffee tables of worry, hide the dirty plates of duty. The flashlight gave me only cones and columns of vision—leprous patches of fallen ceiling plaster, dusty clothes in a corner, an overturned filing cabinet—while my ears concentrated on what I hoped would remain just a four-piece band: my breathing, Vood, the chirping transpo reader, and the erratic percussion of my own quietly crunching footsteps. Any change to that could have meant company. Eventually I was able to concentrate a little in the darkness. The sister pipe was still a plumbing pipe, and it'd probably be toward the back of the building, not the front. Of course, it was almost certain to be in the basement.

Horror movies do have a point about basements. The bowels of a building. The dungeon. In a basement, you are unseen by the outside world, less likely to be heard, and considerable distance from an exit. Even decoration gets abandoned in basements. To some, bald utility and exposed pipes and beams are already violent. But a fortune might have been waiting down those (potentially rotten) basement steps. Crowbar in one hand, flashlight in the other, I followed my genes on down.

Turned out, the only threat was me. I smashed open a plaster wall, threw around the dust and spores, all to the near panic of the beeping transpo. No junkie has ever been more grateful to hold a needle than I was to get the other end of that pipe in my hands. I just barely had the good sense not to kiss it. My lifeline. My artery. The umbilical cord I was more than happy to cut.

47. The Necessary

I WENT FROM DIGGING IN another basement to digging through
mouldy files at a Wayne County records office. That archival real-estate
work is the closest I've ever come to wedding vows. *Do you this tax-
foreclosure take to honour and cherish…?* Little paper riders were clamped
all over the building's deed with the stapling equivalent of handcuffs.
Triangles of thick, encasing paper had been machine-pressed over corner
staples to fix stern, proprietary tax liens onto the deed. Thank you,
American racism and global hyper-capitalism. Thank you. Thank you.
Thank you.

You grow up in bed with an elephant, you get to know the sound of
its snores. On the radio, local news could be from Windsor or Detroit.
In the D, radio news always included arson and one mayoral scandal or
another. When people had to leave the city to go make money elsewhere,
and the city eventually couldn't afford to repossess any more abandoned
buildings (however ornate), the local coffers obviously lacked for taxes.
*Dear Mr. Mayor. If you're not too busy locking out your own council or
doing jail time, I'd like to make you an offer on one of your derelict buildings.*
Failure had never looked so good.

Heading home, I sat at multiple borders. I started off with a digital-
camera-like instant nostalgia, remembering already the pipe in my hand
of a just a few hours ago. But then it ceased to be just a pipe. Kate's trim
calf muscles. Her lithe upper arms. The whole, exciting point about
wanting someone is that we don't choose to want. We don't decide. We
know. The smell of her. The sound of her laugh. A quarter century of
personal experience had made our bodies into keys and locks, ropes and
pulleys. My lips hadn't yet forgotten the feeling of her bottom lip sucked

and held between them. My hand still knew the arc of her hips, a dozen intimate fits. In memory, my thighs could scissor into hers. I had to see her. I know, I know—too little, too late. But work at the casino and you'll see gamblers as shaken by winning as they are by losing.

All these years later I haven't changed my mind about how the heart wants. My eventual preference for tough, childfree women—that's magnetism, not a decision. The brain gets heard at a point. Eventually it can get us out of the arms of someone other parts of us foolishly want to be in. The parliament of emotion is always vulnerable to its upsetting by-elections and dicey non-confidence votes. The pregnancy was heart and head for Kate and me. She knew what she wanted, if not why, and I knew what I didn't want and told myself I knew why. None of these messages was clear and sudden. Genuine knowledge is a war, not just one battle.

While I was inching forward in the lines for the bridge and then Customs, I pictured Kate finishing her afternoon class then heading back to the apartment. Our apartment. I hadn't been there in a week. The me of me and the me of us barely knew each other anymore.

Space—a word nearly as vague as *thing*. *Something I've been meaning to tell you. I'm in a different space now. She needs her space.* I told myself I'd been giving Kate space, that my arguments and horniness weren't what she needed. And hey, I'd already been exiled from the decision. My half-forsaking our apartment had just finalized the details, crossed the Ts on a contract she had written. But she was pregnant. Literal and figurative space had never mattered more.

It's easier to recognize that you don't want to be somewhere than it is to itemize all the reasons why. Windsor, Ontario. Bottom of Canada in more ways than one. I shouldn't have been there but couldn't be who I was anywhere else. Brampton, Oakville, London—sure, I'd have signed on to be another C-minus dad. Down here, I scored much higher as a smuggler.

I'd always admired that when Kate knew what she wanted to do, she did it. No hesitations. When I got to the apartment I knocked before using my key. Two steps in I could see she'd moved out. Her bookcase was gone, and mine had gaps like a defenseman's teeth. Her teapot, her floor lamp, her desk. Poof. No more bras on chair-backs. Not a skirt, flip-flop, or tall boot to be found. No more yucca-berry rainforest polymer shampoo. When a woman takes her shampoo, she's gone for good.

Of course I knew this was coming (so have you). Breakups, affairs, walkouts, and harsh dumpings—they're only surprising in the beginning. Really it's the mechanism, not the action, that's the surprise. That first tidal wave of sadness isn't surprise. It's admission, confirmation. No, this did not last. All things must indeed pass.

. Thankfully we never let a *now* insult too much of our *then*. She sailed her ship, and I chose to stay behind. She left her Christmas-present dresser, with nothing remaining in it save a note on top. No *I thinks*. No *maybe*s. No *later*s.

> *The willing*
> *and hopefully qualified*
> *doing the personally necessary*
> *for the potentially grateful.*

Until this blog and your very, VERY welcome search, her note has echoed your grandsire's for me alone. Here, look at both of them.

48. The Earthly Paradise

BUYING A BUILDING IN ANOTHER country is pretty much
a textbook example of self-inflicted tedium: skimming, inefficient
bureaucracy in notarized triplicate. I won't linger on inspections, water
damage, the nine permits necessary to buy and renovate the Detroit
building, or the five I needed to open a coffee roastery and café. When I
finally owned the building, I didn't celebrate by dousing my second dusty
basement in champers. With two deeds in my name, I opened the pipe
on the Detroit side, crossed back, descended Gran's stairs and opened up
Bill's pipe. I leaned my face into the valve and inhaled. Darling, I smoked
America.

I was fifteen casino-busy months between my pipe hunting B&E and
the opening of The Earthly Paradise, café and loft living for the status-
hungry of Detroit. My tenants had to want to live near the constant smell
of roasting coffee beans (superb olfactory mask that it is). Artisanal food
on the ground floor, bamboo flooring and milk paint in the loft condos
upstairs. Young, professional couples upstairs and daily packets of green
in the basement. Once again gender was my sword and shield. The auto
industry is probably the worst place going to see the gender income gap
(no wonder they deserve billions of our taxes). His four-year degree
in engineering somehow earns him at least twice what her four-year
degree in HR or marketing does. When it came to showing around my
apartments, though, I knew who held the strings. Low-emission this,
carbon footprint that, tuck a recycled paper pamphlet into her left hand
with its one or two rings.

The Earthly Paradise. I thought of calling the place *Ontario Farm III*,
but if I wasn't going to be sentimental with you, I wasn't with the biz

either. I took the title from Antoine de la Mothe Cadillac's 1702 account of the area he would one day run by slinging booze. I hung a portrait of the old liar on the café wall above his own words:

This river is scattered over, from one lake to another both on the mainland and the islands with large clusters of trees surrounded by charming meadows. Game is very common, as are geese, and all kinds of wild ducks. There are swans everywhere, there are quails, woodcocks, pheasants and rabbits, turkeys, partridges, hazelhens and a stupendous amount of turtledoves. This country is so temperate, so fertile and so beautiful that it may justly be called 'The Earthly Paradise of North America.'

I didn't tell anyone save Reese about how Cadillac stole the coat of arms driving by our front windows. Live and let lie.

As for Gloria, we mended—to a degree. With Gran and Kate gone, who else? Not long after Kate left, Glore tried to tell me that if I wound up in prison I'd be dead to her. Words. Words. Words. My gamble, here and there, is that if the stakes are high enough there's usually a second chance. Curiosity may indeed kill the cat, but sometimes satisfaction brings her back.

49. Send

YOU WERE BORN ON THE twenty-third of April in Women's College Hospital, Toronto. Unlike Kate and presumably Gail, I didn't know you were a healthy girl until the next day. Medea Walker Chan. At first that was an island name, you and Kate cut off from the world. Less than two years later it became Medea Walker Chan-Briggs. Fine by me. Carve a name into timber or a state document, it's a story waiting to happen.

I've kept my eye on you since before you were born. It wasn't very expensive to get photos of pregnant Kate coming and going from Gail's. Mystery One solved, I just waited. At the hospital itself, well, only the idiotic would try to bribe a maternity nurse. They're all coo for the wee uns, all teeth for anyone else. But hospitals are employee dense. Porters, custodians, technicians, maintenance—plenty of people pushing carts. My guy walked around with a wad of cash, a stack of phone cards, and a great sense of who to proposition and how. I've had pictures from afar and some details: which schools, the dance lessons, piano.

I freely admit that for years I wished you weren't a girl. Not out of vanity, though—no gender identification blah-blah. I've been afraid that as a girl living with a father slippage, an unseen bio-dad and a loving stepfather, you'd be more likely to blame yourself and become another doormat in heels, your mother be damned. That or you'd become a different kind of casualty, another smart, privileged girl who falls for a series of charismatic parasites. Which'd be worse, you the simp or you perpetually falling for some whiskered cad allergic to fidelity, honesty, and the rent cheque? If you'd been a guy, you'd almost certainly have grown up reckless and defiant. Frankly that could have happened if I'd been around or not.

I worried that you had been told about me and that you hadn't. For a long time after your parents' wedding I figured I was another buried secret. There's always a price to be paid for living outside the law. Your parents knew I wasn't going to show up to a two-lawyer household demanding my "rights" when they could have put me in an orange jumpsuit with one phone call. Besides, you were actually getting parented—quiet nights after even days. I've seen photos of you and Scott since he was pushing you in a stroller. Decent guy, I'm sure.

The Kate before she left me definitely would have told you about sires versus fathers, but of course the Kate that raised you was a different woman. Even when I was hopeful she would tell you about me, I had no idea when. When to topple/enlarge your world? Four years old? Six? Twelve? When your sister was born I lost hope again. Why rock the family VW as it headed down the cottage lane? But your name kept my hope alive. Medea for the first-born and Cassandra for the second. A child killer for the heir and a neglected prophet for the spare. Scott-Schmott: with your name, Kate tipped her hand.

Every day for seventeen years I lived in doubt and hope until you finally found this site and logged in. Seventeen years. At the start I just clicked beads on the abacus, filled bank accounts for me and a trust fund for you. But as the Web deepened and your generation grew up with all of these digi-layers, my hope changed gears. Maybe I wouldn't have to approach you. Why intrude in the flesh when you could pull in this whole story? Keepingthingswhole.ca—viral marketing for one. Your logging in here is a start. If you've heard the poem, you've almost certainly heard it from Kate. Apparently loose lips can raise a few ships as well.

Occasionally I've felt guilty over the years not telling Gloria how much I know about you, not showing her any pictures, but I can't pick at the wound. In the rare moments I've thought of her dying, I've been flooded with guilt. Thankfully there's little risk of that: the old yoga-doing battleaxe, your partial namesake, stages increasingly elaborate and popular plays. Cronus Holdings and I have kept her busy in the theatre where she belongs, calling down the fates under moody lights. But when we had a grey-bearded and limping Voodoo put down I almost caved and told her everything I knew about you. For a time you can't help but think that death is a vacuum and only new life can fill it. I'm glad I didn't show up on your doorstep with Vood's empty collar still fragrant on the floor of my car.

Beckett has a point: waiting *is* absurd. Every night I've typed away at this, every time I've asked what you would make of what I'm doing, I've been simultaneously more and less me, fluid not solid. Waiting for you has been rejuvenating in ways: I am ruled by potential, not just actualities. Thank you for that. Never before has the possibility of judgement already judged me so much. I wound up framing Trevor's *unwilling and unqualified* note, moved it with me from house to house—mirror, screed, proclamation. You might think it's a little too coincidental that I cleaned up only after the post-9/11 paranoia finally died down and my rates resettled. It's been almost a decade since I made an illegal dollar. I sold the first commercial bag of fair-trade coffee east of Vancouver. I own a coffee bean farm in Costa Rica and now try to overgrow the government legitimately. You could work there some summer. Bring a friend. Skype with your mom.

Every story is a staircase. Let me know if ours only goes down. I didn't give you enough when you were a kid. Ask yourself if that really means I can't give you anything now. Is there a statute of limitations on gifts to and from the heart?

Medea, anything's possible if you reach over and hit Send. Lunch. Walks supervised by your parents or a friend. Maybe travel in the future. There's still so much we could try to keep whole.

I'm still waiting for you, Medea, for you alone. Medea. Medea.

Acknowledgments

THIS NOVEL WAS SUBSTANTIALLY ENABLED by a three-year grant from the Social Sciences and Humanities Research Council of Canada. Thanks also to Université Sainte-Anne and the Huntington Library.

Andrew Barrie's *War Underground* and *Beneath Flanders Fields: The Tunnellers' War, 1914–1918* by Peter Barton, Peter Doyle and Johan Vandewalle illuminated tunnel warfare. Various historians attest to German Great-War monikers for Canadian soldiers like "killers of Germans." That phrase is lifted verbatim from the 11 September 1917 entry in the tremendously moving pocket diary of Lieutenant Howard Lawrence Scott (housed at the Canadian War Museum / *Musée canadien de la guerre*). William Williams' list of the fallen are actual tunnel veterans, mostly of the embryonic 170th Tunnelling Company (UK). Marty Gervais's *The Rumrunners* and a September/October 1994 article in *Michigan History* by Phillip Mason sketch Windsor's history of prohibition collusion. Scholarship on the Western marijuana prohibition is vast, and the following were helpful: *The Pursuit of Oblivion: A Global History of Narcotics* by Richard Davenport-Hines, *The Botany of Desire* by Michael Pollan, *High Society* by Neil Boyd, *Reefer Madness* by Eric Schlosser, and *Drugs Without the Hot Air* by David Nutt.

The image of the Canada-US border as a candy store window is borrowed from Mordecai Richler's smuggling novel *Solomon Gursky Was Here*. Michael Stipe describes irony as "the shackles of youth." Quotations from Euripides's *Medea* are from John Harrison's translation published by Cambridge UP. The novel's title is borrowed from Mark Strand's unforgettable poem "Keeping Things Whole." The doubled-edged marriage advice comes from Martin Amis.

About the Author

DARRYL WHETTER'S FIRST BOOK OF fiction, *A Sharp Tooth in the Fur*, was named to *The Globe and Mail*'s top 100 books of 2003. He is also the author of the novel *The Push & the Pull* and the poetry collection *Origins*. Darryl has published or presented literary essays in France, Sweden, Canada, Germany, the United States, India, and Iceland. He was a regular guest on the national CBC program *Talking Books* and reviews books regularly for *The Globe and Mail* and *The National Post*, among other publications.